My Notorious Highlander

Vonda Sinclair

My Notorious Highlander

www.vondasinclair.com

ISBN: **1493505394**
ISBN-13: **978-1493505395**

DEDICATION

In memory of Thistle, Mocha, Indy and Cheyenne. I love you and miss you, my furry babies.

The Highland Adventure Series

My Fierce Highlander

My Wild Highlander

My Brave Highlander

My Daring Highlander

My Notorious Highlander

My Rebel Highlander

ACKNOWLEDGMENTS

Special thanks to Terry, Dana, Vanessa, Nicole, Judy, Eliza, and Derek.

Chapter One

Loch Shin, Scotland, June, 1619

Torrin MacLeod awoke to the sounds of his men talking outside the tent. Dawn had arrived but, being close to midsummer, 'twas still early, around four in the morning.

"Chief," Struan, his sword-bearer, said just outside.

"Aye?" Torrin sat up, his eyes scratchy from lack of sleep.

"Riders approaching."

Having slept fully clothed in his belted plaid, shirt and doublet, Torrin pushed through the flaps of the tent and joined his clansmen. "How many?"

"Six or eight." His brawny sword-bearer narrowed his eyes and squinted into the distance.

Indeed, those approaching through the mist from the south rode along the trail by Loch Shin at a quick pace. "They're in a hurry."

"Aye."

The other six MacLeods in his own party stood at the ready, though they appeared deceptively relaxed. He didn't have to tell them to prepare for an attack. They all well knew anyone could quickly turn into an enemy. He always took his best-trained guards with him whenever he traveled. They'd just left Lairg the day before. After his business there was completed, they'd headed north toward Durness. His good friend and foster brother, Iain Stewart, had wanted to accompany him, but Torrin had left while the man slept off a bad bout of drunkenness from the night before. He didn't need Iain's help on this mission.

None of his men, except Struan, had guessed his purpose in going to Durness. Of course, Struan could read him easily, and he knew Torrin held a keen interest in Lady Jessie MacKay. An interest that had only increased over the last several months since he'd first met her, even though he hadn't seen her again.

She haunted him. Her flaming red hair and her bright blue eyes wouldn't leave his mind or his dreams. Never had he seen such a beautiful lady. She had the presence of a Norse goddess, tall, lithe, and statuesque… almost as tall as Torrin.

Not only were the clan elders hounding him about marrying, but he was ready for a wife. At twenty-eight, he knew 'twas past time for him to marry and sire an heir. His younger brother was already married and had a wee bairn, a lass. He felt left behind. He'd arranged to marry Isobel MacKenzie, but Chief Dirk MacKay, Jessie's brother, had snatched Isobel from beneath his nose. He didn't hold it against Dirk. Torrin had been uncertain of the match anyway. But Jessie… she was a woman he didn't wish to let slip through his fingers.

The riders, swathed in belted plaids, slowed as they approached and eyed Torrin and his men cautiously.

They drew up as they came even with the camp. "A good morn to you," their leader said, his black hair in a queue, and a few days' worth of beard stubble darkening his cheeks.

"Good morn," Torrin said. "You're traveling early."

"Aye, we needed an early start to reach Durness on the morrow at gloaming."

"That's where we're headed as well."

Their leader and two more men dismounted. "Gregor MacBain, Chief of the MacBains." He offered his hand.

"Chief Torrin MacLeod." He shook the other man's hand, noting that MacBain was shorter than him but also stockier. Of course, most people were shorter than Torrin. "Would you like to join us as we break our fast?" He wanted to ask the man what his business was in Durness, but since they'd just met, he didn't want to pry. Likely, the man would reveal his purpose before long.

"I thank you, but we've already eaten."

"It might be good to ride together into MacKay Country. A gang of a dozen or so highwaymen and outlaws troll the area." Torrin wouldn't add that his own brother, Nolan, had joined that gang. It saddened and shamed him greatly.

"Indeed?" Suspicion colored MacBain's tone.

"Aye. Donald McMurdo and Haldane MacKay lead them."

"Och. I've heard of McMurdo, a wily old highwayman who has murdered countless people."

Torrin nodded.

"And who is this Haldane MacKay?" MacBain asked.

"A lad of around twenty summers but still deadly. The youngest brother of the MacKay chief."

MacBain's dark eyes widened. "Any relation to Lady Jessie MacKay?"

"Aye, her youngest brother. You ken who she is?"

"I do indeed." The man gave a smile which could only be called nasty and cunning. "We were engaged in a trial marriage three years past."

"What?" Torrin blurted the word before he could stop himself, outrage and disbelief tensing his muscles.

The man's smile broadened. "I take it you ken who she is as well."

Torrin wanted to smash his fist into the man's face. "I've met her," he said instead, keeping his response discreet so as not to alert MacBain to his interest in her.

"She is lovely," the man mused.

Torrin had no inkling that Jessie had been in a trial marriage. That meant this bastard had taken her virginity and then cast her off like a worn-out shoe. Had she been hurt by his rejection, or happy to leave him? And why would he send her away? Was she barren or had he simply tired of her?

"So… you're no longer married to her?" Torrin inquired in a light tone.

"She was at my castle for a year and a day, as is customary, but…" MacBain shrugged. "I found someone else and sent Lady Jessie back to her family."

"Ah. So you found a more suitable wife."

"Aye, briefly. She bore me a fine son but she died soon after. I'm now in need of a wife again."

Torrin narrowed his eyes and nodded. Why hadn't the man kept Jessie as his wife in the first place if he was but chasing on her skirt-tails again? He disliked indecisive men.

"A chief must have a wife," MacBain said. "You ken what I'm talking about, aye? Are you married?"

"Nay, not yet. Soon, I hope."

MacBain nodded.

"Well, if you will allow us a few minutes to break our fast and finish packing up, we'll ride north with you."

"We need a rest anyway." He turned to his men. "Water the horses." The remaining MacBain clansmen dismounted.

Torrin's men had the camp mostly packed up and his cook was handing out bannocks within minutes.

While Torrin ate, he eyed MacBain. "I take it you are going to visit Lady Jessie."

"How did you guess?" The man smirked.

Torrin shrugged. He didn't like the cheeky bastard. He'd appeared friendly at first, but once he'd started talking about Lady Jessie and his deceased wife, he'd become highly unlikable. Obviously, he had no respect for women. Nor could MacBain make up his mind.

"Are you going to try to arrange another trial marriage with her?" Torrin took another bite of the bannock, although he was swiftly losing his appetite.

"Aye, she was rather smitten with me, so I'm certain she will be agreeable to it."

Hmph. She damned well better not be. Nay, Lady Jessie was intelligent. She wouldn't submit to being the rushes beneath this man's muddy feet. And if she even considered it, Torrin was bound and determined to change her mind. She deserved a man who would treat her like a goddess. Torrin could do that.

Weeks ago, when Dirk and the MacKay party had stopped for a night or two at Munrick Castle, Torrin had been disappointed that Lady Jessie was not traveling with them. For the second time, he'd asked Dirk for Lady Jessie's hand in marriage, but Dirk had said he wouldn't force his sister to marry someone she didn't wish to. Torrin could understand that. If his younger sister were still alive, he wouldn't force her to marry anyone she didn't want to either. A stab of sadness lanced his gut as it always did when he thought of Allina.

He pushed the cutting emotion away and focused on the beautiful image of Lady Jessie in his mind instead. Every time he thought of her, his mood lightened even though she'd rejected him. She simply didn't know him; that was all. She was skittish and suspicious. But he didn't fault her for it; he didn't trust easily either. He'd simply have to prove his worth to her. She made him want to be a better man.

Minutes later, after everything was packed onto the horses, the MacBains and MacLeods rode north.

Torrin hoped Lady Jessie would not give MacBain one moment of her attention. He didn't deserve it. Was there some other reason he was now going back for her? Torrin was certain it had naught to do with MacBain having any feelings for her.

Jessie's older brother, Dirk, was not in Durness, which prevented a marriage arrangement from being made, but MacBain didn't need to know that. He might try to use it to his advantage, or even try to steal Jessie away. Torrin refused to let that happen.

At midday, the sunlight and blue sky glimmered off the dark water of Loch Stack, near blinding him. They stopped to eat and allow the horses to rest. Torrin was staring at the snowcapped mountains in the distance and thinking about Jessie when MacBain approached.

"Why are you headed to Castle Dunnakeil?" MacBain asked. The bold whoreson obviously had no qualms about prying.

"Business. Land," Torrin said and continued eating. Of course, 'twas a lie, but if he could indeed marry Lady Jessie, he would receive the land in her dowry—land that bordered his own. And a marriage was a business deal in most cases. Still, those things were of little importance to him at the moment. He'd wanted a wife like Jessie most of his adult life. 'Twas as if God had taken the woman from his imagination and created Jessie.

He'd never say that aloud, of course; people would think him mad. At times, he wondered if indeed he was going a bit mad. He dreamed of her often, and she occupied his mind during the day. His primary concern now was protecting her from this wily MacBain bastard.

MacBain sat on a rock near him. "I understand Jessie's father passed last fall. Do you ken her brother, the new chief?"

"Aye, Dirk MacKay is a good man. Fair, honest." *A bride thief.* Torrin held back a grin for, in truth, he was thankful Dirk had stolen his betrothed. Isobel was beautiful, but if Torrin had married her, he would've missed his chance with Jessie. Aye, he had to believe he had a chance with her, despite her resistance.

Torrin glared at the man beside him. Maybe MacBain was the reason Jessie was turned against marriage and men. That had to be it. She would likely be furious that MacBain was back, sniffing at her slippers.

"I'm hoping Chief MacKay will be receptive to my offer of marriage to Jessie," MacBain said.

Doubtful, although Torrin wouldn't tell him this. Let

him find out for himself that things were not so rosy. This would give Torrin an excuse and time for Jessie to get to know him. He wanted her trust… and a lot more.

"Why did you send her home at the end of the handfasting?" Torrin asked.

"Another woman bewitched me. 'Twas not something I planned. But I met Ellen about three months after I'd signed the trial marriage contract. I was smitten with her."

"So you sent Jessie home and married Ellen?"

"Aye, but I waited until the year was up so I wouldn't break the contract without good reason and rile her father. 'Twas difficult as Ellen was with child and I had to keep her condition a secret."

Difficult? Did he not think it was difficult for Jessie, watching her "husband" frolicking with another woman? *Bastard.*

"Lady Jessie must have been hurt and angry," Torrin said, as if only vaguely interested.

MacBain shrugged. "Aye, she glared at me a few times. Gave me the cold shoulder. But I'm certain I can warm her up again."

"'Haps." *Ha.* The man was full of horse dung. Jessie was more likely to dirk MacBain in his sleep than smile at him. And he hoped she would.

"She's a fiery one."

Torrin glared at him, not wanting to hear one more word or he might choke the bastard before they made it to Durness.

"Why are you pursuing her instead of some other lady?" Torrin asked. "Surely, 'twould be easier if you didn't have a history with the woman."

"Her dowry is…" MacBain clamped his lips shut.

"Aye?" Torrin prompted.

MacBain eyed him suspiciously. "Well, I suppose I can tell you. You won't tell anyone, will you?"

Torrin shook his head. "Nay. Who would I tell?"

"I heard that her brother increased her dowry, and added

some land in."

"Ah." Money-hungry whoreson. All he wanted was the dowry. Not Jessie. Torrin knew this happened with a lot of marriage arrangements. Land was important to him as well, so his clan could grow more food and not starve. But for him, the woman he took to wife would be far more important than the land she brought to the marriage.

"You won't tell her I said that, will you?" MacBain's brows scrunched together.

"I barely know her." But he intended to change that, though it might take some time. Besides, he wouldn't need to tell her why MacBain was pursuing her again. She'd know. She was one of the canniest women he knew. He hadn't talked to her much, but he'd watched her plenty during the month he'd been at Dunnakeil last winter. He knew her to be friendly and caring, quick with a smile. Not for him, of course, but for those she was close to. She'd been managing the servants at that time and 'twas obvious everything was spotless.

She would make a perfect wife for him. He looked forward to convincing her of that.

***

During supper at Castle Dunnakeil, one of the guards approached Lady Jessie MacKay at the high table. "We have visitors, m'lady," he said, raising his voice over the roar of conversation in the candlelit great hall.

Halting her knife in the midst of cutting a piece of venison, she glanced up at him with trepidation. *Please don't let it be Haldane.* She couldn't deal with her outlaw younger brother. Although Dirk hadn't exactly left her in charge of the castle, she was the next oldest of her siblings and of the highest rank here. Dirk's sword-bearer, Erskine, and the guards were to handle defense. But if they had noble visitors, she was the one left to entertain them… along with her other brother, Aiden. But his method of entertainment was music. She would have to deal with everything else.

"Who is it?" she asked with dread.

"Chief MacLeod and Chief MacBain," the guard informed her.

"What?" Jessie's mouth hung open. Noticing a few people staring at her, she snapped her mouth closed and tried to contain her shock. Those were two names she'd hoped to never hear again. "Are you certain? Torrin MacLeod and Gregor MacBain?"

"Aye."

"What on earth are they doing here?"

"They would not say, but they're requesting entrance."

"How many men with them?" her younger brother, Aiden, asked beside her.

"Just over a dozen."

"I'll see what they want." Aiden stood.

"Wait." Jessie grabbed his slender arm. "I'll go, too." Why couldn't Dirk have been here at a time like this? He and around twenty-five had left, traveling south, a few weeks ago. They'd been planning to stop by Munrick Castle, Torrin MacLeod's keep. He knew Dirk wasn't here. Was that why he'd come? To harass her about marrying him? "Where is Erskine?" she asked. Her older brother's sword-bearer would ken what to do if conflict broke out.

"Outside," the guard said. "But he wanted your permission before we allowed them entrance. We're fair certain the MacLeods are allies, but we don't ken about the MacBains since… eh…" The guard's face flushed.

"Aye." Since her handfasting with him had gone sour three years past.

"I don't think Torrin MacLeod wants to wage war with you, sister." Aiden smirked, his boyish face taking on a pixie charm.

She rolled her eyes. She could guess why Torrin was here, but MacBain? The man whose castle she'd spent a year and a day at. She'd hoped to never see him again. Of a certainty, at the time, she'd fallen for him, but since being away from him, she'd come to realize what kind of knave he truly was. He cared for no one but himself. Gregor MacBain was incredibly selfish and changed his mind as often as the changing weather in the Highlands. He'd entered into a legal marriage with another woman. Jessie had naught to say to him.

After pushing herself up from the table, she crossed the great hall on shaky legs. But never could she let either of the men outside see a smidgen of weakness from her. They would circle and close in like hungry buzzards.

Stepping into the courtyard, she saw that gloaming had settled over the land with a purple light just after sunset, and a brisk breeze blew in off the North Sea. She, Aiden, and the guard moved toward the iron portcullis.

Erskine joined them, his short brown hair ruffled by the wind. He wore leather armor and carried a sword at his hip. But he did not appear overly concerned. "M'lady." He gave an abbreviated bow. "Both MacLeod and MacBain appear to have come in peace. They wish to speak to you."

Jessie's stomach knotted worse than the ropes used on the galleys. *Saints!* She gave a brief nod, though she did not want to face either man, but for different reasons. She took a deep breath and placed a hand upon the hilt of the foot-long dirk in the scabbard on her belt. She was never without it. Not that she expected to have to use it on either man. But it gave her more confidence.

As they approached the gate, her breathing grew shallower and her sweaty hands more fidgety. She clasped them before her.

Remain calm.

Her gaze landed on Torrin MacLeod first. A wave of panic and something far more disturbing washed over her. The man was just as striking and attractive as the last time she'd seen him, mayhap more so, with his compelling green eyes, long chestnut hair and tall, lean frame. He was one of the few men who towered over her. But looking into his eyes filled her with a mixture of dread, fear, and something she didn't want to think about.

She quickly switched her gaze to Gregor MacBain. His

black hair was much longer than it had been the last time she'd seen him and a scruffy short beard covered the lower half of his face. His dark-brown eyes had once completely bewitched her, but now she could hardly tolerate the sight of him. She had been so young and naïve when she'd first met him.

"Lady Jessie," Gregor said in a cheerful tone, then bowed deeply. His conciliatory smile annoyed her greatly. "I'm so glad to see you, lass."

"What do you want, Gregor?" she demanded.

Torrin snorted, one side of his lips kicking up in a half smile as he watched her with pronounced interest.

Heat rushed over her and she immediately felt even more edgy than before. No matter how disconcerting she found him, she simply needed to ignore Torrin, but remain ever vigilant around him for he was a dangerous man. She had seen firsthand what kind of lethal warrior he was.

"Is that any way to greet your husband?" Gregor cajoled.

"You are *not* my husband," she stated firmly, sending him what she hoped was a cutting glare. "You married another woman."

"Aye, but she passed giving birth to my son. I made a mistake. I never should've left you for her. I ken you must have missed me."

"You're wrong. I hardly remember much about you. And our marriage was not a legal one, so you were never my husband, in truth. 'Twas only a handfasting." She detested the Highland practice of trial marriage for a year and a day, to see if the woman would conceive a bairn, before the legal marriage took place. This, of course, benefited the man, usually a chief who needed an heir. She would never willingly enter into one of these arrangements again. She'd much prefer to remain unmarried and be of service to her family and clan.

Gregor sighed. "A storm is blowing in off the sea. Will you not let us in and feed us supper? What of Highland hospitality?"

"I have no hospitality or sympathy for you," she said, only now noticing the strong wind whipping her hair and cooling her overheated face.

"Allow me to talk to the lady alone." Torrin's tone was low and deep, but most disturbing of all, he never took his eyes off her.

Chapter Two

"*The lady* has no interest in talking to you alone," Jessie told Torrin through the gates. Besides, she wished to go back inside before the storm hit.

Torrin merely gave her that enigmatic hint of a smile again. He then switched his attention to MacBain and gave him a warning look. "Give us some privacy."

MacBain narrowed his eyes. "I think not, MacLeod."

"Would you like shelter during the coming storm? Or do you prefer staying out here?"

MacBain surveyed the turbulent sky. "Very well, then. Let us see if you can sweet talk her into allowing us entrance. But I doubt it." MacBain and his men moved twenty feet away.

"Could I have a moment to talk to her, Aiden?" Torrin asked her brother, his tone respectful.

"Are you in agreement with this, sister?"

"Aye. I'll be fine." She didn't want Torrin to know she

feared him.

Aiden stepped back a good distance, but continued to watch them. Not that he could beat Torrin off her if he decided to reach through the iron bars and grab her. 'Twas likely that Aiden, with his slight frame, weighed only half as much as Torrin did with his warrior strength.

"How long have you been friends with MacBain?" Jessie asked, making sure she stayed more than an arm's length away from the gate. But he had long arms that were thick with muscle.

Torrin frowned, looking more ominous than the dark, cloudy sky above. "I'm not friends with the daft man. They came upon us while we were traveling. Once I heard where he was headed and why, I suggested we ride together. I came to protect you."

Jessie forced an ironic smile. "I have no need for your protection." Besides, that would be like a wolf protecting a herd of sheep. After all was said and done, he'd feast on a few of them.

"Nevertheless… I consider Dirk a friend. He is not here to protect you from this knave, so I felt it my responsibility."

"How could it possibly be *your* responsibility? We've barely spoken."

He allowed an amused look combined with a look of determination. "I intend to speak to you far more, m'lady," he said in a lowered voice.

The feverish chills covering her, head to toe, had little to do with the whipping wind and far more to do with his intimate tone. "Why?"

He raised a brow. "I think we both ken the answer to that."

Aye, she knew he'd asked Dirk for her hand in marriage last winter. "I'm not marrying anyone. Not MacBain, and certainly not you."

His smirking, confident smile made her grind her teeth. Could naught dissuade him from his ridiculous objective?

"Are you thinking I would marry a man with a paramour

and children in the village?"

Torrin frowned, his amusement vanishing. "Who are you speaking of? MacBain?"

"Nay. You."

"I don't ken who has been spreading rumors, but I have no paramour in the village and certainly no children that I'm aware of."

Ha. Of course he would deny it. But her sister-in-law, Isobel, had told her this and the information had come from Torrin's own brother. He'd said Torrin was in love with the village lass.

"Who told you this?" he demanded.

"It matters not." She didn't want to get Isobel into trouble. It wasn't her fault if his outlaw brother had lied. "What is he planning?" She nodded toward MacBain.

Torrin eyed her a moment longer, making it obvious he didn't want to drop the subject of the rumors. "MacBain thinks he can convince you to marry him, a legal and binding marriage this time." Torrin shrugged. "But he has far more interest in your dowry. He is the least trustworthy man I've ever met."

Hmph. He was one to talk. "I would imagine you also have a great interest in my dowry." Torrin had to know that Dirk had added the hundred-and-fifty acres that Chief MacKenzie had given him, which joined his own. Everyone knew he was keen on acquiring that land for crops.

Torrin's dark green eyes were troubled. "'Tis not my main interest."

"Of course not," she said doubtfully.

"I would like for us to get to know each other better, Lady Jessie." His voice was sober and his eyes hopeful.

'Twas true she was not well acquainted with him, but the most significant thing she knew about him was that he'd killed her foster brother, Lyall Keith, eight years past. She'd watched the whole horrific incident take place from her hidden vantage point in the old oak. She'd been sixteen summers at the time and had nightmares for months afterward—nightmares that featured Torrin, hunting her down and killing her, the only witness to his crime. She hadn't known who he was and, without a clue to his name or clan, the Keiths could not seek retribution. What would Torrin do if he knew she'd witnessed his dark deed? She would put him and his clan in danger. He might then be more interested in killing her than marrying her.

Lightning flashed behind her, over the sea, and thunder rumbled.

"A storm is approaching," Torrin said.

"I can see that, but why would I want to allow you and MacBain within these gates?"

"MacBain isn't trustworthy, but I don't believe he means you or your clan harm. My men and I certainly mean you no harm." Torrin lowered his voice. "In fact, we'll act as guards. I've secretly assigned one of my men to each of his to keep a very close eye on them."

"What makes you think I trust you and your men any more than I trust the MacBains?"

He shrugged. "I ken trust has to be earned. And that's what I'm here to do—earn your trust." His expression was so sincere, she found herself wanting to believe him, but she knew too much about him.

"You have an uphill battle ahead of you."

"'Twill not be the first time." The determination in his eyes made her stomach ache and her pulse rate increase.

She switched her gaze to MacBain. Even though he was annoying, he didn't knock her out of kilter half as much as Torrin. "I don't want that bastard anywhere near me."

"He thinks you still carry a torch for him." Torrin sounded amused.

"Ha."

"Do you?"

Against her will, her gaze was pulled back to Torrin and his expression of dark humor. Why did he find her so entertaining? "Of course not. He's a scoundrel who has no inkling how to be faithful to one woman."

"Prove it to him, then, and mayhap he will leave you alone."

"What do you mean?" The fearsome wind off the sea blew her hair into her face and she pushed it behind her ear.

"Prove you think he is lower than a worm, that you despise him, and he will no doubt leave in a hurry." Torrin glanced up at the sky. "But to deny him Highland hospitality, especially during a storm, would bring you down to his level. You don't want to sully the MacKay name by being unfriendly to an ally, do you?"

She rolled her eyes. "How can the most notorious Highlander in these parts ask me that?"

"Notorious?" Torrin's eyes widened. "Me?"

"Aye. Who else would I be talking about?"

"Very well. I ken I have a reputation because of the battles I've fought, but that has naught to do with hospitality."

As far as she was concerned, his reputation had everything to do with the heinous deed he'd performed with cold calculation. Aye, she was certain it had been him, though they'd both been much younger.

"If you appear angry with him, he'll get the impression that you are still smitten with him. But if you seem bored with him, 'twill be clear you've forgotten him. 'Haps he will leave tomorrow. Who knows?"

She could only hope. "Will you convince him to leave tomorrow?"

"I'll do my best."

She prayed Torrin would leave at the same time. Aye, he was too disconcerting by far.

"Very well, but everyone must leave their weapons in the guard house," she said.

Torrin nodded. "Wise move." He winked.

Heat flashed over her like the approaching lightning… along with annoyance at herself that she would feel any sort of attraction to him. The longer she glared at him, the more pronounced his grin. He then turned to MacBain. "The lady has agreed we might enter, but we must disarm ourselves."

MacBain strode forward, his glare switching from Torrin to her, but he didn't immediately remove his weapons. His men scowled and muttered amongst themselves.

Loud thunder boomed out over the sea.

"Search them and make certain they are not armed, save for the knives they need to eat with," she instructed the nearby MacKay guards. "Your men may stay in the barracks this night," she told MacBain. "I'm certain you'll want to be on your way in the morn."

Gregor said naught, but his smug grin told her what he was thinking. He was going to try to win back her hand. 'Twould never happen.

The MacKay guards disarmed the men of both clans outside the gates, then allowed them entrance.

Her gaze darted to Torrin as he handed over his dirk and sword in the leather baldric. She hadn't remembered how tall he was, several inches taller than Gregor, who was about an inch shorter than Jessie. She'd always thought that was one reason he'd not been happy with her. He had to look up at her and likely felt like less of a man. She almost smiled.

She headed back toward the castle's entrance just as the first cold drops of rain spattered her hair and clothing.

Torrin fell into step beside her. "You look very pleased with yourself, m'lady."

"Nay. Why should I be, when two men I didn't want to see have shown up at the gates?"

With a hint of a smile, he sent her an amused glance beneath his dark lashes. If not for his past and what she knew about him, she could see herself being incredibly drawn to him. But obviously, he was not who he appeared to be. 'Haps he had a benevolent side and a monstrous side. Or maybe all the benevolence was an act.

When they entered the great hall, Jessie motioned Torrin and Gregor to the high table. "Please make yourselves comfortable and your supper will be served."

She had been almost finished with her meal earlier, when

she'd been interrupted. But even if she hadn't been, she had no appetite now. She directed the servants to bring their visitors food and drink. Most of the men, aside from Torrin and Gregor, would sleep in the barracks on the opposite side of the bailey. She headed up the stairs in search of the chambermaids. She would have them prepare two bed-chambers for the chiefs in a separate wing from where her own chamber was located. She could only hope they would behave themselves and remain in their rooms the whole of the night.

Gregor MacBain was like a thorn in her arse. She wished she'd never met the man at the Keith's residence. He'd seemed interested in her from that first meeting when she was nineteen summers, and she'd thought him a handsome man. Later, after she returned home to Dunnakeil, he'd sought her out and talked to her father about arranging a trial marriage. Her father preferred they have a legal and binding marriage, but MacBain wouldn't hear of it. He wanted a trial marriage because he needed an heir first and foremost. For that reason, he needed to know if she could conceive before the legal marriage took place.

Her father had gone along with it because MacBain was a chief and baron with impressive holdings to the south. Jessie had not known MacBain, except for the amicable façade he put forth. Being of marriageable age, she knew she would have to marry someone. She wanted a family, after all. MacBain had been her best prospect at the time, and she'd hoped they could grow to love one another.

In the end, she hadn't conceived, or maybe he simply hadn't tried hard enough. They'd shared a bed for three months during their time together, but she didn't know if that had been enough. Embarrassed that she hadn't conceived and feeling like a failure, she'd told people they'd only shared a bed three times.

MacBain had seen and fallen in love with another woman. Or more likely, it was lust. She didn't think the man was capable of deep emotion. But she hadn't known about the other woman for months. MacBain had met with her secretly.

Unfortunately, by that time, Jessie had found herself smitten with MacBain, and his rejection and desertion hurt her deeply. Realizing how naïve she'd been to trust him, she couldn't wait to wash her hands of the fickle man and go home.

'Twas obvious he was back now only for her dowry. She would've known that even if Torrin hadn't told her. MacBain had his heir, but now he wanted funds and more land. He would have to acquire them elsewhere for she would never agree to marry him, and Dirk wouldn't force her to. Dirk was an understanding brother who took her wishes into consideration. After all, he hadn't ordered her to marry Torrin, thank the saints. As far as she knew, Dirk already had an alliance with Torrin, and there was no need to arrange a marriage to solidify it.

Now, she saw that Torrin was just as persistent as MacBain, but she knew him to be twice as dangerous.

***

Sitting at the high table, Torrin glanced around the great hall at his men and MacBain's, but he didn't see Jessie. Where had she gone? He'd hoped she would eat supper with them, but mayhap she'd already eaten. It appeared most of the MacKay clan was finished as well, while they drank ale and talked to the newcomers.

Since Torrin had spoken to Lady Jessie at the gates—the most he'd ever talked to her—he was even more eager to spend time with her. He had not imagined the keen attraction between them. 'Twas real, and he didn't think it was one-sided either. Given her adorable blushes, darkened eyes, and fidgeting hands, he suspected he made her uneasy. He'd wanted to take her hands in his, kiss her knuckles and soothe her.

Thank the saints he'd convinced her to allow them entrance to Dunnakeil. Thunder exploded overhead and lightning flashed outside the arrow slit windows.

Aiden and other musicians played music to entertain them while they ate. At the moment, he was playing a lamenting bagpipe ballad about lost love. It reminded Torrin of when he'd been a lad, eating supper in the great hall of Munrick; their piper had often played the same tune. 'Twas a bittersweet memory, for Torrin had loved spending time with his brother and cousins, but he'd always been on edge, expecting his father to strike him down at any moment. The only time he'd escaped the frequent beatings was during the four years he'd fostered with the Stewarts. If not for that reprieve, he didn't know what he would've done. He might have turned out like his vindictive brother.

Torrin had heard Aiden play before and was just as impressed this time as he had been in the past at the lad's talent with any instrument he touched.

Torrin kept an eye on Gregor MacBain beside him. The man had already guzzled several goblets of wine, then he pulled out a whisky flask and downed a long swallow.

He caught Torrin watching him and gave a mock smile. "I would offer you some, MacLeod, but I only have a wee dram left."

"I have no hankering for whisky at the moment." He had to keep a clear head and protect Jessie from this scoundrel. No telling what he would do once the drink took hold of him.

"Where in blazes did Lady Jessie get to?" MacBain asked. "I want to dance with the lass."

"I have no inkling," Torrin muttered, then took another bite of the tender venison they'd been served. Although he'd love to see Jessie himself, 'twas probably best that she'd made herself scarce if the imbecile sitting beside him was going to harass her. He doubted Jessie would want to dance with MacBain.

"I'll not let her shun me. I'm going to find her." He pushed back his chair.

Damnation. Grinding his teeth, Torrin did the same and trailed after MacBain as he headed toward a narrow stairwell leading up. Torrin wanted to finish his meal, the best he'd had in weeks. MacBain staggered and grabbed onto the rope which served as a stair rail. This couldn't be good. He dragged himself up the stone turnpike stairway. Torrin followed, and although he wasn't trying to hide from MacBain, the man already appeared too sotted to realize he was trailing behind him.

"Lady Jessie!" MacBain bellowed at the top of the steps. "I have a gift for you, my bonnie lass!"

Coming up behind him, Torrin saw that Jessie stood in the corridor talking with a maid. The maid hastened away. Jessie placed her hands upon her hips. "Your room is almost ready, MacBain. But you must be patient."

He stumbled forward. "Nay, 'tis not that. I brought you something special." Awkwardly, he dug into his sporran.

Jessie's annoyed gaze darted to Torrin. A lightning flash through the narrow window lit her hair to flaming red and her eyes to bright sky-blue. Her vivid beauty snatched his breath and ignited excitement within him. How he wished this buffoon, MacBain, was not here. He'd do everything in his power to convince Jessie to allow him a kiss.

Her attention switched to MacBain who held up a pendant, dangling from his fingers.

"This is for you, m'lady." He bowed, then offered the pendant to her.

She crossed her arms over her chest. "I cannot accept any gifts from you."

"What? Are you mad, woman? 'Tis real gold and rubies."

"I'm not interested."

"You're still mad at me," he whined.

Torrin rolled his eyes. Had the man no pride?

"A thoussssand apologies," MacBain slurred. "Hope you can forgive me my past misdeeds."

"I forgive you, but I still cannot accept any gifts," she said, as if bored. "Please go back down to the great hall until your chamber is prepared."

Torrin grinned, glad she'd refused the pendant. Clearly,

she was a woman who could not be swayed by expensive gifts, and he admired her for it. He was starting to like her more with every moment he was in her presence.

MacBain let out an exasperated breath and unsteadily dropped the pendant back into his sporran while he wavered back and forth. "S-save it for later then. I'll change your mind, Jessss-ie. Just you wait and see."

"Nay, I think not."

"You protest too much. Come dance, bonnie lass." He staggered toward her.

"I'm too busy to dance, and too tired besides."

"Nonsense. Dancing will make you feel better." He grasped her hand.

She snatched it away. "Go downstairs to the great hall," she ordered through clenched teeth.

Torrin wanted to intervene and kick MacBain's arse back down the stairs, but considering what a strong woman Jessie was, she would likely want to take care of this problem herself. She had to make MacBain understand she had no interest in him, but considering how daft he was, 'twould no doubt take a while to get it through his thick skull.

"Only if you come with me." MacBain grabbed for her hand again, but she drew back and he teetered into the wall.

Torrin took a step forward, ready to seize the bastard if he became more aggressive.

"You're drunk, MacBain. Go into the guest room and sleep it off." Her face red, Jessie pointed at an open doorway.

"Nay. This is no time to sleep. 'Tis time for dancin'... and lovin'."

"You're mad," she muttered, disgust obvious in her low tone.

Torrin shook his head at how ridiculous the man was. "MacBain, leave the lady alone."

MacBain spun around and swayed, but caught himself just before he toppled sideways. "How long have you been there?"

"Long enough. Come. Let's go downstairs. You're being

a nuisance," he said in a reasonable tone.

"'Tis nay your concern, MacLeod! Leave us be."

"I'll not allow you to accost Lady Jessie."

"I'm not accost-ing anyone," he slurred. "This lady is my wife."

"Wrong!" Jessie said, blue fire blazing in her eyes with the lightning flash. "Go with MacLeod or I will have the guards toss you out into the storm."

"Och. You would treat me in such a way, m'lady?" MacBain whined.

"Indeed," she said firmly.

Torrin rolled his eyes. He'd never seen such a pathetic drunk.

MacBain sent her a glare, then Torrin, before wobbling along the corridor the way he'd come. Torrin followed him, then glanced back at Jessie. She was staring at him, or rather at his plaid-covered arse. Her gaze lifted, connecting with his. Her fiery blush was evident, even in the low candlelight of the corridor. She quickly turned and disappeared into the nearest chamber.

A thrill coursing through him, he grinned. Mayhap there was more hope than he'd realized. He was fair certain she had been eying his physique.

***

Later that night, an urgent voice broke into Torrin's restless sleep. "M'laird."

He opened his eyes to find Luag, the guard he'd posted in the corridor, with his head stuck inside the door and a lantern in his hand. Torrin sat up. "Aye?"

"MacBain left his room."

"Damnation." Torrin leapt up from the bed, still fully clothed for just this reason. "Where did he go?"

"That direction." Luag pointed toward the stairwell.

Torrin rushed after him. If the knave had it in his head to find Jessie's bedchamber, he would break his leg. Hopefully, he was only going in search of a garderobe after his excessive drinking.

A MacKay guard stood at the bottom of the steps.

"Which way did MacBain go?"

He pointed across the great hall to another stairwell that led up.

Torrin hurried up the steps and found another corridor and MacBain, carrying a lantern. He knocked at a door. Rage lit Torrin's veins on fire. Was that Jessie's bedchamber? If so, how had MacBain learned where it was? No one guarded this corridor at all.

"Hell," Torrin said under his breath. Why would she not have someone guarding her door with all these visitors about?

MacBain tried the door latch, and Torrin was ready to break the whoreson's neck. The door didn't budge, thank the saints. Jessie had barred it.

MacBain knocked lightly.

With no storm to cover the sounds of his footsteps this time, Torrin slipped from his hiding place and crept up behind the man.

"Who is it?" Jessie asked from the other side of the thick oak door.

"What are you doing, MacBain?" Torrin said over his shoulder.

The man jumped and turned at the same time, bumping hard against the door. "What the devil are you doing following me?" he growled. At least he seemed almost sober now.

"Protecting the lady," Torrin said, keeping his voice low. "What are you doing?"

"None of your concern. Leave," he commanded through clenched teeth.

Torrin shook his head, giving MacBain his most menacing look.

"Don't open the door, Lady Jessie," Torrin warned her. "MacBain was trying to pay you a midnight visit."

She yanked the door open and her glare in the dim light pierced each of them. "Go, MacBain. I don't wish to see you, day or night."

The man's narrowed gaze remained on Torrin, then abruptly he tried to barrel his way past Jessie, into her room. Torrin caught him by his shoulder-length hair and yanked him back. The man struck out but missed. Releasing him, Torrin punched him in the nose and sent him sprawling to the wooden floor with a loud crash. MacBain growled and muttered curses as he held his bleeding nose.

"Bar the door, Lady Jessie," Torrin warned with a quick glance at her. She wore a plaid blanket wrapped around her with only a sliver of her white smock visible at the top of her chest. He quickly switched his gaze away from the appealing sight, lest he become distracted. "I'll take care of this blackguard."

"I thank you." The door slammed and the bar clunked into place.

Torrin shook his head, glaring down at the imbecilic man. "Are you daft?"

MacBain drew his blood-covered hand away from his crushed nose. "You bastard, I thought you a friend and ally or I would never have allowed you to come here with me."

Annoyance twisted through Torrin. "You didn't *allow* me to do anything. I was on my way here before I ever met you."

"So *you* say."

"I consider the MacKays friends and allies. I'll not let you harm one of them, certainly not a lady."

"I'm not planning to harm her. Do you ken naught about seduction, man?"

Torrin snorted. "If you consider that seduction, your skills are greatly lacking."

MacBain merely glared and shoved himself to his feet. Muttering insults and curses, he stumbled away, holding his broken nose.

Torrin glanced back at Jessie's door, glad she was safe this time. But knowing how sneaky MacBain was, he'd have to be ever vigilant.

***

Jessie opened the door a crack and peered through. She

watched Torrin stride confidently toward the stairwell, marveling at his height, broad shoulders and lean waist. Of course, he was an impressive warrior, but what amazed her most was his protective nature. She would've never guessed it based on what she'd seen in the past.

Although she considered herself a courageous woman, she would never be brave enough to confront him about killing her foster brother. But now she wouldn't be able to rest until she knew the truth. What reason would Torrin have had to kill Lyall Keith?

Silently, she closed the door and barred it, thankful that Torrin had stopped MacBain from taking advantage of her. Not that she would've let the rogue get away with anything. But she'd hate to stab the man while he was trying to crawl between her sheets. Knocking him on the head would've been another option, but she preferred the broken nose Torrin had given him. She grinned.

What was she going to do about Torrin? She paced to the fireplace and added more peat to the coals. What if he decided to stay for days or weeks? She hoped he would stay at least until MacBain left. She appreciated him putting a stop to MacBain's plans.

After removing the blanket she'd wrapped around herself and spreading it over the bed, she slid under the covers, thinking how Torrin disturbed her on so many levels. When she'd first met him last winter, face to face, she'd been near speechless. Immediately, she knew that *he* was the one who'd executed Lyall. She would recognize Torrin's face anywhere —handsome as the devil and just as wicked.

Not only was he a frightening and lethal warrior, an image from her worst nightmarish memories, but she also felt herself strangely drawn to his sinfully attractive presence. How could she be drawn to someone she knew to be a killer?

Since then, she'd gone over and over what she'd seen that day eight years ago. Had she misunderstood it, misinterpreted it? Although she'd only been sixteen summers, she remembered the day clearly for 'twas the most terrifying, traumatizing day of her life.

When she'd heard the men approaching on foot, yelling curses and threats, she'd climbed the old oak and hidden among the branches and leaves. Knowing her bright red hair might betray her, she'd covered her head with her plaid *arisaid.*

The eight MacLeods—although she hadn't known who they were at the time—had chased her foster brother and his best friend across the hilly cattle pasture. They wore various weaves of dull plaids, which would help conceal them among the heather and bracken if they were deer stalking. But clearly they were not deer stalking; they were out for her foster brother's blood. They all carried broadswords, dirks, and targes.

Once Lyall stopped and faced his pursuers, Torrin and one other man had been the only two to approach Lyall and his friend. They were even in number and about the same age, early twenties, but 'twas obvious at first glance the MacLeods were larger and more skilled. Torrin was angry, growling low words that Jessie couldn't understand from thirty or forty feet away. Lyall had denied whatever it was Torrin accused him of. Obviously terrified of the taller man, Lyall had tried to run but Torrin hadn't let him. *Don't force me to stab you in the back*, Torrin had yelled. *Pick up your sword, face me and fight like a man!*

Fumbling, Lyall picked up the weapon while Torrin waited. Without warning, he charged Torrin, the sword aimed at his stomach and Jessie thought he actually might best him. But at the last second, Torrin used his own weapon to knock away the tip of Lyall's blade.

Lyall leapt back. Their blades clashed twice more, then, in two quick motions, Torrin knocked the sword from Lyall's hand and slit his throat. Moments later, his friend suffered the same fate at the hand of Torrin's second.

Holding her breath, Jessie had clamped a hand over her mouth and remained frozen in place. Not only was she terrified of being discovered, hiding in that tree, but also seeing her foster brother slain… she had never seen anything so gruesome. She could do naught to help him. She only had a small *sgian dubh* with her, and if she'd charged onto the field, she would've been butchered in a trice beside her foster brother. Those men wouldn't have left a live witness.

The strangers had quickly disappeared, leaving their victims' dead bodies lying where they'd fallen on the blood-soaked ground. Once Jessie, frozen in fear, could move again, she'd run back to the castle and told her foster father what had happened. She hadn't known at the time that the MacLeods were the culprits, because they'd worn no identifying clothing or plant badges. The Keiths could not exact the revenge they craved. And no one knew the motive for the strangers attacking. Would Torrin tell her if she asked? Or would her life be in danger if he knew what she'd witnessed?

Chapter Three

As they broke their fast, MacBain glared at Torrin MacLeod, sitting further along the high table in the great hall of Castle Dunnakeil. Although he didn't remember much from the night before, MacBain did remember the moment MacLeod had smashed his fist into his nose. Pain had slammed through his head and he'd ended up on the floor, half addled. His head still pained him this morn and his nose ached something fierce.

He'd not yet decided what he would do to MacLeod, but he would exact his revenge. The bastard had a ruthless reputation far and wide. Last year, he'd subdued two other, smaller clans and forced their allegiance to him. Would he do the same thing to the MacKays next? If only he'd brought more men with him, they could easily defeat the MacLeods. He'd have to warn the MacKays that Torrin MacLeod was here to subdue them and take over their lands. Much easier to do while their chief was away.

One thing concerned him even more than MacLeod's reputation—the way he was watching Lady Jessie. Every time she walked through the great hall, MacLeod's gaze followed her with great interest, even lust. The bastard had pretended he barely knew who she was. But now 'twas obvious that

MacLeod wanted her, too. He wasn't getting her! That was a certainty.

When MacLeod wasn't watching Jessie, he was eying MacBain in a highly suspicious manner. *Aye, you'd best not turn your back on me, you roguish whoreson.*

MacBain would simply have to stay until Dirk MacKay returned so they could work out a marriage contract. Even if it took weeks or months, he wouldn't mind. That would give Lady Jessie time to become smitten with him again. But with MacLeod in the way, that might be more difficult. He had to get rid of the lecher somehow.

***

"Have you seen Lady Jessie?" Torrin quietly asked one of the servants, then glanced back over the great hall. No one seemed to be paying him any mind. MacBain had gone outside moments ago.

"Last I saw her, she was headed up the stairwell, m'laird." The maid curtseyed.

"I thank you." Torrin climbed the stairs, wondering how Jessie had slipped past him. She had made herself scarce at breakfast and had not joined the others at high table, or any table. She must have grabbed a few bites in the kitchen.

MacBain's nose was crooked and red, and his eyes turning purplish-blue from the blow Torrin had gifted him with the night before. The other men had teased and ribbed MacBain because they knew Torrin had done the damage and why. Apparently, MacBain had told one of the men the night before and word had spread.

MacBain had done naught but glare while they broke their fast. Torrin had watched him closely, anticipating retaliation. Men had killed for far less.

Now, as Torrin walked down a narrow corridor and up another staircase, he wondered where Jessie was. If she was in her bedchamber, he wouldn't disturb her, but he did wish to speak to her. Clearly, she was avoiding him, though he was unsure why. He'd done naught to anger her. After last night, it should be clear that he wished to help her and protect her.

How could she fault him for that?

After searching the deserted top floor, he headed back down the spiral stair, only to come face to face with Jessie. She let out a squeal and jumped backward, tossing the blankets she carried and flinging out her arms.

Torrin caught her just in time. His hands around her waist, he tugged her back before she could fall.

"'Tis only me, Lady Jessie," he said in a calming voice and drew her to the safety of the level floor and away from the stair.

She released hard breaths, her hand pressed to her chest. "You scared the life out of me. What are you doing sneaking about up here?"

"I wasn't sneaking about. I was looking for you."

"Why?" Pulling back, she eyed him suspiciously.

"You didn't join us at breakfast." That was one reason, anyway. But mainly, he simply wanted to see her and talk to her.

"I was too busy, looking after the kitchen servants and what-not. Was Aiden not a good host?"

"Aye, of course. But he's not as bonnie as you." Torrin smiled.

Jessie's face flamed redder than her hair, then she knelt and stacked the plaid blankets. He picked up the one beside him and handed it to her as they stood.

"I thank you," she said, eyeing him.

"Why do you fear me?" he asked in a low tone so as to not frighten her further.

"I don't," she said firmly, defiance in her blue gaze. "I don't fear any man. I have more than one blade on my person at all times."

His gaze dropped to the foot-long Highland dirk he'd already seen, sheathed and attached to her belt. 'Twas the same size as his own and he had no doubt she knew how to wield it. Where else did she have knives hidden on her delectable, lithe body? When he imagined searching them out, his own body heated. "I hope you won't use them on me."

She lifted a brow in warning. "That remains to be seen."

Fierce arousal curled through him, surprising him. Since when did a dangerous woman excite him? Truth was he'd never known a woman like her. Now, he feared he would have fantasies about her holding him at knife-point and having her way with him. He ground his teeth to keep from grinning at that image.

Coming back to his senses, he asked, "What have I done to you that is so terrible?"

She narrowed her eyes and studied him for a long moment. "Naught. I'm simply not interested in any sort of marriage arrangement. Isn't that why you're here? Seeking a wife?"

Disconcerting heat rushed over him, and he cleared his throat. "I admire you for getting right to the crux of the matter," he said dryly. No other woman would speak to him with such boldness, and 'haps that was one reason he was intensely drawn to her. She had more courage than a lot of men he knew. "And, aye, indeed I'd hoped to get to know you, and allow you to get to know me."

"There is no point." She stepped around him and strode down the corridor.

Her tall, slender body and strong but graceful stride gave him hot chills. And that hair… red waves and braids halfway down her back. He yearned to see that hair spread across his pillow. She would be his wife; he could easily visualize it. Had been visualizing it for seven months. But how to convince her?

Mayhap they had something in common. She'd said she carried blades. Had she been trained in the art of warfare?

She disappeared inside a chamber… and screamed.

Torrin bolted toward the chamber, then slid sideways as he tried to stop at the doorway. "What the devil?" He saw naught in evidence that would frighten her. "Why did you scream?"

"I didn't scream," she said in a defensive tone.

He frowned, wondering if she had a streak of madness.

"I merely… cried out very briefly."

Aha. She would not want to display any weakness or vulnerability around him. "Why?" he asked, forcing himself not to smile as he sauntered further into the room.

"A pigeon was in here. The glass in the window is broken and the shutter is open." She motioned toward it. "The bird startled me, then flew back out. That is all."

"I see."

She headed across the room. "You don't need to slay any dragons for me, Chief MacLeod."

He grinned. "Nor break any scoundrels' noses?"

"Nay. None of those either." She deposited the blankets in a chest on the floor in the corner.

He paced to the window and gazed out over Balnakeil Bay, the cool sea breeze whipping at his hair through the broken glass. The water reflected the blue sky. Cliffs jutted out on either side of the bay and a sandy beach lay below where gentle waves splashed and slid onto shore.

"The weather is much different than it was last winter when I was here." He turned to look at her. "The view from here is beautiful." Although the scenery of the bay was lovely, it couldn't compare to her.

"Aye, indeed." Her attention was focused on pushing the trunk against the wall.

"Have you lived here at Dunnakeil your whole life?" Until last winter, he'd never visited Durness. Although he'd met Dirk and his father when they'd traveled south many years ago.

"Nay, I fostered with… another clan from the time I was seven summers until I was sixteen."

Jessie's stomach knotted for she'd almost forgotten who she was talking to. She'd come close to blurting out that she'd fostered with the Keiths. She could never let down her guard with Torrin, even though he was easy to talk to. While he seemed an honorable gentleman on the surface, she knew that deep down he was deadly.

"I fostered as well, but only for four years."

Fostering was a common practice among Highlanders. She knew the purpose was to form a network of clan alliances. Strange that their paths had only crossed one time prior to last winter.

She eyed Torrin and the thick chestnut hair lying on his broad shoulders. The way he steadily watched her with those perceptive evergreen eyes made her heart thump hard and her insides flutter. Was it fear or something else? A mixture of several conflicting emotions?

What in blazes was she doing alone in a bedchamber with him anyway? Although he didn't carry a sword or dirk at the moment, because she'd had all the visitors disarmed, he did retain his *sgian dubh*. And the small blade could be just as lethal as a large one. But strangely, although she knew she should fear him, she didn't. Each time she came face to face with him, she felt less afraid. Was she mad? She'd seen what he was capable of.

"I'd best check on the servants and see how midday meal is coming along." She headed toward the door.

"Do you enjoy archery?" he blurted.

She halted and turned back to him, wondering at his odd question. His green eyes gleamed with interest… in her. This awareness sent heat rushing over her.

"I've only tried it once," she said.

"So you only like the blades?"

She shrugged. "Why do you ask?"

"I could teach you how to shoot a bow."

That would be a wonderful skill to learn, but she knew 'twas only his ploy to get her alone and spend time with her. To allow her to *get to know him*. So she would want to marry him? Nay. Besides, she trusted him less than any man she'd ever met, other than MacBain. She shook her head. "'Tis unnecessary."

"It matters not. It might be fun."

She knew not what fun was anymore, though at one time she had enjoyed many pursuits. "People would watch, and I'm certain I'd be horrible at it."

"Nay, we'll slip away whilst no one is looking. You'll have no audience."

So, he was not ashamed to admit he wished to get her alone. She narrowed her eyes. "I don't think that would be wise, either."

"Bring a guard or two. Aye, bring two guards and a maid, for a chaperone. We'll have them turn their backs while you shoot at the target."

She could not figure him out. Was he a cold-blooded killer or a gallant bent on courting her? "I don't think 'tis a good idea."

His expression darkened. "We're alone here in this room and I'm not attacking you."

That was true, but mayhap he was trying to lower her guard.

"You don't trust me," he stated firmly. "Why? Do you think I'm like my brother, Nolan?"

Her heartbeat sped up. She'd not expected him to confront her about how she felt about him. And she certainly couldn't tell him why she didn't trust him. To do so could endanger her life. The Keiths would still seek revenge against him if they learned of what he'd done eight years ago. Lyall was to have been the next chief. And his father still burned with the need for retaliation and justice.

"I have no inkling," she said. "I've never met Nolan."

"He's an outlaw. And I'm sure Lady Isobel told you what he tried to do to her. I'm not like him in the least."

Aye, Isobel had told her plenty. Enough for her to know she wanted to have naught to do with the MacLeods. And yet, something about him lured her. The sensual shape of his lips, the intent male interest in his eyes, his tall, lean-muscled body. 'Twas only physical attraction—a dangerous physical attraction, for no corresponding emotion lay beneath it.

"I'm glad you're not like him. Well, I must see to the kitchen servants about midday meal." She moved into the doorway.

"Lady Jessie?" he said in an almost desperate tone.

Startled, she paused, eying him with suspicion. Why would he say her name in such a way? Was he desperate to gain her affection? "Aye?"

"I hope you know I would never harm you. I'm here to protect you." His tone was softer, warmer, and she almost believed him.

Why couldn't he have been someone else? Someone she hadn't witnessed at his most brutal.

She nodded. Strangely, she wished she could trust him. And maybe he was telling the truth now, but that couldn't erase what he'd done. "I thank you."

Male voices echoed down the corridor and loud footsteps pounded toward them. Sticking her head out into the passageway again, she saw MacBain and one of his men charging toward her.

"There you are, m'lady. I've searched the castle for you."

"Why?"

"Because that vile MacLeod is missing, too, and I don't trust the whoreson."

She glanced back into the room at Torrin, who made for the door, a thunderous expression on his face.

"Are you wanting your nose broken again, MacBain?" he asked.

"What the hell are you doing here, in a bedchamber, with Lady Jessie?" MacBain's face turned as red as his injured nose. The area around his eyes was a bruised blue color.

"'Tis none of your concern."

"I wholeheartedly disagree. I came to woo and marry this lady in a most honorable way. You are naught but a rogue set on using her and casting her aside."

"Ha. You are the one who used her and cast her aside!" Torrin accused. "'Tis clear to everyone you will do the same again if given the chance. On the other hand, my intentions are honorable."

Mortified by Torrin's candor in regards to MacBain using her, Jessie wished she could crawl into one of the trunks.

"Well… nay. I'm a changed man," MacBain said,

stretching his neck up as if trying to stand taller. "I have already apologized to her for my past mistakes. No one is perfect, not even you, MacLeod."

Torrin gave a derisive laugh and shook his head. "We'll let the lady decide," he said in a hushed tone.

"The lady has decided she is weary of this daft arguing." Jessie bypassed MacBain and headed toward the stairwell.

"Out of my way, MacBain," Torrin ordered.

Footsteps thudded on the wooden floor behind her. She quickened her pace down the stairwell, eager to be free of these two crowing roosters and have some time alone to think. Just before the last step, her foot caught in her skirts and she tumbled forward, her knee smashing onto the stone floor. Pain shot up her leg.

"Blast!"

"Lady Jessie?" Torrin exclaimed just behind her, then knelt by her side, his arm around her. "How badly are you hurt?"

"'Tis only a bruised knee," she assured him, trying to shrug off his strong, protective arm. Aye, the sensation of his arm around her was warm and comforting, but this only served to heighten her *discomfort*. She attempted to push to her feet.

"Here, let me help you." He removed his arm from around her and offered his hand instead.

Much as she was tempted to take his hand, she could not bring herself to. "Nay. I am well."

He released a breath. "Do not be so stubborn."

"What has happened?" MacBain thundered, standing over them.

"Can you not see? She fell," Torrin snapped.

"Allow me to help you up, m'lady." MacBain reached a hand down.

Annoyance verging on rage twisted through her. "Leave me be, MacBain!" she warned. "Go." She pointed toward the great hall.

"Very well. You had only to ask," he said in a petulant

tone and strode away.

"I'm so sick of him," she muttered, shoving to her feet.

A slight grin quirked Torrin's lips as he rose to stand beside her. "I am as well."

She chuckled at how ridiculous the situation was and Torrin joined in. She liked the sound of his deep laugh.

"Are you certain nothing is broken?" he asked.

"Aye, I'll send for the healer, but I'm sure 'tis only a bruise."

"If I caused you to fall, I'm sorry." The sincerity in his dark green eyes caused her stomach to knot, for she did not understand him. He seemed not at all like the man who had killed Lyall with a lethal mixture of cold calculation and blazing rage. Who was Torrin, really, deep down?

She shook her head, trying to clear her thoughts. "'Twas not your fault. My foot simply caught."

"Well, I hope you're going to your chamber now to have the healer check you over."

"Maybe." She didn't care for any man telling her what to do, even if it was for her own good.

He tilted his head, giving her a mock warning look with a potent dose of sensuality mixed in. "If you don't, I'll be forced to carry you there myself."

Heat and awareness burning through her, she started to tell him that he certainly would not carry her anywhere, but a young chambermaid approached. "Would you see if you can find Nannag and send her to my chamber?" Jessie asked her.

"Aye. Of course, m'lady." The maid hastened away.

Trying to ignore Torrin, she limped toward the great hall and the stairwell leading to her chamber.

"Do you have pain when you walk?" Torrin asked, following her.

"Not much."

"I'm glad. But you should rest for several hours."

She glanced back at him, raising a brow. My, he liked to order people about. But she knew it was only because he was trying to be helpful.

"Do you need help getting to your chamber?"

"Nay. I thank you."

The last thing she needed was Torrin MacLeod carrying her to her bedchamber. She knew not how to perceive him, and the more she talked to him the more confused she became.

***

Just as gloaming was turning to night, Haldane MacKay disembarked from a galleon at Thurso with his fourteen men. From here, they'd take a smaller galley or *bìrlinn* along the north coast to Durness. He smiled, loving the idea of slipping up on *his clan.* They would regret making him the clan outcast and welcoming that bastard Dirk as their chief.

It had only been three days since Haldane and his men had left Inverness and escaped his cousin, Keegan MacKay, and the rest of them. He'd had Lady Seona, the love of his life, in his arms, but then they'd snatched her from him. He would kill Keegan slowly and torturously when he showed up in Durness, making Lady Seona a widow, then he would marry her. Donald McMurdo would kill Haldane's oldest brother, Dirk, as he'd been paid to do, long ago, and the chiefdom would be Haldane's, as his mother and father had always wanted.

If his annoying sister, Jessie, or his whiny brother, Aiden, got in his way, they would be killed, too. Any of the MacKay clan who didn't vow their allegiance to him would be dead.

Haldane fingered the leather pouch of silver and gold coins beneath his doublet that McMurdo had stolen from Dirk over a fortnight ago. It was lighter than it had been; he'd spent a great amount hiring men, some of whom had already died in skirmishes with the MacKays and their allies. But he was determined this money would last long enough for him to take over Castle Dunnakeil.

Behind him, a quarrel broke out amongst his men. When he turned, one scruffy whoreson had his dirk pressed against another's throat.

"Halt! What the devil are you doing, Ferguson?" Haldane

marched back toward them, a lone torch on the deserted docks lighting his way.

"This mangy cur MacGillie besmirched my ma's good name."

"Release him or you'll not get your pay. I didn't hire the lot of you miscreants to kill each other, but to kill MacKays. If you're all dead before we reach Dunnakeil, who's going to fight them?"

Ferguson lowered his blade.

MacGillie smirked and muttered a couple of words under his breath that Haldane didn't catch.

With a quick flick of his wrist, Ferguson slashed out and cut MacGillie's throat. Dark blood spurted from the gash.

"Damnation!" Haldane said, rage consuming him. "Kill that bastard," Haldane told McMurdo, beside him.

The old highwayman, with his long gray hair and scarred, pockmarked face, stomped into the fray. He slit Ferguson's throat in two seconds flat and shoved him to the ground beside his dying companion.

Haldane glanced around, hoping no witnesses lingered nearby. He saw no one in the dusky gloaming, other than his own men. "Leave them where they are. The rest of you, if you kill or even attempt to kill anyone else in this group, this is what you'll get. Do you ken?"

They all nodded and cast wide-eyed looks at each other and the men bleeding to death on the ground.

"Go see about hiring a *bìrlinn*," Haldane said to McMurdo. "And I'll search for more men to recruit to replace these two bastards. We'll likely need several more to defeat the MacKays."

McMurdo nodded and strode off to do his bidding. Haldane liked that the old man rarely questioned anything he told him. And that he was a ruthless killer. Haldane had learned much from him over the past several months.

Now, he was so close to getting everything he wanted he could hardly stand it. All he had to do was kill his brother, his cousin, and maybe his sister, if she tried to stop him from taking Dunnakeil.

Chapter Four

Looking out an open upstairs window, Jessie couldn't help but glare at the spectacle below her in the bailey—grown men acting like stags during the autumn rut. Instead of locking antlers, Torrin and MacBain charged each other with dull swords. At least the weapons were said to be dull, so the men wouldn't kill each other accidentally. Although she had authorized this training session, she was starting to regret it, because at times it looked far too real.

With a fearsome grimace and a loud growl, MacBain rushed Torrin, who easily evaded his blade.

"What's going on here?" a deep voice yelled through the portcullis.

Who was that? At first she thought it might be some of the MacKays returning from their long journey. But, nay, she didn't recognize the dark-haired man revealed by the late afternoon sunshine.

Everyone stopped and stared. Torrin stepped back several paces but kept MacBain within his sights.

"Iain Stewart, is that you?" Torrin called.

"Of course." The man drew close to the iron bars, his

smile evident.

"What the devil are you doing here?"

"Ran off and left me while I was passed out, aye? Some friend you are. I couldn't resist hunting you down and watching you make a damned fool of yourself." He chuckled.

Torrin glanced around, looking a bit chagrinned, his eyes meeting Jessie's for a couple of moments, then he headed for the portcullis. Until he'd glanced up at her, she hadn't realized he knew she was watching.

Who was Iain Stewart, and what had he meant about Torrin making a damned fool of himself? Courting her?

"I hope this skirmish here isn't serious, but if 'tis, I've arrived just in time," Iain said.

"'Tis called practice," Torrin said, then turned to face her again. "Will you allow this knave entrance, m'lady? Although he is a scoundrel of the worst order, I claim him as a foster brother and a friend… sometimes."

"Who is he?"

"Iain Stewart, heir to the chiefdom of Stewart and Barony of Appin."

"Aye, if he allows Erskine to disarm him," she said. He didn't seem like the type who would cause trouble, but she could take no chances with so many different clans visiting, and MacBain being contrary.

Torrin gave a courtly bow, then faced his friend again. "You heard the lady. Give up your weapons."

"Gladly. But I want in on this practice session. Looked like you were losing. And by the way, I have four men with me." He motioned them forward.

"They must all disarm themselves," Torrin said.

More men? 'Twas a good thing their storeroom shelves had been stocked full not long ago.

While the newcomers were removing their weapons, Jessie noticed MacBain whispering to a couple of his men. What was he cooking up? His dark, malicious expression changed to a forced friendly one when Torrin introduced Iain Stewart to him.

"Been at this for days, have you?" Iain asked, eying MacBain with his swollen nose and black and blue eyes.

MacBain clenched his jaw and narrowed his eyes, but made no comment.

"Don't tell me you two are vying for the same lady's hand." Iain grinned, turning to Torrin.

"Not exactly."

Iain laughed.

"Enough talk, MacLeod," MacBain said. "Let's get on with the practice."

Everyone stepped back, leaving Torrin and MacBain in the center of the circle. MacBain launched himself at Torrin instantly. Torrin scrambled to deflect the blade slashing toward his chest.

Jessie held her breath. Though she didn't trust Torrin, neither did she wish to see him hurt or killed.

The practice was quickly shifting from a mock battle to a real one. Should she order them to stop? Would they even listen to her? What if someone ended up dead before this was over?

Jessie raced down the steps, across the great hall, and out into the bailey. She pushed her way through the crowd of male spectators. The two men were in the heat of battle, their blades smashing and clanging. No matter that the weapons were dull; they could still kill. Someone grabbed her arm, holding her back.

"Halt!" she yelled.

Torrin paused, his gaze darting to her. MacBain swung his blade again. Torrin leapt out of the way at the last second, but MacBain continued his assault.

"MacBain! That's enough," she ordered.

But he wasn't listening. His face was a red mask of rage.

"Keep her back," Torrin said.

Erskine held onto one of her arms. "I'm sorry, m'lady, but you must stay back. You'll be hurt."

"Make them stop," she demanded, terrified beyond all reason that Torrin would be killed or hurt badly. But Erskine ignored her just as the other men did. If Dirk were here, he'd order them to cease their battle. What if one of them died while she was acting as lady of the castle? Was it not her responsibility to keep the peace and make sure everyone was safe?

In the next second, a sword flew into the air and Torrin caught the hilt of it. To her surprise, he stood before the slack-jawed MacBain and held up a sword in each hand.

"I win," Torrin said in a dry tone.

Several men laughed and a raucous cheer went up. Not from the MacBains of course; they merely glared, some of them red-faced. His look of shock fading, MacBain glowered at Torrin and those celebrating his victory.

Relief surged through her, and Erskine released her. She wasn't celebrating anyone's victory; she was simply glad no one had been killed. She disliked the way men competed, and she especially hated them fighting over her. Though no one said that was what this *mock* battle was about, she knew it was. Each of them wanted to look superior to the other. The more powerful stallion.

They were ridiculous. She turned and strode back into the great hall.

***

"What the devil have you gotten yourself into, Torrin?" Iain asked in a low voice, as the rest of the chuckling men disbursed in the bailey, leaving them alone to talk. Torrin glanced about for Jessie, but didn't see her, though she had been there minutes ago, demanding that they halt their practice. He was fair certain that she'd been afraid he was going to get hurt. He grinned. That meant she cared a wee bit.

Iain snorted. "Saints, you're madder than a stag in rut."

"I have no need for your lowly opinion on it."

"Who is this MacBain, and why is he so irate with you? I'm certain the bastard was trying to kill you."

"You guessed the right of it. He's trying to win back Lady Jessie's hand, and I'm always getting in his way." Torrin smiled. "You see, they were handfasted for a year and a day, three years past, but he sent her away. Now, he's back for another go, but Lady Jessie wants naught to do with him."

"Canny lady."

"Indeed."

"And beautiful."

"Keep your eyes off her," Torrin warned in a mock severe tone.

"Ha! I couldn't help but look. She stormed through the crowd like a goddess of fire, demanding that you stop the fight."

Satisfaction curled through Torrin. "Aye, clearly afraid I'd be injured."

Iain shook his head. "So, she is smitten with you already, is she?"

"Not quite, but I'm gaining ground."

"Well, you have naught to worry about from me. I would never try to steal your lady."

"I ken it well."

"Why did you hasten out of Lairg so quickly while I was sleeping off the drink?"

"Well, you had that lovely milkmaid with you, and I figured you had better things to do than watch me court a lady."

"Nay, I do not. I sent Mary back to her cows. I'm certain this will be grand entertainment, especially since both your offers of marriage to Lady Jessie have been refused."

Torrin narrowed his eyes. "Laugh at my misery if you will, but I'm determined in this. She will agree to marry me before this is over."

Iain grinned. "I've never seen you so smitten with a lass."

"Nay, you haven't."

"Well, when do I get to meet her?"

***

Jessie stood near the stairwell to the kitchen, overseeing the male servants setting up the tables, as everyone gathered into the great hall for supper. Torrin and his newly arrived friend entered from the bailey and strode toward her. Torrin's friend was only an inch or two shorter than him and built like a trained warrior, although she remembered Torrin had said he was Iain Stewart, heir to the Stewart chiefdom. He wore a belted plaid of a weave she'd never seen before.

Torrin's intense green gaze lit on her. "Iain, I'd like for you to meet Lady Jessie MacKay."

"'Tis an honor to meet you, sir." Jessie curtsied.

"The pleasure is all mine." Iain grinned, his dark blue eyes gleaming with humor. He kissed her hand. "I beg of you, m'lady, please do not break this man's heart." He slapped Torrin on the shoulder. "He's been in a lovesick stupor for months."

She sucked in a surprised breath, heat racing over her, head to toe. *Lovesick?* Surely he exaggerated.

"Bastard," Torrin said under his breath.

Iain snorted with laughter.

"Might I escort you to the high table, Lady Jessie," Torrin asked, offering his elbow. "'Twill be best if you sit far away from Iain."

She took his arm, hoping her fiery blush would subside soon, but her fingers pressing into the hard muscles of Torrin's arm, just above his elbow, ignited another type of heat within her. She was not yet accustomed to touching him, and she found that every time she did, her body reacted in disturbing ways.

"You would deprive me of this lovely lady's company?" Iain protested behind them as they proceeded to the dais.

She was not used to so many men's attention or the compliments they doled out, especially in the last three years. The disaster with MacBain had made her shy away from men. But now, she found she liked the attention, though it made her uncomfortable.

Torrin pulled out a chair for Jessie, then took the one beside her.

"You cannot get rid of me that easily," Iain said, sitting beside Torrin.

"Sometimes he reminds me of a leech," Torrin murmured aside to her.

She gave a slight smile but grew uncomfortable beneath his perceptive gaze. "I thank you for preventing any bloodshed today. I think MacBain went mad for a few minutes."

"Indeed, he was possessed of a battle rage." Torrin shrugged. "Truth is… he wants rid of me in the worst way so he can get to you, but I intend to protect you from the knave."

She didn't truly want Torrin acting as her shield, but she was grateful to him. Still, she could've handled MacBain on her own. "I feared the practice would get out of hand." She glanced down at the low table where MacBain sat with his men—unusual, for he usually sat at the high table as was his right by rank. He gave Torrin an evil look which concerned her greatly.

Supper was served. All the men were especially boisterous with their outlandish stories mixed with plenty of drink. Two men, a MacKay and a MacLeod, acted out the skirmish that had happened earlier, except they used the wee lads' wooden swords and added a more dramatic and entertaining finale. Laughter abounded.

Jessie was too worried to laugh. MacBain and his men remained sullen and kept to themselves at the end of one table. They often had their heads together, no doubt planning some sort of revenge against Torrin.

"You're quiet," Torrin said beside her.

"Are you not concerned that MacBain might stab you in the back when you least expect it? You embarrassed him, and he's likely to seek revenge."

"I'm ever vigilant, and I have good bodyguards." He glanced at the two men standing behind him.

That was all well and good, but 'twas doubtful he could have two bodyguards with him every moment. And what if MacBain and his men attacked at a time when Torrin was outnumbered?

"I'm truly flattered and honored that you're so worried

about my safety, m'lady," Torrin said.

Warmth spread over her. "I simply don't want any bloodshed here at Dunnakeil."

Lifting a brow, he gave her a charming, lopsided grin, obviously seeing through her lie.

She focused on eating and pretended to ignore him, but her awareness of him grew more acute with each passing moment, just as the struggle within her grew more annoying. Of a certainty, he was attractive, but was he a good man or a malicious man?

Jessie excused herself and slipped away to the kitchen. Aside from Torrin making her tense, the great hall was too loud, and now Aiden was playing his pipes, which sometimes screeched at her nerves. She simply craved calmness and quiet, the splash of the sea's waves and the wind rustling through the grasses.

While the men were eating tarts, drinking ale, and listening to Aiden's music, she slipped out the kitchen door, through the postern gate, then hurried down to the golden sand beach. One of her knees was black and blue from her fall the day before, but walking did not pain her.

How much longer would the MacBains and the MacLeods remain at Dunnakeil? She was sick of them vying for her attention. She had been as cold as possible to MacBain, but naught dissuaded him. Short of insulting him and telling him to leave, she had little recourse.

As for Torrin, she could not decide how she felt about him. Every time his green gaze caught hers, something mysterious passed between them. His eyes and faint, enigmatic smiles told her he was a sensual devil. Sometimes she imagined what his lips might feel like on hers. One part of her hated such musings, while another was fascinated by the idea.

She stopped and gazed out over Balnakeil Bay. The sunset was a blend of yellow and orange with wee traces of red at the edges. Incredibly beautiful. She smiled, then imagined Torrin standing beside her, admiring it. She shook her head, ousting that daft thought from her mind. He created too many conflicting feelings within her. She didn't understand him. On the one hand, he seemed like a good man, honest, protective, but on the other, she knew what she'd seen all those years ago. It was him who'd chased Lyall and killed him. Of course, Lyall had a sword, but 'twould have been clear to anyone he didn't have a chance against the taller and stronger MacLeod, who'd had no mercy on him, even after he'd disarmed him.

Every time she remembered what she saw, horrid, gruesome feelings overtook her… which did not now fit with the Torrin she had gotten to know over the past few days.

On the beach, she strode toward the cliffs and headland, trying to walk off the tension and confusion. Faraid Head, where Dirk had almost been murdered many years ago, was two miles out. She never walked that far; the high cliffs made her dizzy. The beach here at Balnakeil Bay was far more pleasant. She also loved the beach at Sango Bay with its huge boulders jutting from the sand and would sometimes walk the two miles there to spend a few hours when no one would miss her. With so many guests about now, that was impossible to do.

A thump sounded behind her in the dunes. She turned, seeing naught but the long green beach grasses blowing in the wind. The waves crashing and sliding onto shore with the incoming tide covered most sounds. Sea birds were always about, screeching. The thumping sound could've been a red stag stamping his huge foot. Sometimes she saw them or their tracks on the beach.

How she missed her sweet old deerhound at times like this. Ossian had died just over a month ago. He had been her constant companion, especially anytime she went outside. In truth, she missed him all the time for he'd been a good friend since she'd returned from the Keiths years ago. Certainly more trustworthy than any potential husband she'd ever met.

Few people here at Dunnakeil knew she'd been betrothed when she'd been staying with the Keiths the summer she was eighteen. Of course, her father had approved and signed the documents, but when the groom had run off the night before the wedding, hardly anyone spoke of it afterward.

Was something wrong with her? Was that why men deserted her? Nay. They were all daft sheep. She had no use for any of them. To her, a husband would be like a noose around her neck. Strangling. And then he would kick the block from beneath her feet, leaving her hanging while he ran after some other woman.

She continued forward, past her brother's galleys, their polished wooden hulls gleaming in the golden light of sunset. Where were Dirk, Isobel, Keegan, and the rest of their party now? She had truly not wanted to travel south with them, mainly because she knew they were going to stop at Torrin's keep. But now he was here, which was worse, and he didn't seem inclined to leave anytime soon.

Every time she looked into his eyes, things whirled around inside her like mad. Not just fear, but also attraction. Aye, she'd been highly aware from the evening she met him that she found him physically appealing. But that couldn't change what she'd seen him do all those years ago. Had he murdered anyone else since then?

Running footsteps approached, thumping across the sand. Her heart vaulting into her throat, she yanked her dirk from the scabbard at her waist and turned. Four men charged her, surrounding her. MacBain's men.

"Stay back!" She forcefully slashed her weapon at the closest one. He jumped back, but two more rushed her from the left. She stabbed the blade at one of them, but missed when he leapt out of the way. The other grabbed her arms from behind.

"Let go of me, you bastard!" Still having some movement, she spun the dirk in her hand and jabbed her weapon backward into his gut.

He howled into her ear and shoved her away. "The bitch stabbed me! Grab her dagger!"

She kicked the man in front of her in the groin, sending him sprawling backward and slashed at the next man to approach. She cut his sleeve and he scuttled away.

"Where is that cowardly MacBain?" she yelled. Was he so afraid of her he would send in all his men and remain hidden himself?

Surprising her, another man grasped her knife hand in a strong grip, twisted it behind her back and squeezed her wrist. Pain shot through her arm. She swung her leg around behind, hoping to hook it behind his knee and knock him off his feet, but she missed.

"Bastard! Unhand me!" Grinding her teeth in determination, she held onto her dirk. But the pain in her arm became overwhelming. "Nay!" She could hold the weapon no longer and it dropped to the sand. She screamed and yelled, hoping to alert the MacKay guards posted on the ramparts.

"Calm down, sweet Jessie." 'Twas Gregor MacBain's unnerving voice. He came around from the right and stopped in front of her. One of his men still held her restrained.

"You bastard! What do you want from me?" she demanded.

"I'm not going to hurt you. I but want to marry you so we may have a lifetime of happiness." He gave her a broad smile which was clearly false.

"Do you think this is going to cause me to want to marry you? Nay, just the opposite."

"A lot of men kidnap their future wives. It has a long history of success in the Highlands," he said, his grin now smug.

"Not here. All you want is my dowry, and the land my brother will give you. You don't care one whit about me."

"Now, you ken that is not true, m'lady. I care a great deal about you," he said in a placating tone.

She knew he was lying, for he'd only shown up again after he'd gotten wind of her increased dowry. Why had Dirk done that? Did he want her married off so badly to whoever was greediest? That was the same reason Torrin had come.

He was land-hungry, too. Although 'haps not as much as MacBain.

"Come quietly and no one will be harmed." MacBain glanced over his shoulder, toward the castle. "Bring her to the horses," he told the man restraining her.

MacBain led them between the sand dunes, the high grasses providing extra cover from anyone who might be watching from the castle's battlements.

She screamed again as loud as possible. "Help! Help me!"

"Be quiet," MacBain said through clenched teeth. "You leave me no choice." He dragged a handkerchief from inside his doublet.

"Nay!" She shoved her knee upward into his groin.

"Umph!" He doubled over clutching at his stones, which she had hopefully smashed into dust.

She tried to twist from the other man's grip, but his hands only tightened on her wrists.

Raising up, MacBain slapped her hard across the face. "You witch! Don't you ever do that to me again."

Pain sliced through her cheek. One thing he could be certain of—if he forced her to marry him, she would soon be a widow, for she would kill him.

"Edward! Help him hold her," he commanded.

MacBain's two men held her firmly in place while MacBain tied the gag through her mouth. Ugh! It tasted salty with his sweat. Gagging and coughing, she bent forward, hoping she didn't actually vomit.

"Bring her this way," MacBain said.

She pretended to comply for a couple of minutes. When she felt her captor's hands loosen a tiny bit around her wrists, she elbowed him in the stomach and yanked her arms. One of her wrists slipped from his grip. She wrenched away from him and ran through the dunes, her feet digging into the soft sand.

"Capture her!" MacBain ordered.

Tugging off the disgusting gag and throwing it, she raced through the grasses and gorse bushes, thorns tearing at her clothing and skin, leaving burning scratches. Her right foot sank deep into the sand. She stumbled and fell to her knees.

Blast!

"Ha!" One of the men on her heels grasped her *arisaid* from the back. "Got you, lass."

She slid her hand to her ankle and pulled the small *sgian dubh* hidden there from the sheath. She turned and stabbed his shoulder.

"Ow! Bitch!"

Two more men joined him, tackling her to the ground, almost crushing her beneath their combined weight. One yanked the knife from her hand.

"Get off me!"

"Don't force us to hurt you," MacBain warned, standing somewhere over her while the others held her face-down, the sand cutting into her cheek. She wanted to hurt him. Badly.

"Release me! I refuse to marry you. You cannot force me."

"Aye, indeed, I can." He chuckled. "I only need tell the minister we were in a trial marriage which was consummated. You ken how they hate those trial marriages and want them made legal and binding in the eyes of God as soon as possible."

"That makes no difference." She kicked at one of the men. "No minister would agree that this sort of abuse is allowed."

"I'm not abusing you. Only disciplining my disobedient wife. You're the one hurting yourself by fighting us. Tie her hands and her ankles and carry her to the horses."

"What the hell are you doing?" a deep and forceful male voice demanded.

Who was that? From her position on the ground, Jessie turned her head and looked up at Torrin, standing among the grasses, sword drawn, Iain Stewart beside him.

Two of the MacBain men drew swords. Considering how well-armed they were, all of them had clearly obtained their swords as they'd exited the portcullis at Dunnakeil.

"You stay out of this, MacLeod!" MacBain ordered.

"Nay," he said with deadly calm. "Release her or suffer the consequences."

MacBain laughed. "You only brought Stewart with you. You're outnumbered."

"I knew you were a whoreson the moment I saw you," Iain said.

Two of MacBain's men launched into action, engaging Torrin and Iain in swordplay.

When both of MacBain's men fell, her captors fled.

"Where the devil are you going?" MacBain yelled.

"I'll get them!" Iain chased after the two cowards.

With her hands and feet tied, Jessie could do naught but roll upon the ground like a worm.

Torrin charged MacBain and their swords clanged, sparks popping in the gloaming. MacBain yelped, but she couldn't see if he'd been cut. Torrin was the aggressor, driving MacBain back, but he ran to her other side.

How she wished she could get her wrists untied, or the bindings cut.

Blades clanged multiple times. Someone cried out. A sword flew over her head, and she glanced back to see what had happened. MacBain fell to the sand and Torrin stood over him, the tip of the sword at his throat. A sudden fear seized her and she felt transported eight years into the past. 'Twas like seeing Torrin's sword just before he'd slit the throat of her foster brother.

"Don't murder him!" Jessie yelled.

Torrin sent a quick, dark glance her way then focused on MacBain again. "Should I listen to the lady? Or rid the world of some vermin?"

MacBain held his hands over his head. "I'll go and… and leave Lady Jessie alone," he proclaimed in a desperate voice.

"In truth?" Torrin asked. "Or is this just another lie?"

"I speak the truth. If you let me live, you nor Lady Jessie will ever see me again."

"If we do see you again, I'll take that as leave to kill you.

Get up. We're going back to the castle."

"What about my men?" He motioned to the two lying on the ground.

"You'll have to tell the rest of your cowardly men to come back and fetch them… if Iain let them live."

More of the MacLeods burst through the bushes and grasses, their breathing elevated. "Sorry we didn't arrive sooner, Chief."

"'Tis all under control," Torrin said. "Gordon and Sim, go find Iain and MacBain's two men. They went that way. Luag, see to those lying on the ground."

They did their chief's bidding. One of the MacBain men lying on the ground stirred and groaned. Luag announced that the other was dead.

"Struan, tie MacBain's hands behind his back and take him to the dungeon." Torrin motioned to Gregor, then cut the strips of cloth binding Jessie's wrists and ankles.

"I thank you," she said, sitting up. She was so grateful for his help, she wanted to embrace him, but she controlled the urge.

"Are you hurt?" He took her hands and drew her to her feet.

"Naught but a few bruises and scratches."

"Aye, you have a dark bruise. Did someone hit you?" He surprised her by touching her face.

She started to draw away, but the hot, tingly feel of his fingers sliding over her cheek halted her action. "'Tis naught." She feared if she told him MacBain had struck her, Torrin would kill the man before they reached the castle. "I'll survive."

When he lowered his hand, she was shocked at how much she missed the warmth of his touch.

Even in the dimness of gloaming, she found it difficult to meet his intense and intimate gaze. She so appreciated his help at this moment she couldn't express it or even comprehend it.

"I was on the ramparts when I heard you scream," he

said. "I was praying it wasn't you, but I suspected MacBain was up to no good."

She nodded. "I was merely taking a walk on the beach when his men grabbed me."

"'Tis not safe for you to walk on the beach or anywhere alone now."

"Mo chreach," she muttered under her breath for she loved the outdoors and nature. Walking on the beach was one of the few pleasures left to her. And she refused to allow MacBain to take that away from her.

"My men will escort them off MacKay lands tomorrow, but who knows if he will return? I believe not a word he says."

"Nor do I." Her dirk came to mind and she glanced about, but then remembered she'd dropped it on the beach. Had one of the MacBains picked it up? Her *sgian dubh* should be nearby. Since it was a dark metal, 'twas too dark to see it easily now.

"What is it?" Torrin asked.

"I lost my dirk and my *sgian dubh*."

"I'll help you find them tomorrow."

The MacLeods disarmed the MacBains and bundled all the weapons in a large piece of canvas. 'Haps her knives were among them. If not, she'd have to search the dunes and the beach in the morn, with Torrin's help.

He offered his arm.

"I'll manage on my own," she said, dismissing his offer of help through the dunes, grasses and bushes. It wasn't that she didn't want to touch him—she certainly did. But she was already anxious and on-edge, and he would only make her more so. She was too aware of him and his lean, iron-hard strength. Every time she was near him, her heart pounded harder and her hands grew jittery. What was wrong with her?

They made their way back to the castle, Jessie trying not to touch Torrin or bump into him. But she felt his attention on her. As they walked single file through the bushes, he glanced back at her several times. Making sure she was safe?

His attentive protectiveness confused and perplexed her. Was he truly such a good man? Or was he pretending so she'd let down her guard? She didn't see how he could be a good man after the ruthless way he'd killed Lyall Keith. Though he had let Gregor MacBain live when she'd asked it of him.

As they entered the bailey, she saw by the light of the torches that her clothing was ripped from the thorns and her skirts and sleeves filthy with sand. Her face was also likely dirty. Placing her hand against it, she felt the grit of sand and tried to brush it away.

Concerned clansmen and women inquired whether she was injured, as did Iain, Aiden, Uncle Conall, and several others.

"Nay. I thank you but I am well," she assured them.

Once in the great hall, Torrin asked her, "Could I speak to you in private?"

Och, nay. What now? She did not wish to spend any more time alone with him. Already her nerves were frayed, and it had less to do with the kidnapping attempt than with her rescuer. "Might I change clothes first? I'm filthy."

"Aye, of course." He didn't appear any worse for wear and certainly not as if he'd been in a skirmish. He bowed, then she hastened toward the stairs.

Once Jessie had given herself a sponge bath and her maid, Dolina, had helped her dress in clean clothing and straightened her hair, she descended the steps again.

What on earth could Torrin wish to speak to her about in private? They had been alone, for the most part, on their way back to the castle. Why hadn't he talked to her then? This must be something more important.

When she entered the great hall, he rose from the bench where he'd been sitting, talking to his friend, and approached her. His penetrating gaze swept over her quickly, then came to rest on her eyes. "You look lovely, and except for that bruise, not like you were attacked less than an hour ago."

Her face and chest heated. "I thank you."

"Is there a private place we might talk?"

"Aye, the library," she said, taking a lit candle from a nearby table and leading the way into her brother's official meeting room, off to the side of the great hall. She lit the candelabra on the table while he closed the door.

She faced him, realizing she should offer him a seat, but she didn't feel like sitting herself. And if he was going to talk about marriage again, she wanted to be able to make a quick escape.

"I want to thank you again for rescuing me," she said. "I don't know what I would've done if you hadn't come along."

He gave a brief bow. "There's no need to thank me. I only wish I could've reached you sooner."

"You arrived just in time. 'Tis all that matters."

"I'm glad you weren't hurt too badly. But I must ask… why you said what you did when I bested MacBain?" His expression shifted to that dangerous one she'd witnessed on a few occasions, though never directed at her.

"What do you mean?" She searched his face, trying to figure out what he was talking about and why he was almost angry about it.

"*Don't murder him.* That's what you said when I was holding the blade to MacBain's throat."

"Oh." Jessie drew in a deep breath, her stomach twisting and tying in knots as she tried to compose a reasonable excuse in her head. "I… I simply didn't want any more death. MacBain is a chief and if you were to kill him, there would be consequences. The MacBain clan would no doubt attack the MacKays in revenge."

Torrin crossed his arms over his broad chest, eying her with needle-sharp interest. "Why did you use the word *murder* instead of *kill*?"

Chapter Five

Jessie watched Torrin cautiously, scarcely able to breathe, her heart thundering in her ears. Why had she let him stand between herself and the library door? *Mo chreach.* She glanced down, remembering she had not yet retrieved her dirk, and she only had two blades on her person at the moment. One was strapped high on her thigh, and a smaller one was sewn into the hem of her *arisaid.* She could not get to either of them easily.

But deep down she believed Torrin wouldn't hurt her, no matter what she might say. He'd rescued her from MacBain, after all. Could she tell him she knew he'd killed her foster brother all those years ago? Could she ask him why? Or would it be a grand mistake? Taking a deep breath, she forced herself to be courageous.

"Because… I know. I saw what you did," she said, watching Torrin's face closely.

He frowned. "What are you talking about?"

"Eight years ago in Caithness. On Keith lands."

Torrin's eyes narrowed upon her, giving her that lethal look. "What did you see?"

She swallowed hard and forced herself not to retreat a few steps like she wanted. He must not know how much she feared him. "I saw you murder Lyall Keith."

Torrin shook his head, his eyes reflecting sadness instead of anger or guilt. "I didn't *murder* him," he said in a calm tone. "He'd raped and murdered my sister. 'Twas justice."

Disbelief struck Jessie, knocking her back a step. "What? Lyall did that?"

"Aye. Besides, he had a sword. 'Twas a fair fight."

His unruffled composure confused her, turned everything she knew on its head. Was he telling the truth?

"Did you know him well, then?" Torrin asked.

"He was my foster brother. I fostered with the Keiths for several years. And afterward, I went back to visit often."

"Saints," Torrin hissed. "All I know about him is he was a rapist and a murderer, and my sister wasn't the only one to suffer at his hand."

How could this be possible? She had always thought Lyall kind and trustworthy. "Maybe there was a mistake. How do you ken 'twas him?"

"'Twas no mistake. My sister lived for two days after the bastard raped and beat her. Allina had several injuries and lost a great deal of blood." Pain glinted in Torrin's eyes. "She told us who did it. We'd both met Lyall Keith a week or so before. You see, I'd taken her to stay with our aunt near Lairg. Keith was staying there, too, along with several others. Allina had a mare she was mad about, and she'd gone out to the stables one evening to give her an apple. That's when the Keith bastard and his friend captured her." Anger glinting in his eyes, Torrin shook his head. "When I went back to bring her home, they said she'd disappeared and had been gone all night and half the day. I took a search party out looking for her. We found her knocked out and almost dead in the nearby wood. She was covered in blood and bruises. She was so pale," Torrin said in a near whisper and closed his eyes briefly, no doubt seeing her and reliving the horror of the moment.

Held within the grips of shock and Torrin's palpable emotions, Jessie held her breath.

"We took her back to my aunt's home where she awakened for a short time and told us who'd done this to her," he continued. "We also found a button from the bastard's doublet there in the wood with her, carved with the Keith crest. How I wish I'd come a day earlier so I could've stopped them," Torrin growled through clenched teeth. "I would've torn them limb from limb."

When she imagined the pain and terror his sister must have endured, tears filled Jessie's eyes. And to see his raw pain clawed at her own emotions.

"I am sorry. I didn't know," she whispered.

"Nay. How could you?" he asked in a calmer tone. "I didn't want to kill him. 'Twas what had to be done. The clan and my father expected it. Demanded it. As the future chief, I felt it was my responsibility. Sometimes the only law or justice in the Highlands is our own. If we'd taken it to the authorities, 'twould have been a dead woman's word against the Keith chief's son. Who do you think they would've believed?"

Jessie nodded, knowing that without a living witness to the crime, Lyall would've likely gotten away with the murder. But clans didn't allow such injustice. They took the law and revenge into their own hands. An eye for an eye.

"As I'm sure you recall, we had a skirmish," Torrin said. "He had a weapon and 'twas a fair fight. I'm not to blame for him being a bad swordsman."

Jessie wiped at her eyes. "You're right." Still, she couldn't fathom Lyall doing something so brutal as raping and killing a young woman. Jessie hadn't known him at all.

"Where were you?" Torrin asked.

"In the oak tree. I was fond of climbing trees."

His expression lightened. "How old were you then?"

Her face heated. "Sixteen." Too old to be climbing trees, but she loved them so much she did it anyway.

He gave a curious frown. "You didn't report us?"

"I didn't know who you were. I told them what you

looked like but I didn't know which clan you were from."

"Well, we were careful to hide our identities and our trail. Will you report us now?"

"Nay." She knew the answer without thinking about it. "If Lyall truly did what you said, then he got no worse than he deserved."

Torrin's gaze lit on her again with penetrating realization. "That's why you've been terrified of me the entire time. You thought I murdered your innocent foster brother."

She nodded.

"What do you think now?" he asked.

"I'm not certain."

"Do you believe me?"

Jessie gazed deeply into his eyes as if looking into his soul, and Torrin loved the sensation of it. Her blue eyes were much softer now, and damned if he didn't want to grab her and kiss her. But he must not. He'd had no inkling that anyone, aside from his own clansmen, had been witness to what he felt was justice being served. Certainly, he couldn't have simply let his sister's murderer go unpunished and free to kill others. And it wasn't just the murder, but also the vicious rape and torturous beating he'd given her. No woman should ever be treated in such a way, certainly not his innocent young sister.

"How old was she?" Jessie asked.

"Allina was seventeen summers. Very beautiful. All the lads were smitten with her." His eyes burned and he shook his head. "She was incredibly kind, loving, and helpful to everyone. She didn't deserve such a horrid end. I'll never understand why." Even his abusive father would not lay a hand on her.

Jessie bit her lip. The tears glistening in her eyes struck him on a deep level. She was a compassionate person, and she understood how he felt. He'd never wanted to hold her as badly as he did right now. But he couldn't. 'Twas too soon. She must trust him first.

"I cannot fathom Fate, or why God would allow such

suffering and injustice," he said.

"None of us do," she whispered. "But I can understand why you did it. I know if someone were to murder Aiden or Dirk, I'd want to kill them, too. I'm not saying I would but..."

He nodded. Though he often saw her as a warrior princess, he now knew she was too compassionate to kill anyone, unless forced to, and he loved that about her. "For men, 'tis often different, especially for those of us who have been in battles," he said. "Usually 'tis a case of kill or be killed, you ken? Those are the choices."

"Indeed."

"I hope you won't hold it against me any longer."

She shook her head, but he still saw the uncertainty in her eyes. 'Twould take time to build trust, especially after what she'd believed about him. He could be patient and prove he was truthful and honorable. And he would start with how he dealt with his new enemy.

"I thought we would hold the MacBains in the dungeon until the morn, and then my men will escort them off MacKay lands. Do you agree?" he asked.

"Aye, of course. I never want to see Gregor MacBain again."

Those words thrilled him, but Torrin suppressed a grin. "I'm glad to hear it. I'll tell my men." He moved toward the door.

"Some of the MacKays may want to go with them tomorrow."

"That would be good."

Leaving the room, Torrin felt victorious—jubilant, even. Finally, he knew what was keeping Jessie from him. He hadn't even minded confessing. He was a warrior, a soldier, and as such he sometimes had to kill enemies. 'Twas the nature of it. He wasn't proud of it, but he also wasn't ashamed. Often, he had to do things he didn't want to, but he did them for the sake of his family and clan.

Most of all, he was happy that Jessie understood, that she

could imagine the agony he'd gone through seeing his sister so horribly beaten and dying right before his eyes. Jessie was a caring, intelligent woman—one he was starting to cherish even more than ever before. It wasn't just a physical attraction anymore. Sometimes, when he looked into her beautiful blue eyes, he could hardly breathe. He feared she was capturing his heart.

***

MacBain ground his teeth as he was escorted from the dungeon by one of the MacLeods, his stomach growling because he'd refused to eat the moldy old bread they'd been given to break their fast. Torrin stood in the courtyard, waiting, tall and conceited as if he thought himself a prince. MacBain would see him suffer for all he'd done. And now 'twas obvious to him Torrin MacLeod was after Jessie. Well, he was not going to get her, no matter what MacBain had to do.

"Don't give them their weapons until they're off MacKay land," Torrin said, sending a cocky glare his way.

"Whoreson," MacBain muttered under his breath, but too low for anyone to hear. He knew when to keep his mouth shut. He also knew when to strike out in revenge. 'Twould be soon.

Two of the MacLeods nodded and mounted up. Ten heavily armed MacKays were also waiting in the courtyard. When the guard behind MacBain unlocked the manacles binding his hands, he swung up onto his horse and walked it toward the portcullis.

Where was Jessie this morn? He glanced toward the entrance to the great hall but saw no sign of her. If she wouldn't marry him, then he would make certain she never married anyone.

***

Jessie rushed into the great hall and skidded to an abrupt halt. She'd slept late and the tables were full to overflowing with those breaking their fast. Torrin sat at the high table with Aiden, Iain and several others. With his gaze locked on her, Torrin arose and pulled out the chair beside him.

When she realized how badly she wanted to sit there, heat rushed over her. Still unsure whether or not she trusted him, she cautiously made her way forward. She had gotten little sleep the night before as she'd thought about what Torrin had revealed to her, and what she remembered from eight years ago. She prayed he had told the truth, but there was no way to know for sure.

"A good morn to you, m'lady," Torrin said with a slight bow.

"Good morn." She sat, still feeling overheated.

Iain, sitting on Torrin's opposite side, also greeted her.

"How are you feeling? That bruise on your face is darker," Torrin said.

"'Tis naught. I'm only a bit sore from the scuffle."

"I found your dirk and *sgian dubh* this morn," Torrin said. "I'll give them to you after the meal."

"Oh, I thank you. Were they damaged?"

"Nay, they're in good repair and sharp as razors."

She smiled and a servant placed a wooden bowl of thick oat porridge before her. It held a generous chunk of melting butter and honey, just the way she liked it. With a wooden spoon, she stirred it and asked, "What of the MacBains?"

"Just after daybreak, two of my men and ten MacKays headed out with them."

"Was there any conflict?"

"Nay. All were well-behaved. Since they're outnumbered and unarmed, I'm thinking they'll be as sweet as wee lassies until they reach the MacKay border."

She wondered at his analogy and found it amusing. "Not all wee lassies are sweet."

Torrin snickered. "Surely, you cannot mean yourself."

"I've been told I was a hellion at seven summers."

He grinned. "I can well imagine that… considering what a hellion you are now."

Her mouth dropped open and he laughed, his eyes darkening in an enticing way.

Iain leaned forward, frowning. "Do you not ken 'tis not polite to laugh at a lady?"

Torrin got his amusement under control… barely, his green eyes sparkling with mischief. "I doubt that a hellion would like a polite man."

Heat washed over her and she imagined her face turning as red as her hair. She ate and tried to ignore him. 'Twas impossible, of course, but she could pretend.

Torrin leaned closer. "Pray pardon, Lady Jessie. But I do love the way you carry plenty of weapons about."

Ha. He probably detested it, for it meant if he tried anything, she could well defend herself. She'd best change the subject before the conversation embarrassed her any further. "Do you think MacBain will return?"

Torrin sobered. "'Tis possible, so we must be ready. And because of this, I think it best that I stay until Dirk and his company of men return."

Iain leaned forward. "I'll stay too, m'lady. You'll need me to protect you from this rogue."

Torrin snorted. "You're daft. I've been naught but a gentleman."

"Well… I thank you both for staying to help us. I fear we've angered MacBain greatly and he may seek revenge."

"'Tis true."

The longer Jessie sat beside Torrin, the more aware of him she became. His manly scent of leather, the great outdoors, and the familiar mint soap made here at the castle near entranced her. Somehow, he made the soap smell different and more compelling. His height, the broadness of his shoulders and his overall presence also distracted her from her meal. She could've been eating sand and would not have known the difference.

Her hands jittery, she devoured the porridge as quickly as possible and arose from the table.

"You cannot be finished already," Torrin said.

"Aye, I always eat a light breakfast. Pray pardon, but I must see if the kitchen servants are keeping on task."

She hastened away and down the stairs. In the stone-vaulted kitchen, she glanced around, seeing that everyone was completing their duties, just as they always did. The heat of the kitchen fires was intolerable on her already overheated skin. She exited the doorway into the walled kitchen garden and deeply inhaled the cool breeze off the sea.

She did not understand her reaction to Torrin this morn. She felt as if she'd been in an oven. Of a certainty, she had always been drawn to him against her will. But now that she no longer believed him a murderer, she found him far more appealing. 'Twas as if an invisible barricade had been knocked down. The sensation of sitting next to him had been too intense. She knew not how she would react if he touched her.

His cocky, confident smile and teasing manner tempted her more than she could believe. He could make her smile and blush without any effort at all. Closing her eyes, she remembered and relished everything about him.

"M'lady?"

She jumped and her eyes popped open to find Torrin standing beside her in the doorway. His enticing scent surrounded her.

"Saints! You startled me." And now she was overheating again, even though the morning air was cool.

"I have your weapons." He held up the dirk in one hand and the *sgian dubh* in the other.

"Oh. I thank you." How daft she was to be so unhinged by his presence that she'd forgotten all about her beloved knives. She took them, her fingers brushing against his. The extreme warmth of his skin compelled her to glance up. He watched her with great interest from beneath lowered lashes.

The smoothness of his skin told her he had shaved that morn, and she found herself wanting to stroke her fingers along his jaw line. But her hands were full of weapons. She focused on those and slid the dirk into the sheath that hung from her belt. Next, she bent and, lifting her skirts a wee bit, placed the smaller *sgian dubh* into the sheath strapped above her ankle.

She straightened, appreciating the slight weight of the blades. They gave her more confidence. "That feels better."

Torrin gave a slight, lopsided grin. "Never heard of another woman who loves weapons as much as you do."

She shrugged. "I suppose I'm odd."

"Nay, fascinating and unique."

A blast of heat rushed over her and she lowered her gaze from his scorching one. "Well, I thank you… and I must get back to work."

But he did not move from the doorway so that she might pass. "Surely, you don't still fear me," he murmured.

"Of course not." Nay, 'twas not fear that seized her now, but some foreign sensation she had rarely, if ever, felt before. She did not know the name of it or why it should take hold of her when she was near Torrin. Her hands became unsteady, her heart thudded, and her stomach flipped and fluttered like a crazed bird.

With his dark and observant eyes, he appeared to be trying to read her thoughts. She refused to hold his gaze for more than a couple of seconds; she didn't want him to know her true thoughts. She didn't understand them herself and needed time to think everything through.

"If you would excuse me, Laird MacLeod."

"Please call me *Torrin*."

Again her gaze darted to his challenging one, then away. Of a certainty, she knew he wanted to be on an intimate, first name basis, but she was not sure she wanted to be. Not because he was a murderer, but because he was a man like any other. A man who wished to marry her for her dowry. The only men she trusted were those in her clan.

"Very well," she said.

"Look at me, Lady Jessie," he whispered, placing his fingers beneath her chin and lifting it gently.

Her first instinct was to jump back away from him, but his warm touch captivated her as did his dark, bewitching gaze.

She tried to hide her reaction and that deep down

something that flared to the surface whenever he was near. Instead of removing his hand, he slid his fingers along her jaw line and leaned closer. Her breath stopped and her pulse pounded in her ears.

From six inches away, he searched her eyes. After a moment, he frowned thoughtfully, then drew back, dropping his hand. "I don't want you to fear me."

She didn't fear him, but that didn't mean she wanted him to kiss her. Did it? A kiss from him would no doubt be the most sinful thing she'd yet experienced. But she couldn't indulge. What if he turned out exactly like MacBain? What if she trusted him, fell for him, and then he tired of her? Abandoned her? She could not handle that kind of rejection again.

"Pray pardon." She pushed past him and into the kitchen, but did not remain there. She needed time alone to think.

***

Torrin watched Jessie disappear into the castle. He wanted to follow her and make her see that he was trustworthy. *Saints!* He'd come so close to kissing her, but at the last moment, the fear and alarm in her gaze had stopped him. 'Twas the last thing he wanted to see.

At times, he thought he glimpsed desire in her eyes, or at least a hint of interest. But then something would happen to scare her. She must come to him willingly. He didn't want to force anything upon her, certainly not a kiss.

Besides, he didn't want just a kiss from her; he wanted so much more. A lifetime. Sometimes, when he looked into her eyes, he could see it all, a wonderful future for them. But perhaps 'twas only his active imagination.

He was further disappointed when she didn't appear in the great hall during the midday meal. He didn't go into the kitchen again, searching for her. Clearly, she was avoiding him, and 'haps he should give her some time. Maybe he'd frightened her more than he'd realized that morn.

An hour after the meal, from the ramparts, Torrin spied Jessie sitting on the beach in the sand, her red hair as bright as a flame in the early afternoon sunshine, although most of her was hidden by a large clump of grass. He wasn't overly concerned about her safety, since MacBain and his men were on their way south under heavy guard.

But when Jessie hung her head and wiped at her eyes, he frowned. Was she crying? What the devil?

He made his way down multiple sets of winding stone steps and outside to the beach. Quickly, he strode toward her.

Indeed, when she glanced up at him, her face was wet with tears and her eyes were red.

"Lady Jessie, has something happened?" He dropped to his knees in the soft sand beside her.

"Och." She dried her eyes with a handkerchief, then wiped her nose. "Nay. 'Tis naught for you to be concerned about."

She refused to meet his eyes, but she looked incredibly sad. Was she already in love with someone and that was why she had no interest in him?

"You miss… someone?" If there was another man, he had to know.

She stared down and bit her lip, obviously trying to stop her tears. But it didn't work. She again cried quietly into her handkerchief.

He wanted to put an arm around her and comfort her, but he didn't think she would appreciate that. Instead, he sat beside her on the warm sand and sucked in a deep breath of the salty sea air. If her heart was broken because a lover had left her, he wanted to be the one who was there for her.

"My dog died last month," she said. "He just got old. His name was Ossian, and he was a deerhound. He always went for walks on the beach with me and… everywhere."

"Och. I'm so sorry, lass." Although he was sad she'd lost a beloved pet, he was glad she was not crying over a lost love. Even more now, he yearned to put his arm around her and draw her close, but he feared that would be too much too soon. So he kept his hands to himself.

"I know I'm daft, getting so upset over losing a dog, but

he was my best friend these last eight years."

"'Tis not daft at all. 'Tis indeed heartbreaking to lose a close friend or family member, whether human or beast. I had a dog I loved more than anything when I was a lad, and when I lost him, it almost killed me."

"I'm sorry to hear it."

"I didn't want anyone to know how hurt and sad I was over losing him. I feared they'd see me as weak. I'd walk along the loch or up a hill to be alone so I could cry my heart out." 'Twas true, and this was the first time he'd told anyone.

"'Tis good to know that men cry, too."

"Aye, we do; we just don't want anyone to ken it."

She nodded and drew spirals in the sand with a stick. The sea breeze whipped at her hair. He did naught but enjoy the simple moment in her presence. 'Twas a comfortable silence that stretched out between them. He felt closer to her at that moment than ever before. But he also wanted to take away her sadness and see her smile. He wasn't even ashamed to make a fool of himself to do it.

"Although I'm not too furry, I could be your new deerhound. I could go with you for walks on the beach and protect you."

She gave a short, tear-filled chuckle. "You're mad."

"You could tell me all your troubles, and I would simply watch you with my big sad eyes."

She glanced at him. "You don't have big sad eyes."

"I wouldn't even mind if you scratched me behind the ears or rubbed my belly."

She half-heartedly threw the stick at him and tried to hide her smile. "You are horrid."

"'Tis true, but I made you smile." When she didn't respond, he said, "I could go back and get my bow and a few arrows, then we could walk along the beach that way." He pointed toward the right. "And I could teach you archery. If I don't behave myself, you can shoot me or use one of your hidden blades on me."

She sent a confused frown his way. "Why are you so

determined to teach me how to shoot a bow?"

He shrugged. "I think you would be good at it. You're tall; you have long arms. You remind me of a warrior princess."

She gave him a narrow-eyed look as if he were daft. "Living in a make-believe world, are we, MacLeod?"

He smirked. When it came to her, he likely did, but he couldn't stop himself. "Well, you're always threatening me with those hidden knives you carry on your person at all times. I would truly love to see if you ken how to use them like a warrior."

Lifting an auburn brow, she sent him a challenging look. "You don't believe I can use them?"

"I have no inkling. I've never seen you in action. By the time I came upon you and MacBain, you were already trussed up like a—" He clamped his lips closed.

"Like a what? A boar?"

"Nay, like a tall, elegant stag."

She snorted and leapt up. "Come. I'll show you. We'll go to the end of the beach, near the cliffs where your guards upon the ramparts cannot help you."

He laughed. "Saints! You must indeed be deadly."

"I've hurt a few men but never killed anyone."

"'Tis a great comfort to me," he said in a dry tone and stood, smiling at her cocky attitude. "I'm up for the challenge, m'lady. But surely we aren't going to fight with sharpened blades. I don't wish to hurt you either."

She chuckled and headed along the beach.

Using long, quick strides, he caught up with her. "Are you certain you don't wish me to go back for the bow and arrows?"

"Thinking you'll need an extra weapon to defeat me?" she asked.

"Ha. Not likely."

She gave a confident smile, and he was glad he'd been able to turn her mood from gloomy to merry. He hoped this would be only a wrestling match, where she ended up pinning him to the ground—he'd let her do that. Aye, indeed. His body went on high alert, for he'd long imagined what her slight weight might feel like upon him. Like a dream come true.

"We'll have to use sticks instead of real knives," he said, trying to focus on the issue at hand and not his growing arousal.

"You fear me?"

"Aye, indeed," he said in a wry tone.

She laughed.

He'd love to know where on her body she had the rest of those hidden knives secured. He wanted to take them off her naked body, one by one. How delicious that would be.

"I often see red deer coming from that direction." She pointed toward the grassy sand dunes to their right.

Unexpectedly, Torrin tripped over something, and someone shoved him from the back at the same time. His face plowed into the sand. "What the hell?" The words blasted from his mouth. Spitting out the salty sand, he quickly rolled to his back and grabbed the dirk from the scabbard on his belt. He froze when he didn't see a band of attacking outlaws. Only Jessie stood above him, grinning like a banshee. Of course, he'd known she was the only one near, but he couldn't believe she'd gotten the best of him like that. Damned if she wasn't strong. His warrior skills were slipping, or mayhap he'd simply been distracted with his fantasies of stripping her naked.

"You tripped me!" he accused.

"You mean, I tricked you." Her smug smile was clear, even with the blinding sunlight behind her.

He narrowed his eyes. "Proud of yourself, are you?"

She shrugged, and he pushed to his feet. He'd have to be more careful around her. She was more wily than he'd anticipated. He glanced back at the castle, hoping Iain nor any of his men had witnessed that. He'd never live it down.

"You don't fight fair," he muttered.

"Most Highlanders don't. We're too canny. Fighting fair

will get you killed, you ken?"

He laughed, then faced her with his arms down at his sides. "Are you ready to try it again, then, lady warrior?"

"Nay. I prefer surprise attacks." She backed away from him, moving further along the beach.

He knew what he had to do and 'twas naught more than she'd asked for, knocking him to the ground like that. He ran toward her, his body hunched low.

She screamed and bolted like a deer, flying over the sand. He quickened his pace, caught up to her and grabbed her. With one arm wrapped around her waist, he lifted her off her feet.

Kicking and elbowing, she fought him. He grasped her right hand so she wouldn't grab one of those knives. He hoped she wouldn't stab him, given the opportunity, but he didn't know for certain. She was a hellion… and he loved that about her.

She hooked her heel behind his knee. Losing his balance, he dropped to the sand, taking most of the impact with his shoulder and hip, but he didn't let go. Having captured both her wrists in one hand, he pinned her to the ground, half on her side and half on her stomach.

"Aha," he said against her ear. "Now we're even."

"Don't be so sure, MacLeod," she said through clenched teeth.

Something slammed painfully into his arse. Glancing around, he saw she'd kicked him hard with her bare heel.

He grabbed her ankle and pinned it close to him with his leg, then he tickled her foot with his free hand. She shrieked and squirmed about. With a sudden hard shove backward with her whole body, she flipped him onto his back. He tightened his grip on her wrists.

"Bastard!" she growled like a she-wolf and tried to untangle herself from him.

He laughed but feared she might get the best of him if he gave in to the amusement. He rolled her beneath him again.

She giggled but tried to scream at the same time.

Squirming, she twisted and contorted her body, trying to wrest herself free. All she accomplished was turning to face him a bit more.

Her face was flushed pink, her eyes a glaring flash of blue, while her lips were scrunched with determination.

Damnation, how he wanted to kiss her. But she might break his nose if he did. He chuckled, amazed at how the thought of a violent woman aroused him. He had always thought he wanted a sweet, biddable wife. Now he knew he wanted one who would knock him to the ground unexpectedly.

"Admit defeat, warrior woman."

"Never!" One of her sharp elbows speared him in the stomach.

"Omph. Truce!"

She laughed. "The mighty MacLeod brought down by a mere woman?"

Releasing her, he leapt to his feet. "You are no *mere* woman, but a fierce and formidable one."

She smiled proudly, stood and dusted off her skirts. Her confidence was another thing he loved about her. Her rosy lips teased and taunted him. Again, he was staggered by how badly he wanted to kiss her, but he would wait until she was ready for it.

"I would like to learn to shoot a bow," she said, surprising him.

"Good." Now he simply had to figure out how to convince her to kiss him.

Chapter Six

After a trip to the castle to retrieve his longbow and half a dozen arrows, Torrin and Jessie headed along the beach again. Even though the sun was warm, the cool breeze off the sea kept the day from being hot.

Jessie glanced at him briefly, thinking about their earlier wrestling match on the sand. She had never imagined he would be as playful as a lad. He was a formidable chief, for heaven's sake.

She hadn't realized she was playful either. He must have brought it out in her.

Earlier, when he'd told her about how he'd also lost his beloved dog, she'd suddenly realized, deep down, that he was not that different from her. Of course, he was a man, a chief, and a fierce warrior, but he still had a heart. He was human, just like everyone else. Not the monster she'd always imagined him to be.

Still, just because she'd enjoyed talking to him and rolling about on the sand like a couple of bairns didn't mean she wanted to marry him. She didn't yet know him well, and she didn't wish to fall for another man who would desert her.

But she had to admit, when he'd had her pinned to the ground with his strong, lean body, the heat of arousal had singed her. It had been a long while since a man had touched her. And Torrin was more attractive than most. The wicked thought of what he might look like naked seared through her mind.

Jessie, you wanton wench. Though mortified at her own thoughts, she couldn't help wondering if the muscles of his arms, chest, stomach, and thighs were as sculpted as they'd felt pressed against her. Every part of him had been hard. She had even thought at one point, when his sporran had slid aside, that she'd felt that completely male part of him pressing against her.

The fact that he'd been aroused and hadn't kissed her or tried to seduce her told her much about his character. Aside from that, 'twas clear he'd almost kissed her that morn outside the kitchen, but he hadn't. Why? Had he known she wasn't ready?

Maybe he could be trusted. She glanced up at him again, taking in his steady green gaze, high forehead, solid, angular jaw and chiseled lips. Of a certainty, he was a charmer and a lady's man. He had no doubt seduced dozens of women. He could be the type who indulged in a tryst for a night or a week, then fled. She had no interest in men who changed their minds as often as they changed their shirts.

"Have you shot a bow before?" he asked when they neared the end of the beach close to the cliffs.

"I tried once but was so bad I gave up."

"Och. Never give up."

She smiled at his fierce gaze. "What will we shoot at?"

"This." He held up the short length of near worn out plaid, then pinned it to the high, vertical sandbank with two sharp sticks.

He moved back about fifty feet and she followed to stand beside him. She couldn't help but admire his strong, dexterous hands, long fingers, and muscular forearms as he strung the six-and-a-half-foot bow. Given the warmth of the day, he'd left his doublet at the castle and rolled up his sleeves. Though she tried not to stare at him and his physique, 'twas impossible to ignore his impressive arm and shoulder muscles that shifted beneath the ivory linen shirt.

"Here." He handed her a glove made of thin leather. "You'll need this to protect your fingers."

"Won't you need it?"

"Sometimes I shoot with it, sometimes without. 'Tis likely my fingers are tougher than yours."

She nodded and held the glove while watching him, trying to ignore how warm the leather was from his body heat.

He withdrew a thirty-inch arrow from the quiver. "You nock the arrow like this," he said, placing the feathered end of the arrow against the string while also pulling it back. The front of the bow curved gently. "Most men who have been shooting their whole lives don't take aim. They simply look at the target, and when they release the arrow, it goes where they intended. But since you're just starting, you may want to sight down the arrow and take aim. Line everything up. If there is a fiercely strong wind, you need to take that into account."

"Wind? There is never any wind in Scotland," she said wryly.

Sending her a richly sensual glance, he chuckled. Did he like it when she teased? After drawing his hand back even with his jaw, he released the string and let the arrow fly. It plunked into the plaid in the middle of a green square where two red lines crossed. The sandbank behind the cloth stopped the arrow.

"Now, you're going to tell me 'twas the middle of that square you were aiming at."

"'Tis exactly the one." He grinned and handed her the longbow. "Now you try."

After pulling on the glove, she took an arrow from the quiver and felt very awkward nocking it into the bow. Standing behind her right shoulder, he helped her position it. With great effort, she pulled the waxed linen string back, but not as far as he had. Her arms were shorter than his, and she didn't possess his strength.

"Sight down the arrow," he murmured in an intimate tone that scattered her thoughts for a moment.

Forcing herself to focus on aiming at the target, she let loose the string. The arrow sailed through the air but plowed into the sand a foot in front of the target.

"Och! You see. I'm terrible at this."

"'Tis your first try. We all miss on our first shot. Besides, the bow is a bit too long for you. 'Twas custom built for me with a long draw. Let's move forward a couple of feet."

"'Tis embarrassing," she muttered.

"Nonsense."

Of course, he was more muscular than she was; naturally his shots would be more powerful and the arrow would go farther. She'd always considered herself physically strong, for a woman, but she could never be as strong as he was, with his hard, defined muscles. She had never seen them nor run her hands over them, but she could see a bit of their bulk beneath the sleeves of his shirt, and when he'd had her pinned to the ground earlier, she'd felt them with her body.

"Try again." He handed her another arrow.

Once she had the string pulled back, he stepped in behind her and placed his hands over hers, helping her pull back the string a bit farther. "Now, we're hoping to put the arrow into that green square beside my arrow. This is where I would aim." His warm breath tickled her ear and she suppressed a shiver. "Now, hold it just there, and I'm going to remove my hand from the string."

When he did, her muscles started quivering. She released the arrow. It flew toward the target and *thunked* beside his in the green square.

"You see! You did it perfectly," he said with pride.

"With your help," she conceded.

"I'm glad to help." He observed her with a pleasant, amused expression just shy of a grin.

Her face heated and it had naught to do with the sun. She hated blushing. With her red hair and fair skin, 'twas not becoming.

"Try again," he suggested, handing her another arrow.

She took it and nocked it, determined to prove she could do this. Did she want him to be proud of her? Perhaps so. But mostly she didn't want to look the fool in front of him. She aimed as he had, pulled the string back tight until her muscles ached, then she released it.

The arrow flew faster than her first one and stabbed into the target two inches below the other two arrows.

"Excellent," Torrin said in an astonished tone. "You've made quick progress."

"I thank you." She gave a playful curtsy.

When the sunlight dimmed, Jessie glanced up and noticed thick black clouds approaching from behind the cliffs. "We'd best go back," she said over the rising wind and handed him the bow. She had been so focused on learning to shoot the bow—and on Torrin—that she hadn't paid attention to the sky.

He surveyed the clouds above. "Aye."

After he quickly gathered the arrows and plaid target, they took off at a brisk walk. Moments later, great rain drops splattered Jessie's hair and clothing. Blowing sand stung her face and hands. She sped up to a trot, and he was on her heels, but it was obvious they were not going to make it back to the castle before the downpour.

"The church," she called out over the fierce wind and thunder. It would be a good shelter. It was just off the beach and closer than the castle.

"Aye," he agreed, running alongside her.

Approaching the church, she pushed through the small wooden gate first, ran along the flagstone walkway and shoved open the heavy oak door.

Once inside the small stone building, he closed the door behind them. "The weather here is vicious."

"Indeed. Sometimes the only warnings are those dark clouds," she said, breathing hard.

"I've been out in some bad gales, but this appears to be one of the worst." He lay the bow and arrows on the floor.

Their loud breaths echoed through the church while rain pounded the slate roof.

"'Tis a new kirk, aye?" He glanced around.

Jessie nodded, admiring the polished oak ceiling, the carved pillars and beams. Her favorite were the stained glass windows, not so bright and colorful now since the sun was hidden by the clouds. "My father had it built last year, just before his death."

Torrin frowned. "I was sorry to hear of his passing."

"I thank you." She appreciated his compassionate tone, but it also made her a bit tongue-tied. "Da's tomb is here." She walked toward the front of the church and stopped before a plaque. Griff MacKay's face was carved into the stone along with his name and position. Though she hadn't been as close to her father as she might have been if she'd stayed here all her life, she did miss him intensely. He had been a good man and a much admired chief.

"I remember him." Torrin smiled. "A jovial and boisterous man with red hair and blue eyes."

"Aye. And very tall and strong." What a great warrior he had been when she was small. Sadness caught in her throat. She swallowed hard. "When I was a wee lass, he would carry me around on his shoulder, and I felt like I was on top of the world." Her eyes burned with tears.

"I know you must miss him," Torrin said in a quiet tone.

"Aye. 'Twas never the same after Da remarried. Maighread wanted me out of her sight. 'Twas one reason I was sent to foster with the Keiths. I was never as close to Da after that."

Torrin's gaze dropped. "At least your father cared for you."

"Yours didn't?"

Torrin shook his head, his face taking on a morose expression she had not seen from him before. "Nay. He was a tyrant. He beat my brother and me every chance he got. I tried to protect Nolan from his wrath but it rarely helped. As we got older, Father focused most of his abuse on Nolan, for he was always displeased with him. I think that's why he became an outlaw. He turned out just like Father, being vile to people. Or mayhap 'twas simply in his blood."

"You're not like that," Jessie said, just above a whisper. Was he? Though she hadn't known Torrin long, she was fairly certain he wasn't as ruthless as she'd first thought.

Torrin shook his head. "I'm more like my grandfather. Levelheaded. I like to think things through before doing anything drastic." He stared directly into her eyes. "I don't make rash decisions. That should tell you something."

She glanced away, unable to hold his intense gaze for more than a few seconds. "What should it tell me?"

When he remained silent for a long moment, she found it necessary to meet his gaze again. What she saw in his eyes was as turbulent as the storm overhead.

"Asking Dirk for your hand was not a rash decision. I'd had plenty of time to think about it, and you, during the month I was here last winter."

Jessie's face heated and she paced away from him, a slight panic making her heart beat harder. "But we didn't talk. You didn't know me."

"'Twas not for lack of trying. You avoided me."

Just as she wished she could avoid him now, but she couldn't venture out into the storm. Refusing to show fear, she faced him. "Well, I'm sure you can understand why now, after what I witnessed."

"Aye. I can. But now that you ken the truth and have gotten to know me, 'haps you will reconsider."

Fear latched onto her. She stepped back and lowered her gaze. "You will have to be patient. I still don't know you very well." Since MacBain's rejection, she'd faced the fact and grown used to the idea that she would never marry. Given the things that had happened in her past—that first broken betrothal, then the horrid trial marriage—all thoughts of marriage were dark and unhappy. She loved her family and wanted to stay with them, especially since Dirk had returned and her despicable stepmother was gone. She had become best friends with Dirk's wife, Isobel. The past six months had been some of the happiest of her life.

"I've thought about you every day since we met last November," Torrin said, his deep voice barely audible over the rolling thunder.

She'd be lying if she told him she'd never thought of him. But every time she'd imagined his face, she'd experienced a surge of conflicting emotions. Of course, he was devastatingly attractive in a dark and dangerous sort of way, but she'd also thought him a cold-blooded killer. Though she now knew that wasn't true, she still felt uneasy around him. She didn't quite trust him. When enraged, would he switch suddenly and become that man who'd executed her foster brother?

"You're still frightened of me, aye?" he asked, giving her a speculative look.

"Nay." 'Twas a lie, but she didn't want to appear weak. That was something she'd learned with the Keiths. Never show your vulnerabilities. Besides, she wasn't as afraid of Torrin as she was a few days ago.

"I don't believe you," he murmured.

She forced a smile, a brave front. "As I told you before, I fear no man."

"Prove it." His tone was soft but challenging.

"What?"

"Prove you're not afraid of me." Though his eyes dared her, his lips quirked into a faint teasing grin.

"I'm here alone with you, with no one else to protect me should you fly into a murderous rage. What more proof do you need?"

He lifted a brow. "Kiss me."

His soft words stunned her speechless and she could do naught but gape at him. His gaze traveled to her lips, then lifted to delve into hers once again. He was serious… deadly serious.

"Are you mad?" she demanded, once she had the power of speech again. "Nay!" She turned and marched back to the exit door, praying the storm would end soon, not because she was repulsed by him, but because the thought of kissing him threw her mind and body into a tizzy. She did not like the sweltering, disturbed feelings he gave her. She was a strong, independent woman, and he wanted to take away her power and control. She knew he could do it easily. 'Twas one thing she'd become more and more aware of over the past couple of days.

"Coward," he murmured just behind her in a teasing tone.

Should she run out into the storm, or be brave and face him? "This is a church, in case you haven't noticed. 'Twould be sacrilege," she whispered.

"Are you thinking God cannot hear you if you whisper?" he asked.

"Nay, of course, 'tis only…" What? She didn't know, but she couldn't kiss Torrin in a church… or anywhere.

"Kissing is not a sin," he said in an intimate tone that made her crave exactly what they were discussing.

"Some would disagree with you for it incites…" She snapped her mouth shut.

"Incites what?"

She bit her lip refusing to utter the word *lust* to him. *Saints!* He did make her lustful. The last time she'd felt that way, with MacBain, it had resulted in naught but embarrassment and a shattered heart.

"I thought you a brave lady… but alas, 'tis not true."

"Don't tease me, MacLeod," she warned, sending him a glare that she hoped would make him back down.

"Why not? 'Tis fun." He smiled. *Blast!* He had a beautiful and compelling smile.

"For you, I'm certain," she muttered, annoyed with herself because of her response to him, and annoyed with him for prickling his way beneath her skin.

"I will make the kiss fun for you as well," he promised. "The added benefit is that I won't tease you anymore, once you've proven your bravery."

"You are naught but a manipulative rogue."

He grinned, a look of pure mirth, and she could not look away. "I'll not argue with that. Would you kiss a knave in the… nave?"

Before she could help herself, she snorted with laughter, for they were indeed standing in the nave of the church. Reverend MacMahon would castigate them severely if he were to hear their conversation.

Torrin glanced around behind himself, then whispered, "No one will see us."

"God will see us," she reminded him, hoping he would cease his pursuit.

"God sees us wherever we are, not just in churches."

She blew out an exasperated breath. "You are mad. Why on earth would I want to kiss you? You're but a thorn in my side."

"Well, there are many reasons. There is naught thorny about a kiss, except 'haps my beard stubble." He scrubbed a hand against his roughened cheek. "I did shave this morn, but alas it keeps growing," he muttered.

She bit back a smile and eyed his short stubble, wondering just how rough and scratchy it was. Her lips and the skin of her face tingled with anticipation of feeling his manly texture. But, nay, she couldn't.

"A kiss would tell you whether you should like me or not," he said, his eyes darkening in a seductive manner.

"How so?" she asked, trying to maintain some semblance of decency in a church. "'Twill not be a judge of your character."

"Nay, but it will tell you whether we suit. If you like the kiss, you might like to get to know me better." His confident look told her he was certain she would like any kiss he gave.

"And if I don't like it, will you leave me alone and cease your pursuit?"

For a moment, he appeared crestfallen and solemn. "Aye. If you insist. But you cannot lie. I'll know it if you do."

Her stomach knotted, for she feared she'd just agreed to

kiss Torrin. "I don't lie. I never lie."

He smirked. "Let's see if you do." Taking her hands, he stepped closer. She backed against the door, her pulse pounding against her throat.

If only she could open the door and escape before he reached her, but 'twas impossible. Besides, she wasn't certain she wanted to escape. Maybe a kiss from him truly would tell her whether she should like him or not. She had hated that first kiss from MacBain and that should've told her to run the other way.

"Listen." She glanced at the ceiling, hoping to distract Torrin. "The storm is passing."

"Good." But he wasn't distracted. Instead, he was focused on her eyes and her lips. He leaned closer, his mouth hovering over hers. His breath warmed her skin. She liked his scent—a mixture of leather, sea air, and masculinity—and now 'twas luring her closer.

Needing to end the suspense now, she reached up and pressed her lips to his. *Saints!* His lips were both soft and firm. His scent threatened to disorient her. Startled at her response to him, she pulled back, breaking the kiss, but he came with her.

"'Twas not yet a proper kiss." His lips captured hers again but this time with total possession and domination. Of a certainty, 'twas a rogue's kiss, and it threatened to seduce her. He slipped one hand into her hair and with the other, he cradled her face. She found her own hands caressing the hard muscles of his back.

His actions compelled her to open her mouth and she did, inviting ever deepening kisses. Sinful kisses that made her forget where she was… forget everything but him. His tongue flicked against hers, stroked with fiery erotic movements such as she'd never experienced before. His taste was even more bewitching than his scent and it made her imagine wicked things. The two of them in her bed, their naked skin sliding.

A moan reached her ears and she realized she'd made

that shocking sound. He growled an even louder moan in response and the kiss grew fiercer. Pushing her against the door, he consumed her mouth with fire and passion.

Abruptly, he pulled back, breathing hard, watching her. "Now tell me, Lady Jessie, did you enjoy that, or nay?" he asked in a low murmur.

What? He expected her to talk now? After that? His green eyes were dark as a pine forest at gloaming. His heated look dared her to deny it.

She nodded, then shook her head.

"Which is it?" He darted a glance down at her lips again as if he might want to make a meal out of her. Some part of her wished he would.

"Aye," she whispered.

"And what does that mean? You want another?"

"Nay."

He gave her a crooked grin and moved closer. "You said you didn't lie."

'Twas true; she was lying. She grasped the plaid that crossed his chest and pulled him closer. He made a sensual purring sound and took possession of her mouth again.

Her arms around his neck, she couldn't get close enough to him. With his hands at the small of her back, he drew her tight against him, and she was certain the hardness she felt pressed against her lower belly was not his sporran.

He pulled back an inch, gazing into her eyes, his heavy-lidded and dark with passion. "We suit very well indeed, m'lady, as I knew we would from the first moment I saw you."

Clearly, he was hinting about marriage again. Fear shot through her, along with a good dose of mortification. She yanked her arms from around his neck, unable to believe she'd indulged in such a sinful kiss in a church. The good reverend might make her marry Torrin if he learned of it.

She turned, jerked open the heavy wooden door, and ran outside. Most of the gale had passed and only a light mist of rain and a breeze remained. She strode quickly along the walkway and through the wooden gate of the stone-walled kirkyard.

Torrin's footsteps sounded behind her, but she ignored him and headed toward the castle. Of a certainty, she'd enjoyed the kiss, but that didn't mean she wanted to marry him. He was too pushy and domineering by far. She had found contentment living here with her family and clan. Why alter something that wasn't a problem?

She had wanted a family of her own once, during her first betrothal and even when she'd been in the trial marriage to MacBain. But when that faux marriage had shattered upon the rocks, some of her dreams had died. Maybe she was barren as MacBain had accused. And if so, why would Torrin want to marry her? He needed an heir.

She stopped and turned. Almost running into her, Torrin grasped her arms, steadying them both.

"I'm barren," she said. Her throat tightened and closed and tears burned her eyes. She tore herself away from his hold and ran toward the castle gates.

"Jessie," he called after her, but she didn't stop.

There, she'd told him the truth, the reason they couldn't marry. They didn't suit at all because he needed an heir more than anything, and she couldn't provide one.

***

A quarter hour later, Torrin knocked at Jessie's bedchamber door. The woman he wanted for his wife was not barren. 'Twas impossible. He refused to believe it.

Her kiss had bewitched him. Once his lips had touched hers, he'd been certain she was the only woman for him. Never had a kiss affected him so profoundly. 'Twas not only the lust which had consumed his body, but his heart had somersaulted within his chest. She was the woman he'd dreamed of the whole of his life.

He knocked again.

"Who is it?" Jessie's muffled response came from inside the room.

"Me. Torrin."

"What do you want?"

"To talk." That much should be obvious to her.

"There is naught to talk about," she assured him in a firm voice.

"I disagree," he growled. They had plenty to talk about. He had imagined her as the mother of his children for more than six months. And now, to suddenly be told that wouldn't be possible was a blow to his vitals.

"Did you not hear what I said outside?" she demanded.

"Of course, I heard. 'Tis why I'm here now. How do you ken 'tis true?"

"How do you think?" she practically yelled through the door. "When I was with MacBain, I was unable to conceive a bairn."

"*Iosa is Muire Mhàthair*." He detested the sound of MacBain's name, and to once again imagine the bastard lying with Jessie gutted him.

A chambermaid approached along the corridor. Once she had disappeared into a room, he turned back to the door. "Let me in. I want to talk about this in private. Servants are passing by."

"How grand," she muttered. "Gossip will be all over the castle by morn." She removed the bar from the door and opened it. "Very well. Do come in, m'laird. This is not at all scandalous," she said in an impertinent tone.

He slammed the door closed and barred it. When he faced her and saw the unshed tears glistening in her eyes, annoyance pounded through him. Not annoyance at her but at the situation. "Mayhap MacBain is not as virile as he thinks," he said.

She shrugged. "He was able to sire a son with his lovely *wife* after that."

"How many times did you lie with him?" Torrin hated the image in his head of Jessie with that whoreson. It made him want to break MacBain's nose again, along with a few of his limbs.

"I didn't count. 'Twas three months."

"Were you not in the trial marriage for a year and a day?"

"Aye, but he lost interest and found a prettier lass to secretly spend his nights with."

"There could be no prettier lass than you," Torrin muttered, remembering how her hair had shimmered like red flames in the sunlight today, and her eyes had rivaled the bright blue sky. Now, in the dimness of the room, the colors were more subdued but no less beautiful.

"I thank you, but..." She shook her head, tears dripping onto her cheeks.

He wanted to hold her in his arms, brush all her tears away, then kiss her, but he was unsure what her response would be. Seeing her cry was like a punch to the gut. "I should've hurt MacBain worse than I did. Should've broken both his legs."

"Nay. There was no need. I just hope he stays gone."

"Why did you not leave him when he turned his attention to the other woman?"

"I had no proof. Besides, 'twas against the agreement I'd signed. I had to stay for a year and a day, no matter what, other than physical abuse of course."

"He didn't abuse you?"

"He never hit me, if that's what you mean. But he could be rather insulting at times. My father regretted making the arrangement, but there was naught either of us could do until the year was up, because MacBain kept the other woman a secret. There were rumors, but I didn't know who she was at the time. Only later did I find out he married her soon after I left."

Torrin paced before the small fireplace where a low fire burned. "Well, simply because you lay with MacBain off and on for three months and didn't conceive doesn't mean you're barren."

"'Haps you're right. But you're a chief and will want an heir. I'm certain marrying me would be a risk you wouldn't wish to take. And I refuse to sign another trial marriage agreement. Men have no concept of what that does to a woman."

Some called the trial marriage handfasting, and he could see the benefit of it. But now he tried to imagine the situation from the female viewpoint… from Jessie's viewpoint. 'Twas indeed a precarious position for a woman. A marriage might hinge on whether or not she was able to conceive. In any case, he wouldn't ask that of her. He wanted a real marriage. "I'm sorry you went through that. I can tell 'twas hard for you and it left some lasting damage."

She nodded, gazing into his eyes with a bit more trust than before. "'Tis not something I want to experience again. I've had two broken engagements. The first time, I was betrothed to one of the Keith allies, but he disappeared the day before the wedding and I never saw him again."

"A daft fool," Torrin muttered. What was wrong with these imbecilic men? Not only was Jessie a stunningly beautiful woman, she was also strong, tall and proud. A warrior princess? A goddess? Aye, indeed.

"Mayhap he had a premonition about—"

"Jessie," Torrin chided softly. "Don't say it. You're not barren."

"You don't know that."

"Neither do you. There's only one way to know for sure." Aye, he was ready for the challenge.

Jessie narrowed her eyes, glaring at him, but now—since the kiss—he saw more than just her ire. The way her pale blue eyes darkened told him she was more than interested in his suggestion. The way her hands had dug into his hair and held his head had told him she'd relished the kiss.

"Would it be so terrible?" he asked.

"For you, nay."

"You enjoyed the kiss near as much as I did. You cannot lie about that. And I can guarantee you will not leave my bed unsatisfied."

"Must you be so vulgar?"

Wry amusement came over him. "I was but speaking the truth, m'lady. And furthermore, I promise to give you pleasures such as you have never experienced before."

"'Tis but a game to you, aye?" she snapped. "This is my life we're talking about."

Frustration and need gored him. He knew he was right; he simply needed to prove it to her. "You want to live your whole life never knowing whether or not you're barren?"

She shook her head and stared into the fire's embers for a few moments. "It matters not. Birthing a bairn might kill me anyway."

Fear sliced through him. Every man's worst nightmare—the wife he loved dying while trying to bring their child into the world. "Why do you say that?" he demanded.

"My mother died giving birth to me. 'Tis not that rare."

"I'm sorry. I didn't know."

"For a long time, I felt I was to blame."

"Nay. How could you be?"

She shrugged. "I know these things happen sometimes and no one is to blame."

"You're a healthy, strong woman. I'm certain you will be able to birth many bairns." He prayed she could, for he wanted no one else to be the mother of his children. He'd been imagining her as his wife for months. He'd even wondered what their children might look like. Would they have a son with flaming red hair, or chestnut brown like his? 'Haps several with each. Lasses, too. He'd imagined them living a long, happy life at Munrick.

A knock sounded at the door.

"Who is it?" Jessie asked.

"'Tis me, Mariana, m'lady. I had a question about supper."

"I'll be right out."

"We'll continue this discussion later," Torrin said in a hushed tone so the maid wouldn't hear.

"'Haps." Jessie gave him a warning look, but he wanted naught more than to kiss her and carry her to that bed and prove to her she was not barren. But this was a tricky situation he'd never imagined before.

What if she truly was barren? Would he marry her anyway and give up the chance of producing an heir?

Chapter Seven

Torrin stood on the castle's battlements overlooking the sea, his mind consumed by what he'd learned earlier. The bleak sky with the low-hanging gray clouds and cool, damp air that followed the storm didn't help his mood. He glanced aside when Iain came up the steps.

"What's wrong with you?" his friend asked.

Torrin was unsure if he wanted to reveal how he felt at the moment.

"Your frown tells me the lass is proving impossible to seduce." Iain grinned.

"She is a wee bit stubborn, but so am I."

"'Tis true. Once you set your mind to something, you never give up until you have it."

Torrin nodded, for he meant to have her. "I'll tell you something if you promise not to tell her or anyone about it."

Iain sobered and leaned an arm against the shoulder-high merlon of the stone battlements. "Of course. When have I ever been a gossip?"

Torrin drew in a deep breath of the cool salt air. "She thinks she is barren and refuses to marry me because she knows I need an heir."

"Damnation," Iain muttered, frowning. "She thinks this

because of the trial marriage to MacBain?"

"Aye. They were intimate for three months and no bairn resulted, so MacBain abandoned her for someone else."

"What if 'tis true? You cannot deny that you need an heir."

"Indeed. The clan elders may have my head if I knowingly marry a barren lady. But at the moment, I want her more than an heir."

"Saints! You've gone and fallen in love with her, as I feared." Iain gave an amused smirk.

Torrin shrugged, but deep down he was certain his friend was right. "I know not. I have never felt this way before."

"I have," Iain admitted, though he did not appear comfortable doing so.

"You? In love?"

"Aye, she was a lovely lady, but she loved someone else and went off to marry him instead. End of story." Iain shrugged.

"When was this?"

"Years ago. It amounts to naught now. I've almost forgotten her, but at the time, 'twas hellishly hard to give her up."

"I'm surprised you've never told me about this before. We've known each other since we were lads."

"Aye, but there were times we didn't see each other for many months at a time. Besides, 'tis not something a man likes to talk about."

"You're right." Torrin sucked in a deep breath of the fresh air, trying to clear his head. "I know not what to do."

"The answer will come to you, I'm certain. 'Haps in the middle of the night. Or in the morn."

Torrin nodded as he gazed down at the beach where they'd spent several enjoyable moments talking and shooting the bow. And wrestling. That had been his favorite part, aside from the kiss. He relished anything that put him into physical contact with her.

"Did you at least steal a kiss?" Iain asked.

Torrin's gaze darted to his. He wasn't the type to brag or share too much of his exploits.

"Ah, you did, aye?" Iain guessed. "I trust the kiss measured up to your expectations?"

"Surpassed them by miles." That kiss was the single best thing he'd yet experienced in his life. When he imagined taking her to his bed, he could scarce breathe. He was certain the physical pleasure would be astonishing, but the experience would be about far more than that for him. 'Twas as Iain had said—he was falling for her. He only hoped she would feel the same way. If that kiss was any indication, she was strongly attracted to him. That was a start. Now, he but needed to show her how he felt about her, prove himself trustworthy and convince her to not worry about the future.

"I'd rather not think about the problems anymore," Torrin said. "I just want to… spend time with her."

"Aye. 'Tis what you should do, then," Iain said.

Torrin wanted to make her forget all about this hindrance, if that's what it truly was. It could be a lot of worry for naught. He wanted to learn everything about her. And, aye, he had to admit he wanted to explore every inch of her body and make love to her for hours. After that kiss, 'twas clear to him they could set the bed sheets afire.

He wanted to make her smile and laugh and sigh and cry out his name in pleasure.

"I have to figure out how to make her forget her troubles and have some fun," Torrin said.

Iain grinned. "'Tis the best solution I've ever heard."

"I have an idea for a gift that might cheer her up."

***

"I need for you lads to do something for me," Torrin said in a low voice to three of his men, Sim, Luag and Gordon, in the courtyard that evening.

"Aye, Chief," Sim responded, his dark eyes glinting curiously in the dim glow of the sunset.

"Tell no one of your assignment," Torrin warned them.

They nodded in a very solemn manner.

Torrin lowered his voice even more. "One of my distant cousins in Scourie raises deerhound pups. His name is Angus MacLeod. I want you to go get one for me. A healthy pup with a lot of gumption." He held out his hand, filled with silver coins.

Luag quirked his brows as if Torrin had gone daft, but accepted the money.

"'Twill be a gift for the lady. She lost her beloved dog not long ago."

"Ah." Luag nodded as did the other two.

He hoped the pup would make her smile. She didn't smile nearly often enough.

"Also, while you're out, make sure MacBain and his men haven't returned. You may run into Struan, Fionn, and the MacKay guards who escorted them south. You can leave in the morn after breaking your fast. If anyone asks, you're simply going to look for your clansmen. I want the pup to be a surprise for her."

The three smiled and nodded their agreement. They were well aware that Torrin was trying to convince Jessie to marry him. He hoped this would work to soften her up a bit more. If not, he knew not what he would do next.

***

The following afternoon, Torrin walked along the battlements, his gaze scanning over Balnakeil Bay, the beach, and the sand dunes leading out to the headland. No one was about. He was disappointed to see that Jessie was not sitting on the beach today. He had scarcely seen glimpses of her since their serious discussion yesterday. She was well and truly avoiding him now.

Although Torrin liked Dirk MacKay just fine, he hoped the man didn't return soon. He needed time to grow closer to Jessie first. Dirk would wonder what in blazes Torrin was doing, staying this long. His excuse for now was that he was protecting Jessie in the event MacBain returned, wanting revenge. Once Dirk, Keegan, and the rest of them showed up, he would no longer have an excuse to stay for they could protect Jessie. Of course, Dirk had left Erskine and a garrison to protect both her and Dunnakeil, but Torrin wanted to help out.

His stay here wasn't just about convincing Jessie to marry him anymore. He was feeling something he'd never felt before. He didn't know what he would've done if MacBain had spirited her away and married her. Probably killed the whoreson.

But he didn't want to kill anyone. He much preferred that MacBain stay far away.

Torrin paced along the battlements to the opposite side of the castle where he gazed out over the green hills dotted with gray rocks and black-faced sheep. He remembered his last conversation with Jessie. It had been beyond serious, which had obviously caused her anxiety and worry about her future. What they needed was to simply relax and enjoy themselves. Life did not have to be solemn all the time.

He'd reveled in the wrestling match and the archery lessons he'd given her the day before, but most of all, he'd relished the kiss. 'Haps he shouldn't have kissed her in the kirk, but 'twas his only opportunity and he didn't want to pass it up.

'Haps that bastard MacBain had not bedded her very many times within those three months. Sometimes many months or a year passed before a woman was with child. Dirk and his wife, Isobel, had been married seven months and she didn't appear to be with child when they'd stopped by Munrick a few weeks ago.

Although he wanted children, Torrin would still marry Jessie even if she was barren. He wouldn't tell her that. Not now, anyway. She wouldn't accept his decision. She would think he was being impulsive or that mayhap he would change his mind later and send her away. But the truth was he was well and truly smitten with her.

And, nay, he would not change his mind later. He had never felt the way he did now about a woman. He had not lost interest in her during the seven months since he'd met her. In fact, his interest had only grown and deepened from instant physical attraction to something powerful he'd never experienced before.

He frowned down at the ground far below and the woman dashing away from the castle. Was that Jessie? Her head was covered, hiding her hair, and she faced away from him. But the woman was tall and slim, and she moved exactly like Jessie. She must have slipped past the guards and out the postern gate, and was now headed away from castle, in the opposite direction from the bay. Where was she going? She normally walked on the beach, but she was not headed that way now. Nor was she walking at a leisurely pace. Nay, she was practically running. When she glanced back over her shoulder once, a lock of her copper hair gleamed in the sunlight, and he got a glimpse of half her face. Aha, 'twas indeed Jessie. Why was she slipping away?

Trying to escape him? Or had something happened?

Torrin rushed down several sets of winding steps until he reached the bailey. Not having a key to the postern gate, he asked the guards to open the main portcullis for him. They also gave him his basket-hilt broadsword, for he might need it to protect Jessie.

Once outside the walls, Torrin ran toward the east. She had already disappeared from sight, difficult in this flat landscape near the shore, but gorse bushes grew here and there in small groves. Once he passed a group of them, he saw her plaid-covered head disappear behind another cluster of bushes. He was determined to catch up to her without her seeing him. She wasn't traveling toward the village, and he needed to find out what she was up to.

They must have walked for more than a mile when he lost sight of her. Muttering curses, he glanced this way and that, then ran forward. The rocky shore and a drop off lay ahead. Had she gone in that direction? *Saints!* Had she fallen off the cliff?

His heart rate soaring toward the sky, he quickened his

pace.

Once at the edge, he saw it wasn't a cliff, but simply a steep bank of sand about thirty feet high. Beyond it was a small golden sand beach with black boulders protruding here and there from the sand. He lay down and belly-crawled to the edge so she wouldn't notice him. Aye, indeed, she was descending a rock and sand path along the edge of the bank. What in blazes was she doing here?

He scooted sideways and hid himself better behind a clump of thistles. He was wicked for spying on her, but he had to protect her. Not that he truly expected anyone to be all the way out here, a mile or more from the village and further than that from the castle.

She strolled along the wee beautiful beach, which was enclosed and cut off from other areas of the coast. Cliffs jutted out on each side, making it very secluded. He could understand why she loved this place. 'Twas one of the loveliest spots he had yet seen. To add to its appeal, a slight breeze blew in off the sea, but 'twas a warm summer day.

Jessie perched on one of the boulders and gazed out to sea. Was she daydreaming? He hoped she was thinking of him.

Moments later, she got to her feet and walked further along the shore, her gaze searching the tops of the cliffs and sand bank. He ducked. Had she seen him or sensed his presence? He kept his head down and hoped she didn't notice his plaid.

She hastened to the far end of the strip of sand, which was more concealed behind the large rocks. Though she disappeared from sight, he hesitated to crawl closer to the edge for fear she might spot him.

She appeared again, wearing only her white smock. Hiking it to her knees, she ran into the water.

"Saints," he hissed. She was going swimming? He chuckled, but forced himself to be quiet. Not that she could hear him over the waves crashing into the boulders below. What an adventurous spirit she had. It only made him fall harder for her.

How lovely she looked, her fiery red hair streaming down her back as she waded deeper into the water reflecting the blue sky. She disappeared behind a black boulder.

A swim would be perfect right now. While she was hidden from view, he took the opportunity to slip down the bank along the narrow trail she had used earlier. He hastily removed all his clothing and left it on the dry sand behind a rock, then crept between the boulders. The sun-warmed, wet sand felt good against his bare feet. Then the edges of the cold surf washed over his toes. He often took swims in Loch Assynt, so he was accustomed to cold water. It appeared Jessie was, too.

He waded into the water and peered around the last boulder. When her back was turned, he slid beneath the water and swam underneath a wave. When he emerged twenty feet out, she happened to be facing him. Her eyes wide, she screamed and swam toward the shore.

"Jessie! 'Tis only me," he called.

But she didn't listen; she kept moving quickly toward the beach. Once the water was shallow enough, she ran, probably difficult wearing that smock. She tugged its hampering weight from around her ankles and quickened her steps. He wished she would remove the blasted garment.

He followed her, splashing through the shallow surf.

"Let's go back in," he called over the roar of the waves.

She stopped and turned to face him, her wide-eyed gaze dropping to his groin. She sucked in a sharp breath and covered her eyes. "Put on some clothes, MacLeod!"

Halting ten feet away, he grinned and crossed his arms over his chest. "'Twould be much better if you'd simply remove yours." Although he did appreciate this view. Her wet smock had become more transparent, and her hard, rose-colored nipples showed through the material. But he wasn't going to tell her that. Sexual heat rushed over him despite the cool breeze blowing over his bare, wet skin.

"Are you mad?" She faced the other direction, grabbed

her *arisaid* from the stone and attempted to belt the plaid about her waist.

"I think you are the one who is mad, wearing a drenched smock beneath your other dry clothing. Makes no sense. You should remove it all and lay it on the rocks to dry."

"You followed me!" she accused, refusing to look at him.

"Aye. I had to protect you, after all. MacBain could return." Although he doubted the bastard could return this soon. Torrin's two men and the MacKays who had escorted the MacBains south had not returned yet.

"I need no protection."

He shook his head at her stubbornness. "You didn't mind that I came to your rescue last time."

"Leave me be." Carrying her shoes and three sheathed knives, she strode away from him along the beach, dodging the massive black boulders which protruded from the sand, but he followed. She glanced back, catching his eye, then started running. Abruptly, she tumbled onto the ground with a short shriek.

"Saints! Are you hurt?" He knelt by her, one knee drawn up to conceal his tarse, so she would at least face him.

She turned to her back and leaned up on her elbows. "My foot! I stepped on something sharp."

"Och. Let me see." He lifted one of her bare, sand-covered feet. 'Twas a long, slim and elegant foot, much like the rest of her body.

She sat up, glaring at him. "The other one."

"Ah." He examined her other foot but saw no sign of blood. "Where does it hurt?"

"My heel."

"I see no injury to it. I think you'll live."

She narrowed her eyes, her gaze skittering over his naked chest, then looked skyward. "Where are your clothes?"

"Over there somewhere, but it's much nicer without them today. You should try it. The sun is warm. How often have you gone naked outside?"

"Never." She lowered her voice. "Well, except when I

swim sometimes."

"Indeed? You swim naked?"

Her blush deepened. "A couple of times."

"I'm shocked, m'lady," he teased with a smile. Saints, how he loved the image in his head of her swimming naked like a goddess of the sea. "You are a wild and brave lass, are you not?"

She shrugged. "Some would say *wayward.*"

"I like a wayward lady."

At the moment, the way he knelt, his leg hid his shaft, but the problem was it was rapidly rising to its full height. She made him hard so quickly, so easily, every time he was in her presence.

"Don't give me that look, MacLeod," she said firmly.

"What look?"

She pointed at his eyes. "That one."

Could she see the raw need and desire written upon his face? He hoped so. She'd driven him mad for the past several days. "I can't help it," he said in a low tone. "I hunger for you."

Jessie swallowed hard as she held Torrin's dark, passionate gaze. In the bright sunlight, his lashes halfway hid his deep green eyes, but 'twas clear they reflected profound sensuality. His sculpted muscles were lean and elegant. He appeared iron-strong but not too bulky.

She had seen his shaft moments ago, just for a trice, when he'd emerged from the water, before she'd slammed her eyes closed. She could not see that part of his anatomy now, unless she moved closer to him. Which she was definitely not going to do. What gall he had to gallivant naked in front of her.

At the moment, his eyes bewitched her and she did not want to look away. Besides, his body aroused her. She glanced down at his chest and the defined muscles there. The rippled ridges of his abdomen intrigued her. She had only seen glimpses of naked men or lads before, some, like MacBain, in half darkness. But observing Torrin now, in the daylight, so close… he was a divine work of art. She found herself wishing she could touch him, run her fingers over those muscles and see how hard they were.

He was like a god of the sea who had just emerged from the depths. His dark, wet hair brushed his broad shoulders.

His eyes turning predatory, he slowly moved closer, crawled alongside her and captured her mouth. Giving up the fight with herself, she lay back on the warm sand and slid her hands around his neck into his cool wet hair. He tasted salty, like the sea, and his tongue delved boldly into her mouth. Her body quickened as if awakening from a long sleep to feel the bright sunlight burning into her… and Torrin burning into her.

Aligning his body with hers, he slid his hand around her derriere and dragged her tight against him. Oh, saints! He was hard. She knew what this was all about; she'd lain several times with MacBain during their trial marriage, but never had she been ravenous for him as she now was for Torrin.

One of his bare legs slid between hers and he lay half on top of her. His mouth and body felt divine on hers as if something about the two of them was perfectly harmonized.

His kisses were seduction itself. Not too forceful, but still highly confident, his tongue flicking against hers, teasing her. He knew what he was doing, and he was so good at it.

Before she knew it, her belt was unclasped and her *arisaid* loose beneath her like a blanket upon the sand. His thumb grazed lightly over her nipple through the wet smock. She stifled a moan at the flash of white-hot pleasure that blasted through her. With every kiss, she wanted another, deeper kiss. She wanted him to devour her, consume her, and burn her up with his passion.

His erection felt large against her lower belly. Before she realized what she was doing, she brushed her hand down the hard, rippled muscles of his abdomen, and clasped his hot, rigid flesh. She gasped… and he growled. With a dark, feral look in his eyes, he broke the kiss and pulled back an inch. He clenched his teeth and waited, daring her, challenging her with his midnight gaze.

But she didn't remove her hand. She stroked down his stone-hard shaft, savoring the sleek feel of his skin.

In a flash, he was fully over her, yanking her smock upwards. Abruptly, he halted, breathing hard, his forehead against her. "Damnation, Jessie," he growled. "Is this what you want?"

Her heart pounded against her throat so hard she couldn't speak.

"Tell me what you want." He lifted his head and scrutinized her face.

"Aye," she whispered, almost ashamed of her weakness. She was never weak. She always spoke her mind and did it with firm conviction.

"Aye, what?" he demanded.

"I want…" She searched his eyes. Could she trust him? Though she was unsure of most everything else, she knew without doubt that she wanted him in a most carnal and physical way.

He muttered a curse. "You're driving me mad," he warned. "Tell me before I die of wanting you."

"You. I want you, too," she said, her voice and hands shaking. Her body's need for him overrode all else. 'Twas all she could think of.

He closed his eyes and released a short breath. When his eyes met hers again, something about his expression had softened, but also intensified. "Are you certain?"

She had never seen such passion in anyone's eyes before. So much, she was lost for a moment. "Aye."

"You want me to take you, right here, on the sand?"

She suddenly remembered they were outside in broad daylight. Glancing around, she noticed they lay between two giant boulders, which shielded them from most of the cliffs and high banks surrounding the bay.

"Aye." And she wished he'd be quick about it. With every moment that passed, something inside her ached ever more strongly. With each beat of her heart, need drummed more fiercely inside her.

He sucked in a deep breath and slowly pushed her smock up her thighs, then sat back on his heels. Glancing down, she couldn't believe how his impressive shaft stood proud and upright. Aye, she wanted him. And she knew with certainty she'd never wanted MacBain in such a powerful way.

Torrin hissed a curse; he was observing her most private parts just as she was his. Her first instinct was to close her legs, but she couldn't. He was sitting between them. But more importantly, she wasn't afraid of him, nor ashamed.

He moved over her again, his elbow on the ground by her head. He gave her a fiercely erotic kiss while the tip of his shaft brushed against her most intimate spot.

"Aye," she whispered, widening her legs. He moaned, nudging against her, into her. She drew in a breath and held it.

"Breathe, Jessie," he whispered.

"I am." Her voice was uneven.

"Look into my eyes."

She did, unable to believe the depth of emotion she saw there.

With a gentle but persistent thrust of his hips, he pushed deeper. A stitch of pain caught her and she gasped.

He halted. "Did I hurt you?"

"Nay, 'tis only… it has been a long while since…"

He nodded, his look darkening. "Just relax and trust me. I'll make you forget about him."

Torrin was right; a moment later, he was the focus of her existence. His scorching kisses mimicked the erotic moves of his body. He surged into her and away at an ever intensifying pace. Naught but pleasure and need ricocheted throughout her entire body. She no longer remembered who she was, only that she never wanted him to stop what he was doing.

Cold water from Torrin's wet hair dripped onto the sun-warmed skin of her face and neck as he pounded into her. Hot shivers spiraled through her, along with pleasure that darted and whizzed along her limbs.

He growled in her ear and slowed.

"Nay, keep going," she begged.

"Saints, lass," he hissed and moved his hand between their bodies. When he stroked her, she thought she would explode. She cried out, holding her breath with the increasing sensations. Nay, she could not breathe while he did that… whatever he was doing with his thumb, circling some especially sensitive spot. It felt like magic.

He slid deep, then away. Something inside her caught like throwing whisky on a fire, and she burst into flames. Her body bowed and shoved against his, beyond her control. What was happening? What sorcery had he worked on her? She knew she was screaming but couldn't stop. His mouth closed over hers, muffling her cries and his body ground against hers, deep into hers, over and over, the most perfect feeling in the world. She held onto him, grasping him to her, never wanting him to let go.

He roared in her ear, his body shuddering forcefully against hers.

A moment later, he breathed a curse and collapsed on the sand beside her, rolling her to face him, pulling her tight against him. "Saints! That was heaven on earth," he whispered between harsh breaths.

"Aye." 'Twas true. She didn't understand what she'd felt—that moment of pure bliss that had taken her breath and her mind—but she was too embarrassed to ask him about it.

Observing her a long moment while they caught their breaths, he grinned. "You have a beautiful smile."

She hadn't even realized she was smiling, but indeed she was incredibly happy for the first time in a very long time. Of course, her family made her happy, too. But even with them, she sometimes felt lonely or incomplete.

But Torrin had given her joy such as she'd rarely experienced. And why shouldn't she take her happiness where she could find it? She was no longer a young lass, needing to keep her virtue intact for some future husband. If she was barren, a tumble on the sand wouldn't matter. And if she wasn't… if Torrin got her with child… she didn't know. Did she wish to marry him? Before today, she hadn't thought so, but after what they'd just shared, she was certainly tempted. The emotion and passion in his eyes had held her spellbound. But would he lose interest and desert her as the other men had? Just the thought of it sent an ache through her stomach. If she fell for Torrin and he rejected her, she would never recover. There were too many unanswered questions and unfortunately she couldn't see into the future.

"Come, let's go for a swim." He stood and helped her up.

Her face heated, for she still couldn't get used to his naked body, despite what they'd just shared.

"But you must get rid of this first." He bent and raised the hem of her smock, but her arms prevented him from lifting it over her head.

"Nay! What if someone should come along?" She glanced up at the cliffs and the high bank surrounding them.

"Do you see anyone? We're over a mile from the village and further than that from the castle."

She bit her lip. His suggestion was tempting. How glorious it would feel to swim in the sea naked. She hadn't done so since last year.

"We'll spread the garment over this rock and it will dry in the sun and breeze by the time we're done swimming."

She glanced around, making sure no one was above them looking down. "Oh, very well." She lifted the smock over her head. He took it from her and spread it over the boulder.

His gaze skimmed over her, then lingered on her breasts. "Saints. You are the loveliest of sights."

She suppressed the urge to fold her arms over her breasts. "You're not so bad yourself, MacLeod."

He gave her an amused smirk. "Come. It's been a while since I swam in the sea for any length of time. And today's a rare warm day."

He dove under the water and she didn't see him for several moments, until he emerged thirty feet away. Not to be outdone, she took a deep breath and dove beneath the waves. Seconds later, she grabbed onto him and rose above the surface.

"I don't ken any other lady who could do that," he said.

She savored his compliment, but at the same time, it made her wonder. "Do you ken a lot of ladies?"

"Nay, not that many." He grinned.

Jealousy arose, unbidden. "Liar. I'm certain you have known many in the Biblical sense."

"I remember none of them."

"I don't care for insincere sweet talk."

"Nor do I. I've not so much as looked at another woman, much less touched one, since the night we met."

She searched his gaze, looking for insincerity, but could find none. Either he was telling the truth or he was a very skilled liar.

"I knew then that I wanted you and no one else would suffice."

Why? How? She had a thousand questions to ask him, but she didn't wish to get into any serious discussions now.

He grasped her around the waist as her toes barely touched the sandy bottom. When he lowered his mouth to hers, she slid her arms around his neck. His salty, sweet kiss was like the best of treats.

He trailed his tongue down her throat and, lifting her into the air, fastened his hot lips onto one of her nipples. She gasped as fiery arousal blasted through her.

Torrin pulled Jessie's long legs around his waist and strode from the water with her. Damnation, he must have her again. *Now.* It had only been a few minutes since his release but he was already fully aroused again. The first time with her had been astounding, earth-shaking, and far beyond his wildest dreams. He could've never imagined such pleasure as that which crashed through him with his release.

Gently, he lay her on the sun-warmed woolen plaid—her *arisaid*—their bare, wet skin sliding together.

"Saints, Jessie. I want you again," he said against her

luscious lips.

"Aye. Take me." Between kisses, she whispered those sweet words in a desperate tone that only aroused him more.

After positioning himself, he pushed into her slowly, gradually, savoring each glorious inch. Her delicious, wet heat enveloped him. He looked into her dark blue eyes, seeing more passion than ever before. Though it might be sacrilege, he prayed that she could love him, that she would need him as much as he needed her.

During their first time, his own desire had nearly consumed him. Now, he wanted to give her more of his attention.

When he started moving, she cried out and held on tighter around his neck. "Aye," she breathed against his mouth. He captured her beautiful lips and devoured them. His body near went up in the flames of sexual pleasure.

She lifted her hips, boldly meeting each of his thrusts. Damnation, he was fast becoming addicted to this woman. They'd only indulged a few minutes ago. And he feared twice in one day would never be enough for him.

'Twas as if the first time had only been an appetizer and this was the main course. She accepted his scorching kisses, taking everything he was giving and eager for more. Thank the saints, she was a passionate woman who loved carnal pleasures. Or maybe 'twas their special connection and *him* that fired her up. He hoped.

"So damned good, Jessie," he growled against her mouth.

"Aye. Amazing," she hissed.

Her obvious enjoyment and her ardor for him sent his arousal blazing toward the sky faster than he would've liked. Nay, he had to pace himself and give her more pleasure than she'd ever thought possible. She wouldn't even remember MacBain's name by the time he was through with her this day. Torrin wanted her addicted to the pleasures he could give her. He wanted her to need him and think of him night and day.

Pausing, he moved down and drew her puckered nipple

into his mouth while cradling her breasts within his hands. Her breasts were not overly large, nor were they small. Just the right size, to his way of thinking. Beautiful, creamy and perky with rosy pink nipples.

He moaned and switched to her other nipple. As he suckled it, she shoved her hips upward, imbedding him deeper. The sudden decadence of the move gripped him, and he growled. He wished he could bring her to climax several times before he reached his own, but he wasn't sure he could endure it this time.

After licking his thumb, he slid it between their bodies to stroke that highly sensitive pleasure point, that wee rigid bud just above where he slid. While caressing with his thumb, he thrust harder and faster. The expression on her face was beyond blissful. How he loved watching her at the peak of passion.

Her nails dug into his shoulders, tighter and tighter until she screamed, her body flexing hard and bowing upwards. Her nipples grew even harder and he suckled at one while pounding into her at the height of her pleasure. He held back his own release as long as he could. Once hers ebbed, his own crashed in on him, consuming all thought except how much he loved this woman. Aye, she was his, and he was never letting her go.

The pleasure drained away, bit by bit, and he slowly came back to himself, breathing hard. Saints, he felt like he'd climbed a mountain.

"Jessie," he said between hard breaths. "You are amazing."

She giggled, and the playful, happy look in her eyes told him all he needed to know right now.

Lying down beside her on the warm sand, he kissed her and held her close in his arms. The smile would not leave his face and his heart beat with joy and victory. Aye, she was his now, and she would soon realize that of her own free will. He didn't need to use words to convince her of anything. She would feel it when the time was right. He would show her what a joy life could be.

He drew back. "How about another swim? That one was cut short."

She smiled. "Aye, I'm ready to cool off."

He stood, then took her hand and helped her up. Hand in hand, they ran toward the water. He loved how fearless she was, going naked just as he was. She was a good swimmer, too.

For an endless time, they played in the water, splashing each other, swimming and jumping waves. Torrin grabbed her and kissed her every chance he got, and each time aroused him more and more. Soon, he would need her again, and he hoped she would need him as well.

Movement on the beach caught his attention. He blinked the burning salt water from his eyes. Around a dozen men were lined up along the beach. Were his eyes playing tricks on him? "What the hell?"

Jessie turned abruptly. "Who is—? Haldane?"

Chapter Eight

"That little bastard." Rage twisted through Jessie, and she started from the chest-deep water toward her youngest brother, Haldane, an outlaw who knew better than to show his face here.

"You're naked." Torrin grabbed her arm just as a wave crashed over their shoulders.

She muttered a curse and slid behind him while looking over his shoulder. "Haldane!" she yelled over the crashing waves. "Take your men and go!" She pointed firmly. Though Haldane was an adult and was by no means small, he was four years her junior. She'd always ordered him about, but he'd rarely obeyed her, or anyone.

Even at this distance, she saw his satisfied smile. He shook his head, his bright copper hair and short beard gleaming in the sunlight.

"That gray-haired man beside him is McMurdo," Torrin said.

"Aye." Jessie had seen the infamous highwayman only a few times in her life and knew he had killed at least eighteen people, maybe more, including her cousin. Plus, he had come close to killing Dirk.

"We can wait all day," Haldane called, crossing his arms

over his chest.

"What do you want?" Torrin demanded.

"My sister is going to gain us entrance at Dunnakeil."

"You're wrong, Haldane!" she yelled.

"What are you going to do about it? I have your clothes and your weapons. There is no escape from Sango Bay except up this bank, unless you have a galley somewhere. Or maybe you can swim for a couple miles in the sea."

"Oh, that bastard," Jessie growled between clenched teeth. "I could choke him." He was right; there was no exit from this bay except behind Haldane and his men. Sheer cliffs enclosed the two sides. "Leave now, Haldane! Or I'll throttle you."

He laughed. "I doubt that, sister. You and your lover are outnumbered. We're armed and you are not."

Her blood ran cold and the chill sea water wasn't helping any. The sun was descending in the western sky, and the wind was growing cooler. How long had she and Torrin been here? Clearly, they should've left an hour ago.

"Leave our clothes at the edge of the water and turn your backs!" she commanded.

Haldane did as she said, leaving their clothes in a pile just beyond the surf, turned his back, then he said something low to McMurdo. Several more of the men faced the bank, but not McMurdo.

"Turn around, McMurdo!" she demanded.

He shook his head. "Are you thinking I've never seen a naked woman afore? Trust me, I've seen a few." His nasty grin revealed several missing teeth.

"Ugh."

"'Slud!" Torrin said. "We need to turn the tables on them."

"Aye. But how? There are a dozen of them and only two of us."

"I'll think of something. Come, let's get dressed. Stay behind me."

How mortifying to have to depend on Torrin to shield

her from the view of the outlaws. Gil, a young archer who was formerly a member of the MacKay clan, stood on the hill with his arrow aimed at her and Torrin. With her wet hair hanging over her breasts, at least she was partially covered. Torrin bent and retrieved her smock, then helped her put it on, along with the rest of her clothing, uncaring of his own nudity.

She eyed the outlaws while Torrin dressed. Most of them faced Jessie and Torrin again, vile grins on their unshaven faces. Their unkempt hair and dirty clothing told her what sort of men they were—desperate outlaws just like Haldane. Where had he rounded up such a ragtag group? 'Twas hard to believe her wee brother had turned out so horribly. Their father would be mightily ashamed of his youngest son.

Haldane held her three knives in his hands. She should've kept one of them strapped to her thigh, but she'd known the salt water would rust it. Truth was it would've done her no good. One knife against twelve was naught. Saints! What could they do?

Wait! She remembered she'd sewn a small knife into the hem of this *arisaid*. She'd never had to use it and had almost forgotten it. But it would be difficult to retrieve. She couldn't simply grab it. She would have to unravel the hem first.

"Good to see you again, Chief." Haldane smirked. "So, you've seduced my whorish sister, have you?"

Torrin launched himself at Haldane, but the two men flanking him stepped forward, their blades poised to slit Torrin's throat.

He halted and Jessie grabbed the back of his shirt. "Pay him no heed. He's but trying to provoke you."

"I don't need you, MacLeod," Haldane boasted. "We can put you out of your misery right here. I only need my sister to convince the guards to open the portcullis at Dunnakeil. The only reason you're still alive is that, being a chief, you might be worth a lot of ransom money."

The look in Torrin's narrowed eyes turned lethal and Jessie knew he would have his revenge. He'd already decided.

Of a certainty, he had always been kind to her, but she'd seen how deadly he was to his enemies. If he'd had a sword in his hands, he would've likely cut them all down.

"Leave him be. We'll both go peacefully," she said to appease her brother.

"Aye, you will. Or I'll kill you both," Haldane said.

She frowned, wondering if Haldane could indeed kill his own sister. If not, he would order McMurdo to do it. And she had no doubt he'd kill Torrin if he caused any trouble. Haldane was just like his mother—soulless and coldblooded.

"Both of you, up the bank," Haldane ordered, motioning with his sword.

Torrin took her hand, leading her up the sandy pathway. Though she truly didn't need his help, she accepted it because she loved touching him. He was her only comfort in this treacherous situation. She prayed that Torrin, being a warrior and chief, would come up with a brilliant plan of escape. Or maybe she could, if she put her mind to it. But two against twelve? The odds were overwhelming.

At the top of the bank, Haldane turned to Torrin with a smirk. "By the way, Dirk killed your brother."

Torrin halted, his gaze dark and deadly. "What?" he growled.

Jessie's stomach sank. Was it true?

"Aye, Dirk MacKay, the chief of the MacKay clan, killed Nolan MacLeod. He is your brother, is he not?" Haldane said in a lighthearted tone. How could he enjoy delivering such horrible news to anyone?

Torrin frowned. "Aye."

Jessie tightened her hold on his hand. "He might be lying just to rile you."

Haldane laughed. "I'm not lying, sister."

"Did you witness it?" Torrin asked.

"Nay. But Nolan was with us and then, after a skirmish we had with the rest of the MacKays, he vanished. And good riddance. He was never any help to us."

"He made off with Dirk's woman." McMurdo shook his

head, his long gray beard blowing in the wind. "I knew that was a death sentence."

"Lady Isobel?" Jessie asked, her heart leaping into her throat at this news of her best friend. "Nolan attacked Lady Isobel again? Was she hurt?"

"He snatched her from the tent, put her on a horse and rode away with her. Dirk chased after him, and that was the last we saw of Nolan," McMurdo said.

"Was Isobel hurt?" Jessie asked again.

McMurdo shrugged. "We saw her again later with Dirk. She didn't appear hurt, but then Gil shot Dirk in the calf with an arrow." He gave an evil grin.

"I'm hoping he's dead with fever," Haldane said in a hard voice.

"Nay," Jessie said, worry for her older brother clutching at her stomach. He was strong. Surely, he could overcome such an injury. Couldn't he?

"Damn," Torrin muttered. Thinking his younger brother might be dead ripped his heart out. But with the way Nolan had turned corrupt, Torrin had expected him to meet a bad end. For Jessie's brother to have killed his brother… seemed ironic and strange. And he had no doubt Nolan was dead if he'd done what McMurdo said. Dirk would've had no mercy on him for 'twas clear Dirk loved Isobel beyond all reason.

Jessie watched him warily. "You're not going to seek revenge, are you?"

"Nay. If Nolan kidnapped Lady Isobel or hurt her, he deserved what he got. Dirk wouldn't murder someone outright."

"Nay, he wouldn't."

"Did they bury him?" Torrin asked the outlaws.

Haldane shrugged. "Time to go." He strode forward, joining several of his men.

"I'm sure Dirk would've had him buried if he is indeed dead," Jessie said. "We have no proof of it yet."

Torrin nodded. Aye, without doubt. Still, it didn't stop him from remembering Nolan as a wee lad, being slapped and abused by their father. But he couldn't think about that now. He had to focus on how to get himself and Jessie free of Haldane and his men. They were all well-armed and obviously ruthless. Haldane had hired a bunch of outlaws with no loyalties and no qualms about killing anyone for two pence.

"Move along, you two," McMurdo said behind them, his sword raised.

If Jessie wasn't with him, he'd break McMurdo's neck and grab his sword, then he'd run the rest of them through or cut their throats, one by one. At least, as many of them as he could. He was outnumbered, aye, but they were all scrawnier and weaker-looking than him. But he would do naught to put Jessie in danger.

Torrin took her hand and strode forward to catch up to the others. Why the devil hadn't he realized the potential danger of being trapped in that secluded bay? The lure of seducing Jessie had blinded him to everything else. He'd been daft.

When they didn't head toward the castle, Torrin bristled. "Where are you taking us?"

"To a safe place until we get the lay of the land." Haldane gave him a sinister grin.

What did the sneaky bastard have up his sleeve? Mayhap he knew the MacKay guards were likely to shoot him and his cohorts full of arrows before he could make any demands.

Following a roundabout path, over rocky hills and through stands of prickly gorse bushes, Haldane and his men were clearly avoiding the village and the few crofts scattered about the area.

Torrin studied Jessie as he helped her over a huge rock. She appeared concerned and somewhat afraid. Her own little brother was a ruthless outlaw just as his had been. He'd never feared Nolan, but he didn't know everything he'd done either. Haldane was no doubt a murderer, and his partner, McMurdo, certainly was.

An hour later, gloaming was descending upon the land

and thick clouds were moving in from the west, further darkening the evening sky. They stopped at a dilapidated byre just off the narrow trail.

"Inside, both of you." Haldane waved Jessie and Torrin toward the doorway.

"'Tis dark in there," Jessie said. "There may be vermin."

"Do you think I care? Get inside," he ordered.

"Can you at least give us a lantern? 'Twill be dark soon," Jessie said.

"Nay. Don't be such a coward."

"Bastard," she muttered.

Haldane pushed her, and she slammed into Torrin.

"Keep your hands off her!" Torrin said.

"Shut your gob, MacLeod. Or you'll end up like your brother. Now get inside." Haldane shoved him toward the doorway into the dark stone structure. His first instinct was to shove back, 'haps even grab Haldane's sword, but he knew not what the outcome would be.

Inside, he did a quick survey of the building. It contained no windows and only one doorway. The thatch was old and full of holes, but still mostly intact.

"MacDonald, tie them together, sitting back to back," Haldane ordered.

He entered with the lantern, along with two more men, and did as he was told. First, he bound each of their wrists together behind their backs with strips of wool plaid, then he made them sit on the hard-packed, damp dirt floor, wrapped a rope around their torsos and tied a knot in it.

Torrin couldn't fight them now with Jessie present. Besides, he didn't like the odds. Once Haldane left them there, maybe they'd have a chance of escaping.

"How are you feeling?" Torrin asked Jessie, once the men left.

"Not so good."

He tried to glance around at her, needing to look into her eyes, but that was impossible, tied back to back in the dark. "Are you in pain? He tied the ropes tight."

"Nay, no pain, but… How will we escape?" she whispered.

"We'll think of something."

They listened to Haldane and his men outside, most of their mumbled words too low to hear, then things grew quiet.

"They must have gone," Torrin said, keeping his voice low. "Let's see if we can stand and move closer to the door. That way, we can see how many guards he left. Push against my back."

She pushed back hard, while he did the same, and soon they were standing. Stepping sideways, they inched closer to the door, then Torrin saw him—the man with a scraggly brown beard pacing back and forth on the trail. Was he the only guard Haldane left? Or was another one patrolling behind the structure?

"Let's move to the back wall," Torrin whispered. Once they did, he said, "Now, let's see if we can find a jagged stone to cut this rope with." They rubbed against the rocks, most of which had been laid with the smooth side toward them. But then the rope snagged. "There's one." Torrin placed the rope that was wrapped around his upper arm against the roughened edge and sawed against it. "Is this hurting you?"

"Nay. But I don't feel I'm helping very much."

"You are." He rubbed the rope against the rock with all his strength. He had to do this for Jessie. He had to free her before her unpredictable brother did something insane. The rock was not as sharp as he would've liked. In the dark, he couldn't even gauge his progress. Still, he kept sawing the rope until he was near worn out from using the same muscles over and over.

"Saints," he hissed.

"Is there something I can do?" she asked.

"Nay." He had to sever the rope, but could he do it before Haldane returned?

***

Haldane and ten of his men quickly crept along the trail toward Dunnakeil.

"Remain quiet," he whispered. "If the portcullis is open, we'll slip in. If not, we'll see how many guards are patrolling the battlements, and we'll ken what we're up against."

They didn't yet know how many men MacLeod had brought with him, two or three, or a whole regiment. He also needed to know if the clan was out searching for Jessie. 'Twas suppertime and they'd be looking for her soon. Once he had this information and complete darkness fell, so his men could hide better, he'd bring Jessie to the castle and demand entrance… if they didn't want to see her killed before their eyes.

Earlier in the day, Haldane and his men had left their stolen *bìrlinn* at Smoo Cave. What grand luck that they'd come across Jessie and her lover frolicking in the bay. Haldane snorted, disgusted with his sister. He'd never known her to be a wanton, nor had he expected that match up. 'Twas clear MacLeod was besotted with her, considering how he'd helped her along on their journey through the brush and boulders. He might cause a problem when Haldane separated Jessie from him and brought her to the castle.

"You may have to kill MacLeod," Haldane whispered to McMurdo.

"I thought you wanted to hold him for ransom. You're near out of funds, are you not?"

"I'm thinking he'll be too much trouble for that, especially when I separate him from Jessie."

"He's a chief," McMurdo warned. "His death won't go unnoticed. Every MacLeod in Assynt will be hunting us down."

"Do you think I care? Once I'm chief of the MacKays, I'll have a large fighting force of skilled warriors."

"Won't do you any good if the MacLeods attack and kill half of them."

"You let me worry about the rest of the MacLeods. All you have to do is kill Torrin MacLeod, and then if Dirk shows up, kill him, too."

"Whatever you say," McMurdo muttered in a resigned

tone.

Aye, McMurdo would obey his every command. The old man wanted that tomb inside the church too badly to oppose him.

"Why is it you wish to be buried in the church?" Haldane asked.

McMurdo gave him a dark and deadly look from the corner of his eyes, the menace clear even in the gloaming. "The why of it is not your concern, lad."

Even though Haldane ordered McMurdo around a lot, he didn't dare anger him. He knew the grizzled highwayman could turn against him in a trice. And if that happened, Haldane might be dead in two seconds. Or, if McMurdo let him live but deserted them, the MacKays would be much harder to defeat. McMurdo might be ancient, but he was still lethal. Mainly, Haldane needed him to kill Dirk, for his older brother was a formidable opponent, a highly trained and skilled warrior. He had to be taken out before Haldane could be chief.

Once they took possession of Dunnakeil, they could easily accomplish the rest. He would force each member of the clan to obey his command… or die. Their choice.

As they neared the castle, Haldane saw naught out of the ordinary. 'Twas just as it had been the last time he was here several months ago, except fewer guards were patrolling the battlements. He only saw three at the moment, their dark silhouettes clear against the gray sky.

"Hide in the bushes," he told his men in a loud whisper. They silently vanished. He slipped through the bushes until he had a view of the portcullis. 'Twas closed. "Damnation," he muttered.

One man's voice echoed within the bailey. That's when he noticed a large number of men assembled. They might be organizing a search party for Jessie and MacLeod.

How many men were gathered there? He saw a few he didn't recognize. He'd seen most of the MacLeods several months ago when he'd gone to Munrick. For a certainty, they weren't MacKays.

Haldane and his men might have to hide out and pick them off one by one as they fanned out in their search. 'Twould be easier than charging them in battle.

"Come. Let's slip back to the byre," he whispered to his men. "MacDonald and Douglas, you two stay here, well hidden, and count how many men they have. If you get the chance, secretly ambush them one at a time, slit their throats, and hide the bodies."

The two men nodded.

He had to get back to the byre and move Jessie and Torrin further away until they'd thinned out some of the guards. Nay, they'd move Jessie and kill Torrin.

***

Though she didn't want him to be captured, Jessie was glad Torrin was with her. He was working hard to get them loose, and she wished she could help, but she couldn't get to her wee knife with her hands tied.

Torrin's back was warm, solid, and comforting behind her. "Pull hard against me to tighten the rope," he said. "It's starting to fray and unravel."

She leaned away from him, the ropes pressing tightly into her flesh. He continued scraping the rope against the stone. And then it loosened.

"Aye. There we are," he said, quiet triumph in his voice as the rope binding them back to back unwound and fell away. Now they only needed to remove the tight strips of wet wool plaid that secured their wrists behind their backs.

"I'm going to try to break the strip of plaid around your wrists. Tell me if I hurt you."

"Very well."

Although Torrin's wrists were still bound, he moved his fingers over her wrists and the bindings. He tugged at the material from both sides. "Am I hurting you?"

"Nay." It felt tight but not painful.

After a few moments, the material ripped in the silence. "Thank the saints," she whispered. "Now let me get my knife and I'll cut you free."

"What? You have a knife?" Shock was evident in his loudly whispered words.

"Aye. 'Tis hidden."

"Where?"

"Sewn into the hem of my *arisaid*." She bent and worked at the seam, ripping the thread from the wool material. "'Tis not easy to retrieve, but it has come in handy for the first time ever."

"I'm going to have to use that trick."

When he turned his back to her, she cut the strips of plaid binding his hands.

He sighed and rubbed his wrists. "I thank you. I'm beyond glad to have you as an ally."

She smiled in the darkness, wishing she could see his face. She'd never imagined she would feel so safe with him… protected, even. She relished the deep, rich timbre of his voice, more obvious in the darkness.

"Can I use your knife?" he asked.

"Aye." She handed it to him. "What's your plan?"

"Och. 'Tis tiny. I'm going to disarm the man guarding us. Hopefully, I won't have to kill him. Will you hold it against me if I do?"

"Nay. We have to do what we can to escape, else Haldane may kill us both."

They crept toward the door but hung back. 'Twas lighter outside than inside. Now two men lingered upon the trail.

Torrin drew back. "So, there are two of them. One must have been behind the byre earlier."

"Aye." She bent and picked up a rock. "I'll take care of one of them."

"Are you mad?" Torrin demanded in a harsh whisper.

"I can knock him on the head."

"Nay. You remain in here, in the far corner. If one of them comes after you, then you bash his skull in good."

Typical man orders. "Very well, MacLeod. Have a care, will you?"

"Aye, indeed. How about a kiss for luck?"

Her face burned in the darkness. "Nay. 'Twill distract you."

"Och. You're right. We'll save the kisses for later when we're celebrating our escape. Stay over here, then." His strong hands on her shoulders, he guided her toward the corner.

She waited, watching as he halted at the door, peered out, then slipped outside.

She hastened toward the door, crouched low and looked out. Where had he gone? She didn't even see him. The two guards paced along the trail. She drew back and flattened her body against the wall. Where on earth was Torrin?

Seconds of silence dragged by in which she barely breathed. A shrill squealing sound echoed from behind the byre. It sounded like an animal, an injured rabbit perhaps.

"Go see what that was," one of Haldane's guards said.

"Sounded like supper." He strode out of sight and behind the byre. A thump sounded and someone cried out.

"What the devil?" The other guard followed him, sword drawn.

Blast. She hoped Torrin grabbed the first guard's sword, so he'd be better armed.

Curses echoed. Swords clanged.

Please protect Torrin, she prayed. Taking her rock, she ventured outside and peered around the corner. The two men were engaged in swordplay. But they didn't seem to notice the first guard on the ground stirring. *Saints!* She had to do something. Before he could notice her, she crept forward and bashed the rock against his head. He grunted and flopped to the ground.

"Jessie, get back inside," Torrin ordered.

When his opponent glanced at her, Torrin took advantage and sliced his blade across the man's chest. He stumbled back, but then charged toward her. Still low to the ground, she ducked and smashed the rock into his knee.

He cried out and crashed to the ground next to her.

Torrin grabbed her arm and helped her stand. "Move

away from him."

She leapt back, and Torrin kicked the unmoving man's sword away.

"Is he dead?" Jessie asked.

"Hopefully. I ran the bastard through when he tried to grab you."

"In truth?" She hadn't seen that.

"Aye." Torrin bent and held his hand before the other man's nose. "He's no longer breathing."

Jessie picked up the discarded sword. "I might need this."

"You ken how to wield a sword?" he asked, surprise evident in his voice.

"'Haps not as well as you, but I've had some training." She noticed a large dark stain on Torrin's shirt sleeve. "You're injured!"

"'Tis naught but a scratch. Come. Let's head toward the castle. Is there another route we could use so as to not run into Haldane and his crew?"

"Aye. I'll show you." She led the way around a rocky outcropping and along a narrow trail. When they neared Dunnakeil, low voices rumbled nearby. She ducked behind a gorse bush and he followed suit. The sounds moved along the more oft used trail leading away from the castle. It also led to the byre.

"Haldane may have left one or two of his men to watch the castle. We'll have to be careful," Torrin whispered.

"Aye."

But they also had to hurry or Haldane would discover them gone and start searching for them.

They both stood at the same time.

Again, she was thankful Torrin was with her for she would've been much more afraid had she been alone. She didn't want to tell him this now however. She didn't wish to distract him. They had to approach the castle with much caution even though they were still not on the main trail. The wind off the sea made it difficult to hear any movement in the bushes.

Closer and closer they drew to the castle, to safety.

"Stay behind me," Torrin whispered and got in front of her.

"Why? Do you sense something?"

"Aye." He crept forward one step at a time. "Watch my back."

She felt honored that he trusted her so much. Holding onto the plaid at his back, she turned her head and took a long careful look behind them. Seeing naught in the dusk, she faced forward again, then her gaze searched along the sides of the trail. Just in front of them, the bushes had near overgrown the trail. The deep gloaming only provided enough light to see indistinct outlines of the dark bushes and gray sky.

A shout sounded behind them. Her heart vaulted into her throat.

"Damnation, they've discovered our escape." Torrin grabbed her hand. "Come, let's run the rest of the way. We can't fight all of them."

Holding hands, they dashed through the bushes, the thorns tearing at their clothing. The bushes behind her shuddered and someone grabbed her left arm. She screamed and struck at the person with the sword in her left hand. Since she wasn't left-handed, her blows were weak.

Torrin leapt around her and struck out at the man. She was immediately released. She couldn't see what Torrin was doing in the dimness, but his opponent yelled out and fell into the bushes.

"Come, let's hurry." Taking his hand again, she ran as fast as she could. She tripped over her skirts and started falling, but Torrin caught her and lifted her into his arms. "Hold on around my neck, and I can still use my sword."

She did as he asked, unable to believe his strength, but he was a warrior through and through. They approached the curtain wall, then ran along it toward the portcullis and guard house.

Bushes shook behind them and she saw a few glimpses

of pale-colored shirts. "They're getting closer. Hurry," she said.

Torrin increased his speed.

"Guards!" she yelled. "'Tis me, Jessie. Open the gate."

Upon reaching the portcullis, they did not find it open, but several guards lingered outside, along with Iain and his men.

"What the devil is happening?" Iain asked.

"Haldane and his band of outlaws are on our heels," Torrin said. "Get Lady Jessie inside!"

Just then the gates opened and Torrin pushed her through. She refused to let go, trying to drag him in after her, but he tore away from her. "Go inside the castle! They have arrows."

"Nay! Torrin!" she yelled, clutching her hands onto the closing bars, but he was off with Iain and the guards, charging to confront Haldane and his men.

She ran up the turnpike stairs into the guard house to gain a better vantage point. The guard stationed there eyed her sword.

"What is happening out there?" she asked him.

The clang of blades answered her question. By torch-light, the men fought. Two men fell and she couldn't tell who they were in such dim and wavering light.

Please protect Torrin. Against her will, she had grown to care deeply for him over the past couple of days.

A shout resounded and several men ran away—Haldane's men. The MacKays gave chase but moments later, they returned. Where was Torrin? Her eyes searched the dimness. She ran down the steps of the guard tower and into the barmkin. She met the men at the portcullis as it was opened. Torrin walked beside Erskine and Iain. Her eyes searched Torrin for injuries but found none, other than the one he'd sustained earlier on his arm. She stood still, forcing herself not to run to him. She didn't want him to know how much she cared.

"They fled like a pack of rabbits," Torrin told her.

"Was anyone injured?"

"We killed two of them—men none of us knew," Erskine said. "All the MacKays, MacLeods and Stewarts are well."

She released a sigh of relief, and they all proceeded up the steps and into the great hall. She stopped and faced Torrin. "You need to have the healer look at that cut on your arm."

"Very well, but it has stopped bleeding and is naught to worry over." His lips quirked into a slight smile.

"Still, I wouldn't want you to catch a fever because of it."

"I like that you're worried about me," Torrin murmured.

"Jessie, what happened?" Aiden rushed toward them, a guard on either side of him.

She sent him a dry smile. "Our wee brother has returned to wreck more havoc on us all."

"Haldane's back? Saints! I tried to come out and help but they wouldn't allow it." He motioned to his two guards. "Erskine told them to keep me inside."

"'Tis for the best. You don't want to go anywhere near Haldane. He'd kill either of us in a heartbeat. He wants Dunnakeil and the chiefdom at any cost. He was going to use me to force the guards to open the portcullis."

Aiden's brow furrowed. "I can't believe Haldane has turned against his own family like this," he said in a saddened tone.

"I'm very disappointed in him, to say the least. He's become the most malicious outlaw you could imagine, and he seems to enjoy it. I've never seen him smile so much." She knew the situation had to be hard for Aiden to accept. He and Haldane had always been the closest of the four siblings, being full brothers and near the same age. He had to be concerned about Haldane and what would happen to him if the MacKay guards ever caught him.

"I wish Dirk was here," Aiden said, looking more anxious by the minute.

"As do I. But he isn't, so we must hold Dunnakeil until

his return." She wouldn't tell Aiden that Dirk had been injured on his travels. She didn't want him to worry even more.

"We held supper since we didn't ken where you were," Aiden said. "The men were getting ready to go out and search when you showed up. Where were you when he captured you both?"

"I'd simply taken a walk to Sango Bay." Remembering how she'd been naked with Torrin at the time, she hoped the dim lighting in the great hall hid the heat she felt flushing into her face.

"And Chief MacLeod was with you?"

She glanced aside at Torrin. He had stepped a few feet away to talk to Erskine.

"Aye, he'd followed me. Said he was protecting me in the event MacBain returns."

Aiden gave a sly grin as if he knew Torrin's true motive. "I'm glad he was there."

"So am I. Without him, I couldn't have escaped Haldane."

"Now that he has rescued you… twice, mayhap you will consent to marry him, hmm, sister?"

Chapter Nine

Later that night, Jessie soaked in a large wooden tub filled with hot water and lavender soap. 'Twas heavenly and luxurious. All her muscles ached from where she'd been marched across the moor, then tied up. The skin of her wrists was still red and raw from the bindings.

Thank the saints she and Torrin had escaped Haldane and his cronies. If they hadn't, she or Torrin, or maybe both of them, could've been dead by now. How could her own brother have turned into the most nefarious outlaw in the Highlands?

A knock sounded at her door. Probably the maid.

She lifted her head. "I'm not finished yet. Come back later," she called, wanting to soak some of the soreness out and rest a while.

The door latch lifted and someone stuck their head in. *Torrin!* A shock went through her system. What the devil was he doing coming to her bedchamber? Everyone in the castle would find out they'd had a tryst. She grabbed the smock lying by the tub and drew it over her nude body.

He quickly slipped inside and closed the door, then barred it before she could utter a sound.

"I didn't say you could come in." Her tone was not as

biting as she'd hoped.

He leaned leisurely against the door and gave her a lazy, seductive smile. "I didn't ask."

Her pulse thumped in her throat. "You must go."

"Why?"

"Just because we… doesn't mean…" she faltered, unsure about saying such brazen words to him.

"What? I'm not sure I follow." He sauntered forward, removing the brooch holding his plaid in place at his chest.

"What do you think you're doing?"

"Undressing." He unclasped his belt. It dropped along with his plaid.

Unable to believe he was getting naked in her bedchamber, she realized her mouth was gaping and snapped it shut. What if someone had seen him enter her chamber? He slid the linen shirt over his head and tossed it, leaving him bare.

She swallowed hard, her eyes tracing over his long, muscular body, the likes of which she'd never imagined and certainly never seen before today.

His lengthy shaft was growing erect. The memory of their joining earlier that day overcame her and she could scarce breathe.

"I love the way you look in that tub," he said, kneeling on the floor beside her. His dark green eyes in the candlelight mesmerized her. "I've already bathed, but I wouldn't mind doing so again." Leaning forward, he slid his hand along her cheek and captured her lips. His tongue teased her lips apart and slipped into her mouth. She opened, shocked to realize she wanted to devour him. He tasted of peaty whisky and his own unique essence, which further rendered her senseless.

He moaned and she became aware of her hands fisting in his thick hair. Surprised at her brazen response to him, she immediately released him.

He pulled back, raising a brow. "'Tis a big tub. Mind if I join you?" Without waiting for her to answer, he stood and stepped into the tub. Pulling her legs out of the way, she caught a glimpse of muscular thighs, his erect shaft and his rippled abdomen as he sat opposite her. Oh heavens. Just a glance at him set her body on fire.

He sank into the water and sat back. "Ahh. Feels good, aye?"

She had never imagined bathing with a man before, but she supposed 'twas not much different from swimming naked in the sea with a man. She had a feeling she was going to enjoy it just as much. How shocking she was. If the maids learned of this, they'd be gossiping. But she couldn't run him off; her lust-filled body wouldn't allow her to. Damn him for bewitching her.

Reclining, he watched her with half-closed eyes. "Jessie?"

She nodded.

"What are you thinking?"

"How much I hate you."

He snorted. "Liar." He studied her intently. "You like me. You liked what we did today on that beach. And I sure as hell did."

Heat rushed over her, scalding her more completely than hot water ever could.

"Aye. 'Twas a tryst," she admitted. "But that doesn't mean 'tis going to happen again."

He lifted a brow, looking suddenly serious, determined and a wee bit intimidating. "Come over here." Grasping her hand, he tugged at her.

"Nay! You cannot simply order me about. Maybe you're used to doing that with your other women, but I'm not them." She resisted, trying to pull her wet hand from his, but he held her in place.

"Stop arguing," he said softly. "I have no other women. Do you want the maids or guards to start pounding on the door, wondering what the ruckus is?"

"Nay." She dropped silent and still, her gaze darting to the door briefly.

"Well, then, behave yourself." He gave her a light, playful slap on the arse.

She ended up on her knees between his legs, a very enticing position, with her hands on his broad shoulders.

"I mean to have you, Jessie MacKay," he murmured, his breath teasing her lips and his hands caressing her derriere. "And not just once or twice."

She pushed against his shoulders. "Until you tire of me."

"I'll never tire of you." His words were spoken with quiet conviction.

She wished it could be true. "You cannot know that."

"I know my own mind. And I know you. 'Tis clear to me that you want the same thing."

Dropping her gaze from his, she remained silent, many emotions conflicting inside her. Of a certainty, she enjoyed lying with him, but a woman could not base her most important decisions on such things. She wanted to take a chance on him, but what if, after she trusted him, after she loved him, he put her aside for another woman? She could not bear it. She was strong, but not that strong.

"Do you not?" he asked, sliding his hands up her sides, leaving hot chills along the way.

"Naught is clear to me," she whispered, stifling a shiver.

"Allow me to show you something very clear." He kissed her and she felt as if her insides were melting like hot pastry filling. And his kisses were just as sweet and sinful.

She fell against him, her breasts flattening against his hard chest. He lifted her, placing her knees on either side of his hips. Her most sensitive parts pressed up against his hard shaft. She gasped and his moan vibrated her chest.

What kind of wicked magic was this? She could not believe the lust that immobilized her when he touched her like this. Her secret feminine parts ached to have him.

His hand and forearm beneath her derriere, he rose from the tub. When he turned, her head spun. He strode across the floor and lowered her to the bed. Her hands were tangled in his hair.

"I ken what you need, m'lady," he whispered.

Him. He was the most decadent treat she could imagine.

He kissed down her throat to her chest. His beard stubble prickled over her breasts before he took her nipple between his lips and suckled. Sharp need lanced through her. She arched her back, offering herself shamelessly.

After lavishing both her breasts with sensual torture, he kissed down her stomach and flicked his tongue into her navel. His hot hands framed her hips and he scraped his teeth over her hip bone.

"I want to devour you, lass."

The passion in his tone sent feverish quivers through her.

He brushed his lips over her mound and her hands fisted in his hair. Nay, he couldn't do that. Could he?

He pushed her legs apart and then her nether lips. His hot tongue stroked over her. What on earth? She didn't know or care, but she loved it. She heard herself cry out, then bit her lip to keep quiet. No one could know what sinful delights she was indulging in with Torrin. His tongue and his fingers worked magic. Unintentionally, she thrust her hips toward him, yearning for more. Craving his shaft. His moan vibrated her flesh. He slid a finger into her, then two, stroking in and out while his tongue swirled around an especially sensitive spot.

Saints! That most astounding sensation was coming over her again. Her lungs refused to draw in more breath. The tingles circled through her and then exploded. Every muscle in her body clenched onto the pleasure, trying to hold onto it. She felt as if she vaulted toward the moon.

Seconds later she came back to herself, gasping for breath. How could he make her feel such volatile and blissful sensations? Things she'd never imagined and certainly never experienced before him.

"Torrin, you devil," she breathed.

"Aye." He chuckled, rising onto his knees. "Are you ready for more?"

"I'm not certain," she teased. "I think you've worn me out."

"Hmm. I wonder." He stroked the tip of his shaft over her most sensitive flesh.

She hissed in a breath at the intense sensation. At the same time, need flashed through her. Unintentionally, she lifted her hips toward him.

"Aye," he whispered, tempting her with more wet strokes. He nudged himself into her, then away.

"More," she said, aching deep inside.

"Are you certain?"

"Aye, Torrin. Please."

"Mmm." He wrapped his arm around her thigh and thrust his hips, embedding himself within her. He moaned deep in his chest, while pleasure, endless need, and the feeling of completeness encompassed her.

More, more, more.

He suckled at her breasts, first one, then the other, as he started moving.

Her arousal heightening, she buried her hands in his hair and arched up to meet his powerful thrusts. Growling, he besieged her body as if he couldn't get enough. Erotic decadence ran rampant through her.

Torrin could hardly believe he was making love to Jessie. Each time felt like an amazing dream, but the pleasure and need for more which consumed him told him 'twas indeed real. Her eagerness was beyond anything he could've imagined. Her pale blue eyes darkened with desire set him off like flame to gunpowder. Her hands in his hair pulled, sometimes painfully, but he didn't care. He wished she'd bite him and leave her mark on him.

He'd thoroughly enjoyed feasting upon her moments ago. Her sweet essence was like strawberries and honey, but twice as addictive. Driving into her tight depths felt like something he'd waited for his whole life.

Digging her nails into his shoulders, she sucked in a hissing breath and arched her neck back. How he loved bringing her to the peak of carnal delight. Watching her, gauging her reactions, he waited until she was on the precipice, her breath held, then he increased his pace with sudden intensity. Muscles deep within her clutched at him, caressed him. *Saints!* He couldn't endure it. His release blasted through him like a cannon. Fiery, explosive hedonism that burned up his thoughts and rationality. He consumed her mouth as the last waves of pleasure rippled through him.

Damnation, naught had ever felt so good. Not just physically. But for the first time in what seemed like years, he felt true happiness and found himself smiling like a fool. "I've dreamed of this since I first saw you over six months ago," he said, lying beside her.

"Hmm," she said.

"I knew we'd be perfect together."

"I did not know such… intense pleasure was possible," she said in a shy tone, refusing to meet his gaze.

"In truth?"

She shook her head.

"You mean the climax?"

Lifting her gaze, she searched his eyes, then nodded.

He smiled, then compressed his mouth into a line, trying to hide how pleased he was. "Am I to assume MacBain didn't ken how to bring you to climax?"

She shrugged a slim shoulder. "He didn't. At the time, I didn't ken anything about it. I thought that was all there was to it."

Torrin snorted. "I knew he was a daft bastard."

"Indeed. I don't want to think of him anymore."

"Nor do I, for a certainty."

When she stroked her fingers down his chest and abdomen, exploring him, his heart warmed. He wanted to kiss her head to toe. It wasn't simple lust he was feeling now but something much deeper. 'Twas the reason he couldn't get her out of his mind. He had to convince her to marry him; he needed her for a lifetime. She meant more to him than the chiefdom of Clan MacLeod or an heir. Alarm blasted through him. Was he mad? He didn't know. He didn't understand himself. All he knew for certain was he didn't want to live his life without her. He'd never imagined feeling this way. He'd heard of men tossing all aside for a woman, but could never comprehend it. Now he did. Some obsession had overtaken him… body, mind and soul.

He wanted to ask her to marry him now, wanted her promise that she would, but fear gnawed at his gut. She might say *nay* again. He didn't want to ruin this perfect moment. What could he say to convince her?

His one hope was that if he could get her with child, she would agree to marry him. But he didn't care. He'd marry her either way, whether she was barren or could have ten children. And he knew the reason—because he was in love with her. *Saints!* He'd always thought such emotions daft. He was a chief and a warrior; he was supposed to be too hard to feel such things. But it seemed he had a heart after all. His father hadn't beaten it out of him. All of the battles he'd fought… none of it mattered. A lady had brought him to his knees. A lady he'd give anything and everything to if she would let him.

"Jessie?"

Her fingers stroked leisurely over him. "Aye."

His heart pounding, he kissed her forehead. "I want…" 'Slud, he couldn't think of the right words.

"What?" She stroked her hand over his bare hip.

A potent combination of lust and emotion struck him. He took her hand and laced his fingers through hers. "What do you want… in life? What do you wish for most?"

She tried to pull her hand from his, but he tightened his fingers.

"It matters not," she whispered.

"Aye, it matters. 'Tis the most important thing."

"Peace."

"Indeed, peace is a good thing, but you must want more."

"I don't wish to speak of this, MacLeod. If our tryst is over, mayhap you should go back to your own chamber." Pulling her hand from his, she turned onto her side, away from him.

Hell. He'd known this would happen. Why was she so damned stubborn?

He snuggled up tight against her back, his growing erection against her arse. "Our tryst isn't over," he whispered in her ear. "'Twill never be over." He stroked his hand up over her hip, her waist and cradled her breast in his hand. He teased her nipple and sucked her earlobe into his mouth. "I'm hungry for you, and I'll never get enough."

She arched against him, sliding her hand back into his hair and around his neck. He loved the moments when she let go and fully accepted him, even if it was only physical lust. He would get to her heart one way or another.

Rolling her onto her stomach, he pinned her beneath him.

"What are you doing, MacLeod?"

"I'll show you." He spread her legs and stroked his fingers between, finding her wet.

She gasped and arched up in a most inviting way. Lust surged through him, making him want to rut like a wild stag. But he didn't; he teased that sweet feminine spot.

"So wet," he whispered in her ear.

Moaning, she pushed her derriere against him. He wanted to give her exactly what she was craving, but making her wait appealed more. It wasn't that he wanted to make her beg for it; 'twas only that he wished she wanted everything he did. And mayhap she did, but for some reason, she wouldn't let go and admit it.

"Torrin." Her demanding feminine growl intensified his arousal even more.

"Aye. What is it you want?"

"Take me."

"Mmm." He loved the sound of that but not enough to give in yet. He lightly bit her shoulder, his fingers caressing her. She grew wetter and more swollen by the second. Nor did he want her to experience a climax yet. He wanted her suspended in intense arousal a bit longer. Could he make her addicted to him? Could he make her feel as he did, as if he could never get enough of her? Could he make her lie awake at night, burning… craving as he did?

"I want you now," she gasped, her voice breathy. "Please, Torrin."

Damn, he could no longer resist. He positioned himself and slipped into her, the wet heat taking his sanity. He muttered a curse, held her hips between his palms and gave into the pounding need. Never in his life had lust seared him so profoundly. Her moans and whimpers near drove him mad. He but wanted to please her, fulfill her every desire.

He slid his hand over her mound and stroked that wee bud of pleasure. She cried out, then pressed her face against the pillow, trying to muffle the sound. He grinned, wanting to laugh but at the same time, his release threatened. He ground his teeth, forcing himself to wait. Her body clenched onto him, so tight he thought he might die on the spot. She screamed into the pillow but he didn't let up. Nay, he made himself wait. Wait, wait… until no more rational thoughts remained in his head. And then an explosion of fire and pleasure consumed him. No thoughts, just ecstasy and heaven… yet hot as hell.

Moments later, Jessie was asleep, but Torrin was too wound up, going over and over all the possibilities in his mind. If he got her with child, she would marry him. 'Twas likely the only way she'd agree to it.

He slept fitfully for a few minutes at a time. At the first light of dawn, a knock sounded at the door. He leapt up but Jessie didn't even stir. He slipped his long shirt over his head, grabbed his plaid, and unbarred the door. Cautiously, he opened it a crack and squinted into the corridor.

The older man outside the door frowned and lifted his lantern, his red and silver hair glinting in the light of the flame. Hell, 'twas Jessie's uncle, Conall. He and his large family had been moved into the castle last night for safety, so Haldane wouldn't take any of them hostage.

"Good morn," Torrin said.

"I thought this was Jessie's chamber," Conall said in a gruff voice, clearly displeased.

"Aye, 'tis." Torrin's face heated, though he had no idea why. Surely, Conall knew that Torrin wished to marry Jessie. "Has something happened?"

"Aye. Aiden's gone."

"Saints," Torrin hissed. "Did he run away?" *Or did someone kidnap him. Haldane?*

"We know not."

"What is it?" Jessie asked groggily from the bed.

Torrin turned his head, hardly able to see her in the gray dawn light, but kept the door almost closed. "Naught to worry over. Go back to sleep and I'll take care of it."

"Nay. Tell me." She slid to the edge of the bed and grabbed a smock.

"We'll be out in a minute," Torrin told Conall.

The older man gave a brief nod and stepped away.

"Who's out there?"

"Your Uncle Conall."

"Blast," she muttered. "I didn't want him to find us together. What did he say?"

"They can't find Aiden."

"What? Nay!" She hastily jerked on her plaid *arisaid* and belted it. "Where do they think he is?"

"He didn't say." Torrin belted his own plaid about his waist and straightened it as best he could in the dim dawn light.

She hurried to the door, opened it and stepped into the corridor. Torrin followed.

"Uncle Conall, is Aiden gone?"

"Aye. His bodyguard reported it about a half hour ago. We searched the castle top to bottom."

"Do you think he slipped out to talk to Haldane?"

The corners of Conall's mouth slanted downward within his gray and red beard. "'Tis what some of us fear."

She released an exasperated breath. "The lad is daft! Haldane will use him as a hostage, just as he did me. Or kill him."

"Let's not be so cynical yet," Torrin said. "We'll go out and search for him. Haldane won't kill him right away. Like you said, he'll try to use him for leverage first."

"He thinks because he and Haldane are brothers, and they were close until last winter, that Haldane won't hurt him. He is so naïve."

"Aye, that he is," Conall said. "Without doubt, he thinks he can talk some sense into Haldane."

"He doesn't realize how much Haldane has changed. He's turned into a man who is a vicious killer."

Conall nodded, looking disgusted. "Your da is most likely turning in his tomb at the moment."

"I'll help organize a search party." Torrin headed down the corridor.

***

Haldane sat by the fire-pit outside a cave halfway up the side of a mountain, his stomach growling and his mouth watering as he watched the two rabbits roasting on a spit. Thank the saints Gil was gifted with a bow and arrow.

This cave was one of McMurdo's old hideouts and near impossible to get to over rocky, steep terrain. No wonder he'd evaded capture for years. The MacKays would never find them up here.

Haldane arose and paced across the rocky ground. The morning sun was glinting over Ben Hope in the distance and Loch Eriboll lay below, reflecting the blue and gold sky. This was a miserable place. He ground his teeth at having to hide out in these wild mountains. He should already be the MacKay chief. He should be living comfortably in Dunnakeil, sleeping in a featherbed each night, filling his belly with fine foods every day, and sitting by a warm fireplace in winter. 'Twas how he'd grown up and what his mother and father had wanted for him.

"Look who we found!" one of his men called out behind him.

Haldane turned and came face to face with his wee

brother. Victory surged through him. Aiden would be an even better hostage than Jessie had been. He couldn't fight worth a damn and everyone in the clan loved him.

"We searched him for weapons and found none," MacDonald said.

Haldane grinned. "What are you doing here, Aiden?"

"I came to talk some sense into you, brother. What the devil do you think you're doing?" His green eyes glinted with ire, making Haldane want to laugh. Even though Aiden was two years older than Haldane, he was still skinny and small, like a lad. And unfortunately, he was as trusting as a child. Haldane felt sorry for him, and experienced a moment of remorse for what he would have to do.

"What I'm supposed to do," Haldane said. "What Mother and Father would've wanted me to do."

"Nay, you're mad. You're the youngest. You were never destined to be chief."

Annoyance twisted through Haldane. "Wee brother, you don't have the stones to be chief. Dirk is an imposter. And Jessie is a woman. I'm the only one left."

Aiden shook his head, his thin sandy hair blowing in the mountain breeze. "Are you still lying to yourself about Dirk? He is Da's oldest son. I remember him very clearly from before he disappeared."

"Nay." Haldane knew good and well Dirk was who he claimed to be, but he loved keeping up the pretense as his ma had always done. Besides, Dirk didn't deserve acknowledgement as a MacKay. "Dirk has to die. He murdered our mother, Aiden! Don't you remember?"

"He didn't murder her. He killed her in self-defense."

"Ha. That mountain of a man felt the need to kill our scrawny old mother in self-defense?"

"She poisoned Isobel and me and almost killed us both!"

"Not intentionally, not in your case anyway."

"Ma tried to have Dirk murdered several times. Don't you remember, she hired McMurdo to shove him off a cliff thirteen years ago?"

Haldane smirked and glanced aside at McMurdo. The man with the long gray hair and scarred, wrinkled face narrowed his black eyes, his menacing gaze moving back and forth between him and Aiden. 'Twas a sore point with him that he hadn't succeeded in a job he'd been paid a thousand pounds to accomplish.

"And 'tis a job he is determined to finish, aye, McMurdo?" Haldane asked.

He gave a brief nod and continued sharpening his sword.

"Nay," Aiden said, his eyes widening. "You're getting McMurdo to kill Dirk?"

"Of course. He's the best man for the job."

Studying Haldane, Aiden shook his head. "You've become just like Ma."

"If you mean canny and brilliant, aye." Haldane smiled. "I'm glad you came to visit me. Now, I can convince Erskine and the guards to open the gates."

"Wrong. They won't do it."

"Then you'll die, too, along with Dirk and anyone else who gets in my way."

"What happened to you, brother? You didn't used to be like this."

"I came to my senses. That's what." Fury rampaged through Haldane's veins. "If you'd had the gall to stand up and be chief as Ma wanted, I wouldn't have been forced to do this. I supported you. I would've helped you. But, nay. You wished to give it all up to Dirk."

"Dirk is the best chief this clan could possibly have. I'm not suited to it and neither are you."

"I'll be as great a chief as Da was."

"You are mad."

"Indeed!" Haldane grinned. "Madness suits me, does it not, McMurdo?"

He nodded.

Fear lit in Aiden's eyes when he watched McMurdo. Haldane was glad. He knew Aiden didn't fear him. But he should. He didn't want to kill Aiden, but if he was all that stood between Haldane and the chiefdom, he would do it.

In the meantime, he would use him to get inside the gates of Dunnakeil. No way in hell would Erskine, Jessie, and the rest of them allow Aiden to be killed.

"You should give it up, Haldane. You'll never succeed at this."

"There's where you're wrong, wee brother."

"You'll get yourself killed. If you want to live, you should go south and stay there."

Haldane gave a bitter laugh. "I've been south. Dunnakeil is my home and I mean to claim it, no matter the cost."

"'Tis not worth your life."

"Don't worry over me. I'm a big lad now. I can take care of myself." He placed his hand upon Aiden's bony shoulder and guided him toward the fire-pit. The roasted rabbits appeared to be almost done. "Come. Let's break our fast. We have a mission at gloaming."

"What mission?"

Haldane smiled. "You're going to get us into Dunnakeil."

Chapter Ten

"Glad I found you," Torrin told Jessie in an upstairs corridor. "We've looked for Aiden in the stables, the smithy, all the outbuildings and the kirk. No sign of him. The search party is ready to head out."

"I've searched the entire castle for him again, all the places he practices his music," she said, her throat tightening at the thought her wee brother could already be hurt or dead. "'Twas clear to me last night he wanted to talk to Haldane. They've been close their whole lives, and Aiden naively believes his brother wouldn't hurt him. And it could be that he fears Haldane will be killed before he can see him or talk to him again."

Torrin nodded. "I can understand that. I wish I could've talked to Nolan again one last time. It hurts to lose a brother to a life of crime."

"Indeed, it does."

He took her hand and kissed the back. "Don't you worry. We'll find Aiden."

"I'm going with you." Jessie said.

"Nay." Torrin frowned. "If you go, I'll have to protect you instead of searching for Aiden or fighting Haldane."

He was right. Though she knew how to use a dirk, she wasn't a warrior, and she would only be a liability. "Very well.

I thank you for putting your own life in danger to help Aiden."

"If what Haldane said is true, I no longer have a little brother. If I can help save the life of yours, I'll be glad."

Tears stung her eyes. "You're very generous."

He shook his head. "Just doing what is right." After glancing behind himself, Torrin stepped closer, slipped his fingers around her nape, beneath her hair, and kissed her lips. 'Twas a fierce, passionate kiss, but over too quickly.

He stepped back. "We'll return soon."

A bit unsteady on her feet, she braced against the wall and noticed a man's loud voice yelling *MacLeod* from the great hall.

"Have a care," she said.

"I intend to." He gave a lighthearted smile, stroked his fingers along her cheek and kissed her forehead. Then he disappeared down the steps.

She ran further along the corridor and watched out the window as Torrin joined the other men in the courtyard and mounted his horse.

"May God protect him," she whispered, tears in her eyes. *And please let him find Aiden alive and well.*

Though she could scarcely believe it, those were the two men she cared most about in this world… them and Dirk. 'Twas obvious she would care about her brothers… but Torrin? She had never imagined. Sometimes when she relived what they'd indulged in yesterday and last night, she was shocked at herself.

Aye, shocked, but she didn't regret it. Like her father, she had always believed in living life to the fullest when the opportunity arose. But that had left her emotionally bruised and battered. If she didn't fall in love with Torrin, she wouldn't be hurt when he deserted her. But simply imagining that made her chest ache and her throat close.

"Nay," she whispered. *I have not fallen in love with him.*

Have I? Tears filled her eyes.

***

Torrin rode beside Erskine, Dirk's sword-bearer. His position was that of a war-leader, and from what Torrin could tell, the man was highly skilled. Torrin's two bodyguards followed, the only two of his men he hadn't sent on errands. He hoped the others returned soon. Iain rode farther back with the four Stewart men. Twelve MacKay guards and clansmen also accompanied them, including Conall and two of his brawny sons, Dougal and Little Conall. But, truth be told, Little Conall was larger than Big Conall.

First, they visited the old byre where Torrin and Jessie had been held. 'Twas empty. Next, they searched Smoo Cave. Also abandoned, but they found an eight-oar *bìrlinn* on the beach there. Obviously, this had been Haldane's landing point. Two of the MacKays used their axes to chop holes in the boat so the brigands couldn't escape so easily.

"McMurdo is known to have some well-concealed hiding places," Erskine said. "'Tis why he has escaped capture all these years. My father and the former chief often searched for the highwayman. He's as wily as a fox."

Torrin nodded. He'd heard tales of the elusive and murderous McMurdo all his life and knew better than to underestimate him.

The clan tracker, Silas MacKay, a tall, lanky fellow with a receding hairline, rode in front as they left the coast and headed inland. Beyond the byre, Silas veered off the trail onto the moor, got off his horse and examined the grass and other plants. "Looks like they might have gone this way," he called back to Erskine and Torrin.

They all followed him as he walked, leading his horse so as to see the ground and plants better, looking for signs of disturbance. An hour later, they neared larger rocks and crags leading into the mountains, the large expanse of gray broken only by patches of green heather.

"We must be ready. They could be hiding behind any of these boulders," Erskine warned.

"Indeed." Torrin crept forward with them, all the men armed with swords, targes and dirks, though Torrin did not have his own sword; the outlaws had stolen it the day before. Three MacKay archers also accompanied them. Those on horseback dismounted.

The further they advanced into the mountains, the more the path turned to gravel and scree which had eroded off the mountains for millennia. 'Twas impossible to see tracks now, but only one trail existed through this area with the steep mountains on both sides.

Fully aware their horses could be injured, killed, or stolen by the outlaws, they left the beasts with five men and continued on foot. 'Twould be too simple for a horse to break a leg amongst these unstable rocks.

Going by foot also allowed them to creep more quietly along the rough stony path. Torrin hoped they could slip up on the outlaws and catch them unawares. Most of all, he prayed Aiden was unharmed. He didn't know the lad well, but he was Jessie's beloved brother. Daft though he may be for leaving the keep to talk to Haldane. He should've known better, but Torrin could also understand the need to try to talk some sense into his law-breaking younger brother. Torrin wished he could've convinced his own younger brother to change his depraved ways before it was too late.

No use wishing for things he could never have now. A heavy sense of loss kicked him in the stomach and memories of their younger years haunted him.

Damnation! Don't think of it.

The one thing he was determined to have now was Jessie. He simply had to convince her of his worth and devotion.

A scent caught his attention—smoke and roasted meat. He halted, holding up his arm so those behind him would stop. "Smell that?" he asked, his voice hushed. "Their camp is close."

"Aye," Erskine whispered.

Sudden loud clanging and war cries resounded through the rocky crags. A rag-tag group of warriors wielding swords and targes stormed from behind boulders. But Torrin was ready, and the men who stood with him appeared ready as well. Blade clashed against blade.

Arrows flew down from the cliffs above. Torrin lifted his targe to deflect them. A skinny, blond-bearded man wearing ragged trews charged Torrin. He easily warded off the younger man's blows. The miscreant bared his teeth and launched a more determined attack. After landing a few blows against Torrin's blade, the man had worn himself out.

Torrin went on the offense. With two strikes, he drew blood, and with the third, dealt a killing slash. The daft lad had chosen the wrong opponent.

The next man to meet his gaze was McMurdo. A quick glance at the warrior lying unmoving and bloody at his feet stopped Torrin's breath. *Erskine?* Torrin charged forward, intending to run McMurdo through, but the gray-haired bastard fled with uncanny agility up the rock-covered ravine along with the rest of the surviving outlaws after Haldane had shouted the order to retreat.

"Get him! He's killed Erskine," Torrin yelled at the MacKays and chased McMurdo up the mountainside. The smoking campfire came into view, along with Aiden, sitting at the entrance to a cave, a brawny man with a sword guarding him.

"Bring him!" Haldane pointed at Aiden.

The guard picked up the lad, tossed him across his shoulder and ran.

"Bastard," Torrin growled.

Aiden wriggled and fought his captor, but it did no good. The man weighed twice as much as the lad.

Arrows rained down on Torrin and the MacKays, forcing them to use their targes for protection overhead and dive for cover behind boulders; their targes could not shield the whole of their bodies. Once the outlaw archer had stopped shooting, Torrin charged forward again.

"They're getting away!" Torrin sped up but the outlaws were twenty yards ahead. "Give me your bow and an arrow," Torrin ordered the young MacKay archer.

The bow was about the length of his own. Torrin threw down his other weapons, took the bow in hand and nocked the arrow. He aimed, praying he wouldn't shoot Aiden, but if he didn't get that whoreson to release him, he'd likely be dead soon anyway. When the outlaw turned a bit, his side facing Torrin, he released the arrow. The broad-head stabbed into the outlaw's ribs and he fell to his knees. Aiden slammed to the ground as well, but tried to scramble from beneath the injured brigand who was yanking at the arrow and growling like an enraged wolf.

The rest of the outlaws dashed out of sight, but the one he'd downed grabbed for the sword he'd dropped.

Aiden stumbled and fell amongst the rocks.

"Aiden! Come on!" Torrin tossed the bow back to its owner, grabbed his sword, and sprinted forward to help the lad.

Aiden shoved to his feet and loped toward him, while the injured outlaw lumbered forward, growling, his teeth bared.

Another arrow stabbed into the knave's chest. He dropped like a rock and writhed upon the ground, howling in pain.

Torrin quickly glanced back to see that the MacKay archer had fired the shot.

Reaching Aiden, Torrin grabbed his arm. "Hurry. We have to get you out of here."

Aiden was gasping for breath as he stumbled forward. Torrin glanced around, checking for lingering outlaws, but thankfully saw none.

"Help him down the mountain," he told the MacKays.

"Come on, cousin. I've got you." Conall's burly son, Dougal, picked Aiden up on his back and carried him. "Are you hurt?"

"Nay." Aiden huffed and puffed. "I thank you. All of you."

Torrin retrieved his targe and dirk from the ground, where he'd tossed them earlier, and followed.

Minutes later, Aiden insisted on walking, and they rejoined the rest of the search party.

"Aiden!" Conall yelled, his face red. "Are you daft? Leaving the keep that way? You could've been killed. Erskine's badly injured."

"He lives?" Torrin asked, his gaze scanning over Erskine's bloody, unmoving body and closed eyes.

Iain, crouched next to Erskine, glanced up. "Aye, indeed."

"Thank the saints! How bad is it?"

"'Tis a deep sword gash. He's lost a lot of blood."

"Bastards," Torrin growled. "We have to get him back to Dunnakeil." He wanted to tell Aiden he should be whipped for putting himself and the clan in so much danger. But he was the chief's brother. 'Twas Dirk's place to reprimand him. Or Jessie's. He was certain she would rake Aiden over the coals.

Upon seeing Erskine's bloody wound, Aiden squeezed his eyes closed. "I'm sorry. I ken 'twas my fault."

"Aye," Torrin agreed with a glare at the lad.

If Aiden was his brother, he might cold cock him, but they weren't family yet. Instead, he turned his attention to Erskine and knelt beside him. His face was ashen, and he was out cold.

Iain removed his shirt and used it, along with one he'd gotten from one of his men, as a makeshift bandage around Erskine's abdomen, trying to staunch the flow of blood. "We have to get him out of here."

"Indeed." Torrin stood, his gaze searching the craggy granite mountainsides to make sure no outlaws had returned, then the ground closer to him. Two outlaws, besides the one Torrin had killed, lay dead. Their weapons caught his attention. "'Tis my sword and Jessie's dirk," he muttered, snatching up the weapons and shoving them into his scabbards.

One of the MacKays approached with a wood and linen litter. He must have retrieved it from one of the horses, further back, to transport Erskine on.

Torrin prayed they made it back to Dunnakeil in time for the healer to help him.

***

Jessie paced back and forth in the cobblestone bailey, praying Torrin, Aiden and the rest of the men would return soon. They'd been gone all day, and gloaming was imminent. Sunset streaked the sky overhead with pink and gold.

"They're coming, Lady Jessie!" one of the guards called out from the battlements and pointed toward the east.

"Oh, thank the saints." She rushed to the portcullis. Minutes later, upon hearing the clomp of horses' hooves and men talking, she stepped back several paces. The guards raised the portcullis.

Torrin and Aiden entered the bailey first, leading horses. Joy that they were both alive and well near overcame her. Tears burning her eyes, she grinned and rushed forward to greet them. But neither of them was smiling. Instead, they appeared morose and worried.

"What happened?" she asked.

"Erskine was badly wounded," Torrin said.

"Nay," she gasped, her gaze searching among the men and horses pouring into the bailey. Then, she saw Erskine, passed out, on a litter carried by two men. The large makeshift bandage around his abdomen was soaked with blood.

"Oh, saints." She rushed toward them. "Take him into the great hall." Turning, she found a stable lad nearby. "Go get Nannag and take her to the great hall quickly."

"Aye, m'lady." He ran off.

"Was anyone else injured or killed?" she asked Torrin.

"A few cuts and bruises, but naught serious."

That was a relief, but still, Erskine's condition was perilous. He'd lost a lot of blood.

"What of the outlaws?" she asked as they headed inside.

"We killed four of them, but Haldane and McMurdo fled."

Jessie nodded, having mixed feelings about her youngest brother. In order to stop him from his objective, someone would have to kill him. But when that happened, she would be saddened, for he was still her brother.

"By my estimation, Haldane's gang is down to about six men," Torrin said. "They don't stand much of a chance now, unless he hires more men. I'm going to recommend that the MacKays patrol the area in parties of a dozen or so and mayhap they can pick off the rest of them. Haldane wants Dunnakeil, so he won't go far."

***

An hour later, Erskine was resting in a bedchamber. Nannag and her helpers had stitched up his wound and stopped the bleeding. He'd awoken enough to drink a special herbal tea Nannag had prepared.

Jessie prayed he would recover quickly without getting a terrible fever. Leaving the chamber, she found Aiden lurking in the corridor with several others, his head hung dejectedly. Fury at the risk he'd taken and the danger he'd put everyone in burned through her. "I want to speak to you in the library," she told him.

He eyed her warily. "Very well."

"Mind if I join you?" Torrin asked behind her.

She glanced back at him, finding he wore a concerned frown. "Whatever you wish."

Once in the library with the door closed, Jessie asked, "Aiden, what on earth possessed you to slip out? Are you mad? Now Erskine is almost dead because of you. Dirk will be furious."

Aiden pressed his eyes closed. "I ken 'tis my fault but—" He swallowed, his prominent Adam's apple bobbing. "You've never been close to Haldane. You only came back three years ago. He's… my brother. We've been together our whole lives… until last winter."

"I know that," Jessie said, her throat tightening at the emotion in Aiden's voice.

"I was hoping to change his mind… to convince him…"

Aiden shook his head. "He wouldn't listen."

"Of course not. He's beyond redemption." Jessie hated to say the words, but Aiden needed to realize the truth, so he wouldn't do something daft again.

Tears glistened in Aiden's eyes and he hung his head.

Torrin placed his hand upon Jessie's shoulder and squeezed gently. She didn't have to look at him to know what he wanted to tell her—to not be so hard on Aiden. Maybe Torrin was right. Aiden did appear exceedingly remorseful.

"I'm glad you were unharmed," she told her brother in a softer tone.

"I'm sorry." Aiden quickly left the room.

Jessie pulled away from Torrin and faced him. "What? Did you wish me to be easier on him? He put the whole clan in danger."

"You're right. I was furious with him, too. But the lad feels terrible. He just wanted his brother back. I can understand that."

Jessie nodded and pressed her eyes closed. "Well, he's right. I was never close to Haldane. We didn't grow up together. And the three years we lived here at Dunnakeil together, we didn't get along. But I've always watched out for Aiden."

"You're close to Dirk, too, are you not?"

"Aye. I'm four years younger than him, and we had the same mother." When she thought of Dirk, she couldn't help but think of her childhood, a time when things were fun and uncomplicated. "When we were small, we spent a lot of time together. Why do you think I like knives so much? I played with him, Keegan, and the lads who were always in mock sword fights. I just wish Dirk was here now to help with all this."

Torrin gave a slight lopsided smile. "You'd make an excellent chief."

She gave a soft snort. "Hardly."

"You're tougher than some men I know."

Her heart leapt at his high praise. "I thank you, but I had

to be."

"Why?" With a small frown, he tilted his head.

"Life with my foster family was not easy."

"The Keiths?" he said in a bitter tone.

She nodded. "The daughter closest to my age was a real harpy. She was jealous of everything and everyone. My closest friends were the cook and one of the nursemaids. But I did love Lady Keith. She was warm, welcoming and motherly, very different from my own stepmother." 'Twas really the only mother she had known, other than her own nursemaid when she was a wee lass.

"I'm sorry you had a tough time of it," Torrin said. "Did anyone ever hit you or punish you?"

"Nay, thank goodness. My father visited a couple of times a year to check on me, and he would've been furious with them if they'd beaten me."

"I must have been more of a hellion than you were, then," he said.

"Why? Were you punished?"

"Aye, my father used a leather strap—or his fists—on me… and my younger brother."

It pained her to imagine an older, bigger man beating a young Torrin. She could never understand why some parents were abusive. If she had children, she would likely spoil them. "What did you do to deserve that?"

He shrugged. "I can't even remember. He simply enjoyed hurting people. Not just us but the servants, too. Sometimes he would say 'twas how he was going to make hardened warriors out of us."

She shook her head, his story and his sad expression breaking her heart. "'Tis terrible. What of your mother?"

"She died when I was ten summers," he said in a matter-of-fact tone that had to be concealing deep emotion.

"I'm sorry to hear of it." She knew the void and emptiness of not having a mother, but she had not known hers. To lose a mother at ten must have been the worst.

"I was away, fostering with the Stewarts at the time," he

said. "I didn't even get to attend her funeral. Da sent a missive, and that was that. When I returned home a year later, Ma simply wasn't there anymore."

"'Tis tragic," Jessie whispered, tears welling in her eyes.

"'Twas long ago." Trying to shove the emotion aside, Torrin paced to the fireplace, knelt and stirred the coals with the iron poker, then added a brick of peat. 'Twas summer, but with gloaming, the room had grown chill. Thinking about his past always made him crave cozy warmth, for much of his childhood had been emotionally cold.

He didn't know why he'd opened up so much to Jessie. Mayhap because he felt so comfortable with her. He'd revealed more to her about his past than he had anyone in years. But he must forget his past misfortunes and concentrate on the future. His future with Jessie—if she would have him.

"I thank you for rescuing Aiden," she said behind him. "That means more to me than I can say."

Torrin stood and faced her. "You're welcome. He told us on the way back that Haldane had planned to use him to force us to open the gates."

"Of course. Haldane cares naught for him, or anyone, but himself."

Torrin nodded. "I believe Aiden sees the truth of it now."

"I'm sorry to ask, but would you be willing to stay until Erskine recovers or Dirk and Keegan return. I know naught about how to lead a clan, especially during conflict such as Haldane has stirred up. The guards may need your advice and guidance about how to handle it. Of course, there is Uncle Conall and the clan elders who will have their say in all matters, but they cannot lead the men into battle."

"Indeed. I'd planned to. And I thank you for trusting me enough to ask. You do trust me, aye?" He hoped she did after all that had happened.

The fire burned brighter, the flames reflecting in Jessie's eyes, revealing a pleasant expression. "I do now."

He placed a hand over his heart dramatically. "In that case, 'tis the best day of my life."

She smiled. And he thought she was blushing, though 'twas hard to tell in the firelight.

"In truth, your trust means the world to me." Drawing near, he kissed her forehead.

Her fingers curled into his clothing, holding him close. Warmth and gratitude spread through him, along with arousal. Wrapping his arms around her, he kissed her temple. Her hair tickled his lips. Her feminine lavender scent awakened his senses. Drawing back a wee bit, he slid his hand around her neck and into her hair. She lifted her gaze to his, her light blue eyes turned dark. The passion he read in her eyes kicked his heart into a faster rhythm. He pressed his lips to hers.

When she responded, kissing him back with affection and eagerness, he pulled her tight against him.

A knock sounded at the door. Jessie started.

He released her and stepped back. "Now, who could that be?" He strode to the door and opened it.

Sim waited outside. "Chief!"

"I'm glad you've returned." Torrin stepped into the corridor and pulled the door almost closed behind him. "Were you successful in your mission?" he whispered.

Sim grinned broadly. "Indeed, m'laird."

Torrin stuck his head back into the library and asked Jessie, "Could you wait here for a few minutes?"

She frowned a bit. "Why?"

He shrugged, not wanting to raise her suspicions any more than he had already. "I but want to talk to you more," he said, hoping she knew that by the word *talk* he actually meant *kiss*. He winked.

She blushed and clasped her hands together. "Very well. If you hurry." She gave an impish grin.

"I will indeed hurry."

Torrin disappeared out the door, closing it behind him. Jessie wondered how long he would make her wait. And what would they do or talk about once he returned? She did enjoy spending time alone with him, and of course his kisses.

Apparently, the men had returned from escorting the MacBains south. Maybe Torrin would come back and tell her news of whether MacBain had caused any trouble. For a certainty now, she could not go out and walk on the beach with so many outlaws on the loose. She turned, gazing out the window at Balnakeil Bay below. The sun had already sunk below the horizon but 'twas still light enough to see the beach and the cliffs in the distance.

She busied herself lighting the candelabra on the table. 'Twould be dark soon, and she wanted to see the varying expressions that crossed Torrin's face.

Moments later, the library door opened again and Torrin entered, carrying a large wad of plaid in one arm. What on earth was that? When it wiggled, a shock went through her.

"What is that?" she asked.

A whine pierced the air.

"A surprise." He pulled back the plaid and a furry, dark gray head popped out.

'Twas the cutest puppy she'd ever seen. Her mouth dropped open. "I didn't know you had a dog."

"'Tis not mine."

"Whose is it?"

"Yours." Torrin grinned and set the long-legged pup on the floor. It ran to her, its tail wagging like mad. The wee Scottish deerhound was dark grey all over, except for white paws and a white star on his chest.

"I don't understand." Her heart melting, she knelt to pet the adorable and enthusiastic animal.

"'Tis my gift to you. I sent my men to get it in Scourie. I have a distant cousin there who breeds deerhounds. You're lucky; he only sells them to chiefs."

"Torrin." She shook her head, emotion tightening her throat. He was so sweet and generous, but she couldn't become attached to another dog. Losing Ossian had near killed her. Taking a deep breath, she forced the sadness away.

"You shouldn't have. I wasn't planning to get another dog."

Torrin frowned. "Why not? You love them."

"Because… it hurts too much when you lose them."

He knelt opposite her and rubbed the puppy's belly while it squirmed on its back between them. "There's always the chance we'll lose people or animals we love, but we can't let that hold us back from loving them."

Tears burned her eyes. "I know, but I simply didn't wish to get attached to another dog."

"Just as you don't wish to get attached to another man?" Torrin lifted his brows, his perceptive gaze piercing into her.

Though she hated to admit it, she nodded. "I've been hurt enough."

He shook his head and drew his hand back from the pup. It leapt up and loped across the room.

"Jessie." He crawled closer to where she sat on the floor, her knees drawn up, and placed a finger underneath her chin to lift it.

Not wanting him to see her tears, she pressed her eyes closed.

"Look at me," he murmured.

She opened her eyes to find him studying her intently with a sincere gaze.

"I vow upon my life, I'm not going to hurt you. I would never abandon you or send you back to your family once I make a commitment to you."

"You could change your mind in a year or two. Who knows? People change. What they want changes."

His eyes narrowing, he drew in a deep breath and let it out slow. "What I want has not changed since I first saw you," he said in a firmer tone.

"That was only last winter."

"Aye. Seven months ago. If I were not certain, do you think I would be here now?"

"I know not. 'Tis only…" She cared too much for Torrin now. If she accepted his offer of marriage and he tired of her, she couldn't survive it. Tears flooded her eyes. She stood, turned her back to him and stared out the window, not wanting him to see her tears or her weakness.

"So," he said, getting to his feet. "You do not accept me or this wee laddie?" His tone was so disappointed she could hardly stand it.

She wanted to accept them both. She truly did.

"Very well," he said from across the room. The door clicked shut.

Chapter Eleven

Jessie turned and stared at the door Torrin had just closed behind him as he'd left. Of course, 'twas her fault he'd walked out, but at the same time, she realized this was what it would feel like if he abandoned her. She pressed her eyes closed tight, tears running down her cheeks. 'Twould rip her heart out.

But he hadn't abandoned her. He'd simply left the room because he believed she wouldn't accept him or his gift.

"I'm sorry," she whispered. The words echoed in the quiet, empty room.

The leggy pup scuttled toward her and sniffed at her skirt-tail.

She lowered herself to the floor on shaky legs and the pup clambered onto her lap. "What is your name, wee furry beastie?" she asked, trying to keep him from washing her face with his pink tongue. "You are a handsome lad." Already the pup wriggled his way into her heart, just as Torrin had. She couldn't help but smile. Torrin was a sweetheart to give her such a thoughtful gift. She would have to thank him, for indeed she could not refuse the puppy.

"How about Greum?" she asked him. "Would you

answer to that name?"

The pup put his white paws on her shoulder and licked her ear.

"Och, you are very forward just like Torrin." She rolled him onto his back and rubbed his belly. He squirmed and kicked, a happy grin on his face. Playing with him, she repeated the name a few times, hoping he'd come to recognize it quickly. "Are you hungry? I bet you are as hungry as a wild boar, are you not? Come, Greum, and I'll find you something to eat."

She rose and approached the door. Greum scampered at her heels as she left the library and crossed the great hall. Everyone was assembling for supper. She glanced around the room and her gaze landed on Torrin, standing by the fireplace with several of his men. She sent him a brief smile and continued on toward the kitchen, not waiting to see what his response would be. She was sure he thought her daft. And mayhap she was. But she could only do what she felt was right for her.

***

Torrin's attention was completely ensnared when Jessie strode across the great hall, the pup on her heels. She smiled at him, halting his breath, then disappeared down the stairs leading to the kitchen. *Saints!* What did that smile mean? He refused to chase after her and find out. Nay, she would have to come to him this time.

Had she decided to accept the pup? He certainly hoped so. She needed it. She needed something or someone to love, who would love her back. Torrin could do that, but he was unsure whether she would ever accept him. All he could do was try to prove to her, over and over, that he wouldn't abandon her as MacBain had. The whoreson.

Everyone seated themselves as supper began. Torrin joined Conall, Iain and several others at the high table. The men left a vacant seat beside Torrin, but the reason remained unspoken. However, as the food was served, 'twas clear to him Jessie was not going to join them this eve. Although his stomach ached with hunger, he had little appetite. Another seat further along the table also remained empty.

"Where is Aiden?" Torrin asked Conall.

"In his chamber, under heavy guard."

"Heavy guard?"

"Aye, he slipped past the single guard who was watching him last night. So, now he has two."

Torrin doubted he would try to sneak out again, anyway, considering what a disaster last night's adventure had been. "Is he not allowed to join us for supper?"

"Aye, of course. But he said he wishes to eat in his room." Conall shrugged.

Saints! Aiden was always at the high table for meals. The situation with Erskine had affected the lad more profoundly than Torrin had imagined. And he was also likely still upset about Haldane.

"How is Erskine?" Torrin asked.

"He was sleeping when last I checked in on him a quarter hour ago," Conall said.

Torrin nodded, praying that meant he was recovering. After taking a bite of venison stew, he turned to Struan, his sword-bearer, who had joined them at high table. "Tell me of your journey south. Did MacBain and his men give you trouble?"

"Nay, they were quiet and cooperative, but glared at us the entire way. 'Tis clear MacBain is angered beyond reason. I fear he will strike back. 'Haps with a larger force of men next time."

"Saints! 'Tis just what we need," Torrin grumbled.

"At the border, we told them to be on their way," Struan said. "'Twas a tense moment when we threw their weapons down at their feet. At first, we were unsure whether they would grab their swords and attack or not. But clearly, they were outnumbered, and they didn't wish to risk it. We were careful to watch our backs, especially at night when we camped."

"Good work. And I thank you for handling that risky job

so well." Torrin drank a long sip of the bitter dark ale.

"'Twas an honor, m'laird. A few miles south of Durness, we came upon Sim, Luag and Gordon returning from Scourie with a pup, of all things." Struan chuckled. "I thought, what on earth is the chief up to now, sending them to fetch a wee dog? But once they told me 'twas a gift for the lady, it made perfect sense. I take it she liked the wee beastie."

"I think she did." He hoped.

"Of course she did," Iain said, leaning forward, where he sat on Struan's other side. "Did you not see the blinding smile she sent him across the great hall moments ago?"

"Nay, I did not," Struan said, then took a huge bite of stew.

Iain grinned. "'Twas a sight to behold, as if the sun shone at midday."

"This is good news, then, m'laird," Struan said.

Torrin snorted. "He exaggerates."

Aye, he thought she liked the pup, but she had not said so yet. He hoped she would search him out later and let him know. If he couldn't see her tonight, he would miss her terribly. Already, he was addicted to her. Last night had been the best night of his life, and he wanted many more of those.

As everyone was finishing the meal, they looked glum, sipping their ale. The low murmur of conversation was only a quarter of the usual volume, and where music used to fill this great hall, there was silence. 'Twas clear the clan was worried about Erskine, but also missing Aiden and his music.

"'Tis late," Torrin said. "I think I will check on Erskine and Aiden, then retire for the evening."

Iain lifted one brow and gave him a speculative look.

Torrin merely glared at him. *Do not even say what you're thinking.* No doubt it had something to do with Jessie. Torrin rose from the table and bid them good night.

He headed toward the stairs.

"Lad, could I have a word?"

Torrin halted. Was someone calling him *lad*? Only his uncles and the MacLeod clan elders did that these days. Och, 'twas Conall following him. He should've guessed.

"Aye, of course." *Saints!* Was the man going to berate him for defiling his niece? "Would you like to go into the library?" He sure as the devil didn't want Iain to listen in on this conversation if Conall was going to question him about where he'd slept last night.

"That would be good," the older man said.

Torrin proceeded into the room, and Conall closed the door behind them.

"I have great respect for you as a chief and laird," Conall said. "'Twas clear to me today what a great leader you are."

Torrin gave a brief nod. "I thank you for that."

"You've generously helped this clan in many ways since you've been visiting."

"I'm more than glad to help out when I can."

"But… Jessie is my niece and… well, you were in her chamber this morn. Her father is no longer with us, and her older brother is away, so I felt it my responsibility to say something."

"Aye, well, I want you to know, sir, that I want to marry Lady Jessie," Torrin said, feeling almost as if he were speaking to Jessie's father. "I've offered for her hand twice. Dirk has refused each time because he says Lady Jessie refuses. I'm simply trying to change her mind. I think once she gets to know me, she will reconsider and accept my offer."

"Um-hmm," Conall grunted his response and nodded a wee bit, thinking that over. "Well, mayhap *she* is the one I should be speaking to about making this right."

"'Haps." Torrin was unsure whether Conall would help the situation or damage it further if he tried to pressure Jessie into marrying him. "Does she usually take your advice?"

"Aye, of course. All the young folks do."

Naturally, he would say that, but Torrin was still unsure. "She is stubborn, is she not?"

"Indeed. Most of the MacKays are," he said heartily.

"I care about her a great deal, and I truly want her for my wife. I have since the night I met her last winter." Torrin hoped the older man could see his sincerity, and how much Jessie meant to him. "If you can put in a good word for me, I would appreciate it."

"Aye. I'll do that." With a wee smile, Conall offered his hand, and Torrin shook it. "You're a good man, and I'll look forward to having you for a nephew."

"I thank you, sir. That means a lot to me. And I hope it comes to pass."

After he and Conall left the library, Torrin headed upstairs to Erskine's chamber. Several candles lit the room and the ancient, white-haired healer, Nannag, and her two younger helpers sat watching Erskine sleep.

"How is he?" Torrin asked, keeping his voice low.

"He has no fever and his breathing is strong," Nannag said in a paper-thin whisper. "The bleeding has stopped."

"Good. Send someone after me if his condition changes."

"Aye, indeed. I will, m'laird."

"I thank you." He exited the room and headed toward Aiden's chamber on the same corridor as his own but further along and around a corner. Two burly guards stood outside the door.

"I've come to see Aiden," Torrin told them.

One of the guards knocked on the door.

All was silent inside. Anxiety slithering through him, Torrin frowned. Was he asleep, or had he slipped out somehow?

The guard opened the door and barged into the room. Torrin followed. Aiden sat before the fireplace.

"You scared the life out of me, Aiden," Torrin said.

"Why?"

"When you didn't answer, I thought… never mind what I thought."

The guard left the room and closed the door, giving them privacy.

"Did you eat supper?" Torrin asked.

"Nay, I'm not hungry." Aiden stared listlessly into the

fire, his shoulders slumped.

"You must eat something to keep up your strength. We missed you greatly at supper."

Aiden sent him a troubled look, but remained silent.

Torrin dropped into the other wooden chair by the fireplace. "Erskine will recover, I'm certain."

"You don't know that." Aiden's voice was hushed and glum.

"He's stable, thus far, and sleeping."

Aiden swallowed hard and nodded.

"I wish you hadn't slipped out to see Haldane, but I understand why you did."

Aiden sent him a defiant and questioning glance.

"Yesterday, Haldane told me that Dirk had killed my younger brother, Nolan."

Aiden's eyes widened. "Dirk did? Why?"

"Because Nolan kidnapped Lady Isobel from their tent when they were camping somewhere south of Munrick. I'm certain Dirk did what he had to in order to rescue her." Torrin stared at the glowing embers in the fireplace, his eyes burning.

"I'm sorry to hear of it," Aiden murmured.

"Aye. Well… Nolan was an outlaw, so 'tis to be expected. I keep remembering the last time I saw him, outside the walls here. He'd ridden north with us to see what was happening with Lady Isobel, trying to find out why Dirk had brought her here. Once Dirk told us that Nolan had tried to rape her, I couldn't believe it. My own brother?" Torrin shook his head. He especially couldn't believe it given what had happened to their sister, Allina. "After Nolan fled with the outlaws, I knew it must be true."

Aiden frowned, looking troubled.

"Nolan never returned home," Torrin continued. "I didn't get to see him again after he joined Haldane and his gang. I wish I could've talked to him, tried to convince him to change. Even though, likely it would have done no good."

Aiden nodded.

"So, you see, I understand why you wanted to speak to your brother and get him to see the error of his ways. No one can blame you for wanting to help someone you love."

Tears glistened in Aiden's eyes. He cleared his throat and swiped his sleeve across his eyes. "I fear he will be killed, aye. I figured 'twould be my only opportunity to see him one last time." Aiden shook his head. "But he is just like Ma. He will not give up on what he wants, no matter the cost. He is willing to risk his life in his quest to kill Dirk and take over this castle."

"Aye," Torrin agreed. "He is determined, and doesn't care who he has to murder to achieve his goal."

"It kills me to see how he has changed. And now, if Erskine dies because of me… I don't know."

"He's a strong, healthy warrior. I'm near certain he will recover."

"I pray 'twill be so."

"Well, 'tis late. I'm going to bid you good night. Try to get some sleep."

Aiden nodded but didn't look in any better spirits than he had when Torrin had entered. "Good night."

Closing the door on his way out, Torrin shook his head. "Look in on him from time to time, would you?" he asked the guards in a hushed voice. "I'm concerned about him."

They both nodded.

Torrin proceeded down the corridor and around the corner toward his own chamber. When someone moved in the darkened corner, startling him, he halted. The lone candle sconce revealed a female with long red hair.

"Jessie," he whispered, a thrill coursing through him.

She stepped away from the corner. "Were you visiting Aiden?"

"Aye."

"How is he now? I took him food earlier but he refused to eat it."

"He seems near devastated. Nothing like his normally merry self."

Her brows drew together. "Aye. I hope he will get some sleep, at least."

Torrin nodded, studying her eyes, darker in the dimness. "I missed you at supper."

"I'm sorry. I didn't feel in a sociable mood. I sat with Erskine while he slept."

"He seems stable."

"Aye. I'm praying he improves quickly." She appeared distracted for a moment, then her expression lightened. "I want to thank you for the pup."

"You decided to keep him?"

She gave a faint smile. "Aye. I named him Greum."

Torrin grinned. "'Tis a fitting name. Where is the wee rascal?"

"In my chamber, asleep before the fireplace."

"Spoiling him already?"

"Aye."

"I'm glad you want him."

She dropped her gaze briefly. "I was simply… uncertain before. I suppose I'm afraid of risks in some ways. Not physical risks but…" She shrugged.

"I ken what you mean. 'Tis not easy to let go and put your heart out there. There is always a risk that we'll be hurt in one way or another, no matter what we do. But you're a strong and brave woman, Jessie. I admire you more than I can say."

"I thank you. And I admire you also," she whispered, her blue eyes taking on a seductive quality. "You're very generous and thoughtful to give me such a gift. I'll never be able to repay you."

"Och. I think you will." He grinned. "'Twill only take a bit more convincing."

When she frowned and tried to draw away from him, he took hold of her wrist to keep her there. "I'm teasing. I would accept a thank you kiss, though."

"Rogue," she muttered, giving him a mischievous smile.

"I'll not argue with that." He slowly leaned down and

kissed her lips… soft, delectable and tasting of sweet, spiced wine. When she opened her mouth, the kiss quickly turned fiery. *Saints!* He wanted to consume her.

He drew her the short distance to the door of his guest chamber and inside. Pushing the door closed, he leaned against the wood, pulled her body tight to his and deepened the kiss. When her tongue flicked his, lust seared him.

"Jessie," he growled. Shoving his sporran aside, he pulled her hips tight against his own, hoping she felt how badly he wanted her.

Moaning, she buried her hands in his hair and reached up for more of his forceful kisses.

"I need you," he said.

"Aye." Jessie could not believe how fiercely she craved Torrin at this moment. It seemed each time they were together, her desire for him grew to unbelievable depths. She tugged at his clothing, tried with unsteady hands to unfasten his belt.

"Let me," he said, unbuckling the belt. In a trice, his shirt lay on the floor with his plaid. The fire in the hearth revealed the delicious ridges and planes of his muscular body.

"Now, your turn." With a seductive smile, he had her undressed just as quickly.

She shivered, not because the room was cold, but because the look in Torrin's eyes was so hot.

He lifted her and carried her across the floor to his bed, drawing her nipple into his mouth at the same time.

Tremors of delight coursing through her, she arched her back and held him close. He feasted upon her breasts, stimulating the nipples to hard points. His shaft lay heavy and hard as granite against her lower abdomen. She slipped her hand down and traced her fingertips along its feverish length, then squeezed it, eliciting a groan from him.

"You have awoken the beast, now." He sat back on his heels, grabbed her ankle and bit it playfully.

She giggled but in the next second, he was between her thighs, spreading her legs. He stroked a thumb through her moisture, then hissed a curse.

Leaning his long body over hers, he guided his shaft into her, the sensation filling her with intensifying arousal. Aye, she wanted more. Lifting her hips to meet his first slow thrust, she moaned.

With dark, intense eyes, he observed her, gradually increasing the pace. His body completely bewitched her, filling her with magical sensations she'd never imagined possible. When they grew too powerful to bear, she closed her eyes and held her breath. The swirling pleasures crashed and exploded. She wanted to scream, but Torrin's mouth was devouring hers, muffling her cries.

Somehow, he drew the pleasure out, on and on, then he shoved hard against her and held himself there, deep within her, growling between clenched teeth against her ear.

"Saints, Jessie," he hissed. "*Tha gràdh agam ort.*"

She froze. Did he say *I love you*? Maybe she'd misheard.

He collapsed beside her and drew her close against his side.

Mo chreach. He hadn't just told her he loved her, had he?

She listened as his harsh breathing calmed, hoping he wouldn't remember what he'd said. She knew not how she felt about his confession. Did it mean anything, or was he simply caught up in the heat of passion? MacBain had also told her he loved her, and 'twas obvious how that turned out. He'd lied.

She didn't think Torrin was lying, but mayhap those words didn't mean the same thing to men as they did to women.

"I missed you, Jessie," he said between a whisper and a mumble, sounding half asleep. He drew her close into his arms and his breathing evened out. She glanced up at him. Was he asleep already? He must have been exhausted from the long day of searching for Aiden, in addition to the battle.

Remembering how he'd said he loved her, she remained tense while he slept, her mind spinning over the possibilities, along with the problems. She had already feared she was falling in love with him. Regardless of how they felt about each other, she couldn't marry him if she was barren. A chief and laird couldn't have a barren wife. He would likely grow to resent her over the years if she couldn't provide an heir.

Her eyes burning with tears, she slipped from beneath his arm and slid from the bed. She dressed quietly in the firelight, then crept out the door.

A fiery tryst was all they could ever have.

Chapter Twelve

His long gray hair blowing in the strong wind, McMurdo rushed from the edge of the cliff toward Haldane. "A garrison of men is approaching from the south."

"How many and who are they?" Haldane threw down the rabbit bone he'd just cleaned off, breaking his fast.

"Have no inkling who yet, but there are about three dozen."

"God's teeth." Haldane followed McMurdo to the crest of a hill where Gil had been posted as lookout. They stayed low and out of sight. Indeed, a small army approached through the morning mist. Most on horseback. Some on foot. All heavily armed, from what he could see. "'Tis not Dirk's party." Nay, the plaids were unfamiliar and some were dressed in a Lowland style, wearing trews and knee breeches.

McMurdo shook his head.

"We're outnumbered, but we have no quarrel with them. We'll go down and see who they are… and what their mission is." Haldane instructed every man with a bow to guard their backs. "Come." Haldane scrambled down the grassy hillside, stumbling over loose rocks and heather, McMurdo behind him.

When the regiment drew nearer, he and McMurdo

stepped out beside the trail, no weapons in their hands, but close at their sides if needed. The clan's dark-haired leader, riding a fine chestnut stallion, halted and held up his hand. All the men following him stopped.

Haldane recognized him immediately as Gregor MacBain, Chief of Clan MacBain, the man Jessie had entered into a trial marriage with two or three years ago. His daft sister had not pleased the man, and he'd sent her home.

"Chief MacBain, 'tis good to see you again," Haldane called out.

"Who are you?" the man demanded, frowning.

"Haldane MacKay. Lady Jessie is my sister. We met only once." Haldane slowly moved forward and held up his hand for the man to shake.

MacBain narrowed his devil-dark eyes. "My apologies. I didn't recognize you, lad." He dismounted, two of his brawny bodyguards following suit and moving to stand beside him.

MacBain shook Haldane's hand briefly.

"Coming to pay Jessie a visit?" Haldane smiled, trying to be his most congenial.

MacBain eyed him and McMurdo suspiciously. "Aye, indeed. I miss the lass. I was here a week ago, but I didn't see you."

"We hadn't yet arrived. Was Jessie not welcoming?"

MacBain's face reddened, and his gaze turned lethal. "Nay. I tried to convince her to marry me, but she showed little interest."

"Och. 'Haps because… of the MacLeod chief courting her." Haldane had almost blurted out that Torrin MacLeod was frolicking naked in the sea with her, but that might infuriate the man. He needed to keep MacBain as calm as possible in order to convince him they could help one another.

"Aye, MacLeod. The bastard," MacBain said between clenched teeth.

Haldane was thrilled to hear how much MacBain disliked Torrin MacLeod, but he hid his reaction. "We could help you defeat him, and then Lady Jessie would be yours. After I'm chief, she will have no choice but to do what I say."

MacBain's brows shot upward. "You're going to be chief of the MacKays?"

Haldane despised the surprise in the man's tone. "Aye, once this imposter who calls himself Dirk is dead. He claims to be my brother, but the real Dirk died thirteen years ago in an accident."

MacBain nodded. "That's what I'd heard."

"Aye, well, that's what we're doing here—awaiting the imposter's return so I can take my rightful place."

MacBain's expression eased, and he even looked a bit hopeful. "And you wouldn't be against my marrying Lady Jessie?"

"Of course not. You would have my blessing. I'll even increase her dowry once I'm chief."

MacBain's eyes lit up. "Indeed? What is your plan in defeating this Dirk then? I've never met him."

"He and a party of about two dozen will be returning sometime soon. We're not certain whether they're traveling by land or sea. I have lookouts in several places." Well, three places. His men were quickly dwindling but he didn't want MacBain to know that. "When Dirk's party arrives, we'll be attacking and killing as many men as possible. No one is to hurt the women, though. One of them will be my future wife."

"Of course, we would never harm the women."

Haldane hoped the man was being truthful, for he would kill any man who hurt Lady Seona. "Then, we'll need to get inside the castle."

MacBain nodded. "And you will help me get Torrin MacLeod out of my path so I can marry Jessie?"

"Indeed. He's an enemy. He killed one of my men." He didn't want MacBain to know that MacLeod was such a good fighter, he'd killed several more than that.

"We have an agreement then." MacBain held out his hand.

"We do." Smiling, Haldane shook it, unable to believe his good fortune—three dozen strong-looking warriors to add to his shrinking force. They would succeed now in defeating the MacKays and taking Dunnakeil.

***

"Jessie, could I have a word with you?" Uncle Conall asked in the corner of the great hall while everyone disbursed after breaking their fast.

"Aye, uncle. How is Aiden this morn?" She had stopped by to see him earlier but he was in bed asleep. She hadn't wanted to disturb him.

"I've not talked to the lad yet today. He was resting when I dropped in." He lowered his voice. "I wanted to talk to you about MacLeod."

Mo chreach! She'd been expecting this since yesterday morn, when her uncle had come to her room and found Torrin answering her door.

"Let's go into the library," he suggested.

"Aye." She gave a mock smile and proceeded into the room, lit by morning sunlight. He was no doubt thinking she was a harlot, but what could she do about that now? He'd practically caught them in bed together.

Conall closed the door and faced her. When she saw that his expression was neutral… 'haps even pleasant, she relaxed a bit.

"I believe MacLeod is a good man," Conall said.

She nodded, unsure where he was taking this conversation.

"He has helped the clan in many ways since he's been here. He almost single-handedly saved Aiden's life. He rescued you twice and brought you back to the castle after you'd been captured each time."

"'Tis true," Jessie agreed. "He's very resourceful. And I'm grateful to him for his help."

"And you… seem to like him a great deal, aye?" Conall gave a tight smile.

Jessie's face burned furiously. "Aye. Like you said, he is a good man." Not to mention gorgeous and seductive.

"He has asked for your hand in marriage, twice now, has he not?" her uncle inquired.

Annoyance twisted through her. "I'm not yet ready for marriage. I do not wish for a repeat of what happened with MacBain."

"MacLeod is not MacBain," Conall grumbled, a frown pulling his rusty-gray brows together. "The two men are vastly different. MacBain is a viper hiding amongst the rocks. From what I've seen, MacLeod is an honorable man, and he told me he cares for you."

Jessie nodded, but she refused to tell her uncle why she couldn't marry Torrin right now—that she was most likely barren. 'Twas not something she could discuss with a male family member without dying of mortification.

"I will give you some good advice, lass," Uncle Conall said sternly. "Marry the man before he leaves and marries some other lady."

When she imagined Torrin marrying another woman, devastation clutched at her heart. "I will consider it," she said low, not meeting her uncle's gaze.

Conall blew out an exasperated breath. "You are more stubborn than your father," he muttered.

Jessie bit her lip. 'Haps he was right.

"I'm telling you, lass, you will regret it if you do not take him up on his offer." Her uncle turned and left the room.

Aye, she already regretted being unable to accept Torrin's offer. But the situation was becoming impossible. If their liaisons did not result in a bairn, she wouldn't marry him. How could she? She refused to trap him in a position where he couldn't sire his own heir.

Each time she lay with him, the experience became more and more intense. She fell deeper and deeper for him. She did not know what she would do when he eventually left. Her heart would be as empty and hollow as this room.

***

Jessie stood beside Aiden's bed, staring down at his

prone form beneath the blanket. He was covered up to his ears and facing away from her.

"Aiden, 'tis near noon and time for you to rise. You cannot lay abed all day."

"Leave me be," he muttered.

"Aiden," she said more gently. "I'm sorry I was so harsh with you yesterday."

He made no comment. She knew he was a gentle soul and could not handle much scolding.

"Erskine is improving," she said in a happier tone. "I visited with him a short while ago. He was drinking broth and herbal tea." When Aiden didn't respond, she asked, "Are you going to eat with us in the great hall?"

"Nay. I didn't sleep well last night."

At least he had eaten the bowl of porridge she'd sent up by a servant this morn.

A brief knock sounded at the half-open door. She glanced around to find Torrin waiting on the threshold. Looking into his captivating green eyes always sent a flush of heat over her, as it did now, making her recall how intently he looked into her eyes while making love to her.

"How is the lad feeling?" he asked.

Shoving down her excitement upon seeing Torrin, she swallowed hard and said, "I cannot convince him to get out of bed and join us in the great hall for the meal."

Torrin frowned. "Is he ill?"

She shrugged, though she didn't think he was physically ill. She was certain 'twas more of an emotional ailment.

Torrin entered the room and stood beside her. When his arm brushed hers, a hot shiver traveled over her.

"Aiden?" he asked.

"I'm not hungry," her brother muttered.

"Erskine was asking about you," Torrin said.

Jessie sent him a questioning look.

Torrin nodded. "'Tis true. He wanted to make sure you were rescued from Haldane—Erskine was passed out, if you recall—and he wants you to come play a tune on your flute."

Aiden turned onto his back and frowned up at Torrin, searching his gaze. "I don't believe you."

"Och. You think I would lie about such a thing?"

Without answering, Aiden rolled over again, facing the wall.

"Very well, then," Torrin said, his tone resigned. "Erskine will be mightily disappointed that you refused to entertain him. Music soothes the soul and heals the body, you ken."

Aiden didn't respond.

"Maybe we should leave him to his rest," Torrin told Jessie, then winked at her.

What was he up to? Regardless, his mischievous look and that wink sent her pulse tripping along.

"Aye. Have a good nap, Aiden," she said, and followed Torrin out.

The guard closed the door behind her.

Once around the corner, Torrin grabbed her hand.

"What are you about?" Jessie demanded in a quiet tone.

He tugged her into his guest chamber and pushed the door almost closed, but he left a crack and peered out.

"What are you doing?" she whispered.

"I want to see if Aiden leaves his room and goes to visit Erskine."

"Do you think he will?"

Torrin shrugged.

"Did Erskine truly ask him to come and play a tune?"

"Indeed. I asked him if he would like to hear Aiden play and he said *aye*."

"Sneaky devil," she muttered, but she loved the way his mind worked.

Torrin sent her a quick smile, then continued watching out the door. A moment later, a wide grin spread across his face. He opened the door and stuck his head out.

"What is happening?" she whispered.

He drew back into the room and softly closed the door. "Aiden is headed in the direction of Erskine's room. I could not tell if he had a flute with him or not."

"Let's follow him and see if we hear music," she suggested.

Torrin nodded. They exited the room and slipped along the corridor. A few yards from the open door of Erskine's room, they halted. The two men and Nannag talked within the room, though Jessie couldn't understand their words. Then, the soothing sounds of flute music floated out into the corridor. Jessie smiled.

She knew Erskine didn't blame Aiden for being injured, but Aiden had no doubt blamed himself. Now that he saw Erskine would likely recover, mayhap he could forgive himself for his poor decisions.

"Come," Torrin whispered. Taking her hand, he led her back along the corridor. His big hand surrounded and warmed hers, soothing her and giving her shivers at the same time.

"I thank you for helping Aiden," she said. "I've never seen him so upset. Hopefully, he's back to his old self again."

"I hope so." Torrin pulled her into his guest room and closed the door. Considering the attentive way he watched her, he was no longer thinking of her brother.

"And now what are you about, MacLeod, bringing me to your chamber?" She placed her hands upon her hips in a mock severe posture.

"I wish to speak to you," he said mysteriously.

"About?"

"Are you avoiding me?"

"Nay," Jessie said, although, in one way, she wished she could avoid him; in another, she wished to tackle him to the bed right now. "Why would you think that?"

"You didn't break your fast in the great hall, even though there was an empty seat beside me."

"I simply don't want everyone to think… you know… that we're…" She paused, refusing to say the words.

"We're what?" He lifted a brow.

He knew what she was trying to say, blast him.

His expression turned troubled. "You're ashamed of me," he said, somewhere between a statement and a question.

"Of course not! The clan will gossip. They will think we're…"

"Lovers?" he supplied.

A mixture of heat and excitement washed over her. "Aye."

"Well, they will think the truth, then."

She blew out an exasperated breath. "I don't wish everyone to know that."

"You won't avoid me tonight, will you?" he murmured. "I woke up last night and you were gone. I missed you."

"We cannot be caught together again. Uncle Conall already—" she broke off, not wanting to discuss the M word with Torrin.

He sent her a mischievous look. "Conall told me he intended to have a discussion with you. Did he give good advice?"

"I have no need for anyone's advice," she said firmly.

"Ah, well, I figured as much," he said in a mild tone, and was obviously squelching a grin.

She glared at him. "You put him up to that, did you not?"

"Nay! 'Twas all his idea. He confronted me about being in your chamber. I told him the truth—that I wish to marry you." Torrin crossed his arms over his chest and raised a brow.

"And I told him the truth as well—that I cannot marry you. Now, if you will pardon me, I must get to the great hall." She eyed the door, hoping he would let her pass.

"What if you are with child?" he whispered.

Her gaze flew to his, lit brilliant green by the midday sunlight slicing in through the narrow window.

"I'm not." She would know it if she was with child, wouldn't she?

He tilted his head. "How do you know?"

She narrowed her eyes. "If that happens, I'll tell you. In

the meantime, there is no sense discussing it." And getting her hopes up. Aye, she would like naught better than to have children of her own… with him… but she couldn't tell him that. 'Twas like a sweet tart dangling before her nose, while she starved, unable to reach it.

Slowly, he moved toward her, and though she knew she should back away, she couldn't. The sensual look in his eyes was too tempting by far.

He stroked a finger along her jawline, sending tingles traveling down her neck to her breasts, then he leaned in and kissed her lips. The light, sweet kiss urged her to latch herself onto him and demand more… demand all the heat and passion she knew he could unleash on her. She fisted her hand in his plaid and tugged. With a moan, he slipped his arm around her waist and drew her closer. This time, he consumed her lips, flinging her scattered thoughts to the wind like thistledown. He slipped his hands lower, over her hips, and pulled her tight against him. The hard length of him, obvious behind his plaid, made her recall how splendidly he'd made love to her, giving her pleasures she'd never imagined before him.

"I want you," he whispered, then sucked her earlobe into his mouth, before nibbling down her neck.

She shivered. "They're expecting me in the great hall," she whispered.

"Who cares? I need you more. And 'tis obvious you need me, too."

"If we're both… missing," she said, trying to gather her broken thoughts, "they'll know we're together."

He growled and stepped back, his eyes much darker now. "I want to see you tonight. I'll slip to your room after everyone's abed."

The passion in his demanding tone sent spikes of excitement through her. She looked forward to their trysts as much as he did, and she could not deny him.

"How does that sound?" he asked.

"Very well," she said modestly, trying to hide her own

enthusiasm. "But we must keep it a secret."

Lifting a brow, he gave her a wee smile. "I'm good at keeping secrets."

If only she could keep her heart out of the mix until she was with child. But that was impossible. She already loved him so much, just the thought of him abandoning her near gutted her.

***

As Jessie and everyone was gathering for supper, a guard stormed down the stairs and into the great hall, startling her. "Three large galleys are being rowed into Balnakeil Bay!" he announced.

Jessie hurried toward him, excitement buoying her steps. "Is it Dirk and the MacKay party?"

"We're not certain."

She quickly followed the guard onto the battlements to take a look, Torrin behind her. Shading her eyes, she did indeed see the three sizable galleys in the distance. "They didn't leave on galleys," she said.

"Nay, but the MacKenzie chief promised Chief Dirk a galley as part of Lady Isobel's dowry."

"'Tis true," Torrin said.

As the galleys drew nearer, she could see more detail. Their plaids looked familiar and she thought she saw Dirk's red hair shining, and their fair-haired cousin, Keegan, beside him. "I believe 'tis the MacKays." She noticed five castle guards striding purposefully toward the beach. "Are those guards going to warn them that Haldane is lurking about?"

"Aye."

"I'll go down and meet them." Torrin gave her hand a squeeze, then rushed down the stairs.

As the galleys drew nearer, she recognized more of the people aboard—Lady Isobel, Lady Seona—both with dark hair—and her aunt, Lady Patience. What on earth were they doing returning? Part of the reason for the journey was to take Seona and her aunt to their home near Inverness. No matter. She was thrilled to see Seona, for Jessie considered her a good friend. And of course, Isobel, being her sister-by-marriage, was almost like a true sister to her.

Thankfully, Dirk stood proudly in the bow of the galley, as tall and imposing as always. Happy tears filling her eyes, she was grateful he had survived the arrow wound.

Jessie also noticed a couple of Isobel's brothers aboard, along with Dirk's friend, Laird Rebbinglen, or Rebbie, as his friends called him.

Minutes later, some of the guards on board the galleys leapt into the shallow surf and tugged the boats further onto the beach. Luckily, high tide was in. Or maybe they had waited off-shore until high tide.

She watched as the ladies and their maids disembarked and guards escorted them toward the castle. Jessie rushed down several flights of steps and across the great hall so she might greet them in the courtyard.

Torrin waited by the portcullis with Iain, as did several clansmen and guards. When the women were escorted inside, Jessie hurried toward them.

"Oh, Isobel, I'm so glad you've all returned." Jessie embraced her, then turned to Seona. "And I'm happy to see you and your aunt again." 'Twas half true anyway, she was indeed thrilled to see Seona. Her aunt, not so much, for she was a harpy, but the older woman's face didn't appear near as pinched and annoyed as it used to.

"I'm now your cousin-by-marriage. Keegan and I are wed." Seona smiled so brightly, 'twas nearly blinding, and her blue eyes gleamed with happiness.

"In truth? Congratulations! I'm so pleased." Jessie embraced her. "You will have to tell me how this came about when we have more time."

"I will. And this is my younger sister, Talia." Seona motioned to a petite, dark-haired lass of about eighteen summers who stood behind her, a shy smile on her face.

"Welcome, Lady Talia. I'm glad you've come," Jessie said. "Let's go inside where you can rest. I'm sure you're all exhausted from the journey."

The women proceeded across the courtyard, but when shouting and a loud commotion erupted outside the gates, they halted.

Jessie turned to see Torrin and the others bolting through the portcullis. She ran toward them, but one of the burly guards blocked her path.

"Stay back, m'lady! Get them inside," he commanded another guard.

The only thing she could see through the closing portcullis was Torrin withdrawing his sword and dashing toward the beach.

"Torrin!" she yelled, but he didn't even look back. "What's happening?" she demanded of the guard.

"Haldane and his men charged down from the hill."

"Nay!" Isobel tried to get past the guard. "Let me pass!"

"Nay, m'lady. With all due respect, you must go inside. Chief Dirk will have all our heads if you're injured."

"Haldane, that bastard," Jessie said. "Come, ladies, we can see what's happening from the ramparts."

The other ladies followed her into the great hall and up the turnpike stairs to the area she'd been watching from earlier.

A large force of men, all wearing similar plaids rushed the beach.

"Oh, saints," Jessie hissed, dread kicking her in the stomach. "Haldane didn't have that many men." Although she saw Haldane among them. "Who are they?" And then she saw Gregor. "MacBain, you bastard!" she yelled.

"Who is he and why are they attacking?" Seona asked, anguish in her voice.

"He is the man I was in the trial marriage with. He returned a few weeks ago, trying to force me to marry him. He even tried to kidnap me. Torrin MacLeod rescued me and had him escorted off MacKay land. He's returned with his army." She watched as MacBain engaged Torrin in a sword battle not too far from the castle. "This is my fault."

"Nay, 'tis not. Please, God, protect them," Isobel prayed.

Closer to the water, Dirk was enmeshed in a sword dual with McMurdo. All the men were involved in hand-to-hand combat. Wind blew the kicked up sand from the beach, creating dust clouds.

"Is Dirk well enough to fight?" Jessie asked. "We'd heard he was shot with an arrow."

"He is better but still limping," Isobel said, her face white. "Kill him, Dirk," she growled low.

Three of the MacBains had already fallen and another of Haldane's men, thank the saints.

When Jessie's frantic gaze shifted back to Torrin, she saw that blood had saturated his white shirt. But he still battled MacBain.

One of MacBain's men slipped up behind Torrin.

"Torrin! Behind you!" Jessie shouted, unsure if he could hear her with all the wind and noise of battle.

The bastard knocked him on the head with his sword hilt and Torrin fell. MacBain stabbed his sword toward Torrin's stomach.

"You bastard! I'll kill you!" Jessie rushed down the steps, tears blurring her vision.

"Jessie! You can't go out there!" Isobel yelled after her. But she had no time to answer. She was determined to pull Torrin to safety. *Please don't let him be dead.*

She checked that her Highland dirk was in the sheath on her belt.

If Torrin is dead, so help me… MacBain would die by her hand this day.

She ran outside into the bailey, to the closed portcullis. "Let me out!" she ordered the young guard left in charge of the gates. Apparently, all the seasoned guards had joined in the battle.

"Nay, I cannot m'lady. The other guards would string me up."

Jessie pretended to head back inside the castle, but when the guard turned his attention elsewhere, she dashed along the side of the castle toward the small back postern gate.

With shaking hands, she opened it with her key and locked it back. Taking out her foot-long dirk, she hurried along the outside of the curtain wall, trying to stay low and hidden behind the grasses and bushes, her stomach aching more with each step. What would she find when she reached Torrin? Would he be dead from some horrid sword wound? Wiping the tears from her eyes, she approached the place she'd seen him fall. The rest of the fighting had moved to the beach.

Torrin was pushing himself up on his elbow. Saints, his shirt and doublet were drenched in blood.

"Torrin, thanks be to God you're alive! I have to get you inside the walls."

"What the hell are you doing out here?" he growled. His face contorted in pain, he glanced about.

"Helping you, you daft sheep. The faster you come with me, the faster we'll get behind the gate."

Grimacing, he pushed himself to his feet, his sword still in his right hand. She gently placed an arm around his waist, careful to avoid his injuries, and helped him. Glancing around, she didn't see anyone nearby. She helped him closer to the portcullis. Almost there.

Someone shoved them both from behind, and they crashed to their knees.

Mo chreach!

She tried to get her dirk turned to stab their attackers.

"Grab her! Come on!" That was Haldane's voice.

"Bastard!" Jessie yelled. She would gut him if she could get her blade in the right position.

She was still on her stomach when someone dragged her by the feet, away from Torrin.

"Release her!" Torrin shouted.

"Kill him," Haldane growled.

"Nay! Leave him be and I'll go with you." Shoving the hair out of her eyes, Jessie saw 'twas McMurdo that Haldane was ordering about.

Loud clashes and curses echoed as Torrin fended off McMurdo's blade.

She sat up, intending to stab Haldane's leg. But he kicked the knife from her hand and yanked her to her feet. She thrust her fist toward his face. He ducked and slapped her hard across the cheek. Pain lanced through her face and neck, and she swayed.

The earth spun as he picked her up and threw her over his shoulder.

"Put me down!" she ordered, beating her fists against his back.

"Shut your gob," he said, breaking into a run.

Dizzy, she watched the ground speed by underneath her. Haldane's solid shoulder slammed painfully into her stomach with each step he took across the hard-packed sand, near knocking the breath from her. Coming to her senses, she kneed and elbowed him. If only she could get to one of the knives strapped to her calf or thigh, but 'twas impossible to reach them now.

"Are you mad, Haldane? Release me!"

Haldane merely laughed as they headed away from the battle on the beach and through the massive sand dunes.

She noticed someone chasing along behind them. *McMurdo.* Nay! Had he killed Torrin?

Please, God, let him live.

Chapter Thirteen

Torrin pushed himself to his feet, hot pain lancing his side and abdomen from the two sword wounds. Blinking and trying to wipe the sand from his eyes, he saw his archer some thirty or forty feet away, an arrow aimed at one of the MacBains.

"Sim!" Torrin yelled.

When he turned, his eyes widened and he came running. "I'll get you inside the gates, Chief."

"Nay!" he growled. "Give me your bow and arrows." He could stop Haldane from a distance with those. And he damned well intended to slaughter him.

"I'll carry them. Where are you going?"

"Haldane got Lady Jessie! I'm going to kill the bastard." If Haldane killed her… God, he couldn't think of it. He had to get her back. Sheathing his sword, he gritted his teeth and took off running across the upper part of the beach, toward the sand dunes where Haldane had disappeared with Jessie over his shoulder. Considering the pain slicing through Torrin, 'twas more like he limped forward. Still, he moved as fast as he could.

"You're bleeding badly, m'laird!" Sim chased after him.

"Do you think I care?"

"We'll find her. Struan! Luag!" he yelled back to the other MacLeods. "Come!"

Moments later, Iain was running alongside Torrin. "Saints, man! Where are you going? You've lost a lot of blood. We must get you inside the gates!"

"Haldane ran off with Lady Jessie. We're going to get her back," he ground out, trying to ignore the pain lashing through him with every step and the blackness teasing the edges of his vision.

"I'll go. Let them take you back," Iain said.

"Nay! I'm going to kill that whoreson myself." If he didn't pass out first. Saints, he couldn't. He had to save Jessie. If she died, he didn't want to live.

"Hang on, Chief." Struan got under one of Torrin's arms, and Luag the other. They practically carried him through the massive sand dunes as they moved overland.

"Follow the tracks," he said, his vision blacking out for a moment. Nay, he had to stay awake for Jessie. Her damnable brother was a monster and he'd kill her with not a care in the world.

Torrin grew dizzy, and it appeared the sand was turning to grass. Indeed it was.

"There they are," Sim said, pointing with his bow.

In the fading light of sunset that glowed beneath the rose-colored clouds, Jessie's hair was a bright red flag against the green beach grasses as Haldane ran with her over his shoulder. Torrin loved her fiery hair. And he loved the way she pounded her fists against her despicable brother's back. Thank the saints she was still alive and fighting.

"We must catch them," he said through clenched teeth, willing the pain away. He still had time to rescue her.

"Why the devil is he bringing her out here?" Iain asked.

Torrin shook his head hard, trying to think more clearly and keep himself alert. His gaze scanning the undulating landscape leading out to the rugged headland, he figured it out. "Damnation! He's taking her toward the cliffs. When Dirk was a lad, he was almost killed out here when McMurdo shoved him down a cliff."

And McMurdo was with Haldane now, his gray hair and beard resembling dirty wool in the waning light. His clothes were bloody, for Torrin had gotten in a few good strikes before the coward had fled. The archer, Gil, accompanied them.

"I'll kill every last one of them," Torrin swore through his teeth.

"I'll help you," Iain said.

They were all winded when they neared a jagged ravine that cut deep into the headland, high above the sea. His men released him and he forced himself to stand, his knees threatening to buckle. Cold sweat drenched Torrin's clothes, and his side burned like the fires of hell where McMurdo had stabbed him and MacBain had gotten in a deep slice. The two must have missed the vital organs, thank the saints, or else Torrin would be passed out or dead by now.

"We have to get to them on the other side of the ravine," Torrin said.

"Stop right there!" Haldane ordered.

On the opposite side of the deadly narrow gorge, fifty feet away, Gil nocked an arrow and aimed at Torrin. Haldane lowered Jessie to her feet, then stood behind her and held a dagger to her throat. Her skin was deathly pale when her eyes met his. His chest tightened painfully, for he'd not felt such excruciating fear since he'd found his severely injured sister eight years ago in that dark wood.

"Don't move, MacLeod! And keep your men where they are!" Haldane yelled to be heard over the ocean wind. "If anyone comes around this ravine, you'll find your lady on the rocks below."

Torrin glanced around, seeing that Iain stood close behind him but to his left, and Sim kept his bow hidden behind his back and leg.

"What do you want?" Torrin demanded, trying desperately to think clearly. He needed a plan, but everything was going fuzzy.

"We'll have to wait until that Dirk imposter shows up, won't we?" Haldane asked.

What the devil? Torrin frowned.

"He must be wanting to trade her for Dirk," Iain muttered.

"Does Dirk know you're out here?" Torrin yelled.

"Aye. He saw." Haldane grinned.

Rage burned through Torrin that Haldane would find this amusing. "You harm one hair on her head and you're a dead man, Dirk or no Dirk."

"Don't threaten me, MacLeod! I have what you want. You can kiss my arse." Haldane moved Jessie even closer to the edge of the cliff, only a foot remained between her and the drop-off. Waves crashed onto the rocks two hundred feet below.

Blackness and oblivion teasing at the edge of Torrin's vision again, he wavered, but prayed he wouldn't pass out before he could get Jessie safely out of Haldane's clutches.

"If I pass out…" he said to Iain, "or die, promise me you'll rescue her."

"Of course, man. But you're not going to die."

"I hope you're right." Torrin gauged the mad look in Haldane's eyes. Then he turned and glanced behind them, not seeing Dirk or anyone approaching from the dunes. He had his doubts that Dirk even knew they were out here.

A scream sounded, drawing Torrin back around in alarm. Loose dirt and stones slid from beneath Jessie's feet and dropped into the abyss.

"Pull her back from the edge!" Torrin yelled.

Haldane grinned and appeared to be chuckling. God's teeth! He truly was a madman. Torrin itched to end the bastard's life.

Haldane held Jessie by one arm, while she grasped both hands onto Haldane's plaid as her feet scrambled for purchase on the crumbling edge.

"Pull her back, you bastard!" Torrin ordered, his heart thudding in his ears so loudly he could hardly hear anything else.

Haldane shook his head slowly, looking mightily entertained.

Placing his hands behind his back, Torrin motioned with his fingers. "Give me your bow," he murmured low to Sim, hoping he was close enough to hear above the wind.

Moments later, the smooth yew wood slipped into his hand, along with an arrow.

"You, there! Stand back where I can see you!" Haldane shouted.

Keeping the bow hidden behind him, Torrin glanced aside and noticed Sim had moved back and to his right.

McMurdo murmured something to Haldane, who looked frantic for a moment as his gaze darted back and forth over Torrin and his men. "Put the bow down, MacLeod!" he ordered.

"Pull Jessie back from the edge and release her, and I will." With no further need to hide the weapons, Torrin held the bow in one hand and the arrow in the other, down at his sides. He could nock the arrow and let it fly in a second if he had to.

The coward kept Jessie in front of him, like a shield, less than a foot from the ravine. If only she was a safe distance back, he'd skewer Haldane with an arrow.

Jessie slowly lifted her right leg toward her hand, dug beneath her skirt, and took something from her calf. A knife. *Nay!* 'Twas too dangerous. What the devil was she planning?

Torrin's hands clutched the bow and arrow tightly. He had to be ready to shoot quickly.

Jessie carefully moved the *sgian dubh* into position, then stabbed backward into Haldane's belly. He howled and shoved her to the ground beside him. Torrin swiftly nocked and released the arrow. It shot across the ravine and jabbed into Haldane's throat. He gasped and tried to pull it out while blood spurted from the wound.

Jessie attempted to crawl away from him and the cliff's edge, but Gil kicked at her, blocking her path.

"Bastard," Torrin growled. "Give me another arrow, Sim!"

In a trice, he had one in hand and nocked. He let it fly toward Gil, but the lad dove to the ground at the last second, and it missed.

"Damnation! Another," he demanded.

He shot this arrow at Haldane, hitting him in the side, hoping he'd die before he could harm Jessie.

Haldane sank to his knees at the edge of the drop-off, his bloody hands grabbing onto Jessie's skirts. She kicked at him as he started sliding off the cliff.

"Turn her loose!" Torrin yelled, his heart seizing and dizziness crashing in on him again. He couldn't get around the deep ravine in time to pull her back. Sim and Luag took off at a sprint in that direction.

Jessie slid down the cliff face onto a lower rock that jutted out. Using the knife, she cut at her skirts. The material ripped off under Haldane's weight and he fell. She dropped her knife and grabbed onto the rock with both hands, most of her body dangling over the edge.

"Help her back up!" Torrin ordered the two men left standing, McMurdo armed with a sword and targe, Gil with a bow and arrows.

Gil launched an arrow in their direction, and Torrin leapt out of the way. It drove into the ground a foot from him. Gil took off at a fast sprint away from them.

"What the hell is going on out here?" a deep voice yelled behind them.

Torrin turned to find Dirk approaching, limping, a sword in his hand, his red hair windblown, his blue eyes wild and his clothes bloody. Several men accompanied him.

"Tell that bastard to help her back up!" Torrin said, hanging onto consciousness by a thread. Iain grasped Torrin's shoulder. Had he swayed?

Dirk stepped forward, eying Jessie clutching the rocky outcropping with both hands. "Pull her up, McMurdo!"

"Promise me, upon your life and your wife's life,"

McMurdo said, "that you will give me the tomb in the church your father promised me, and I will."

"Aye. Of course! The tomb in the church is yours!" Dirk yelled. "And I'll be glad to put you in it," he growled low.

Hurry, you bastard! Torrin wanted to shout. The lower half of Jessie's body was dangling off the cliff.

"And you'll all let me go free," McMurdo said.

"Aye. You can go free," Dirk said. "Just help her up now or you'll be a dead man buried at sea!"

McMurdo reached a hand down. Clinging to the cliff with one hand, Jessie reached up and grabbed onto McMurdo's hand. He hauled her up to solid ground, then took off, running like a scalded rat.

Torrin, Dirk, and Iain hastened to circumvent the deep ravine and get to Jessie. Torrin glanced across to find her crawling away from the edge of the cliff. Sim and Luag finally reached her and helped her to a safer area. "Thank the saints," Torrin whispered, so much relief flowing through him, the pain vanished for a second.

"Where's Haldane?" Dirk asked, breathing hard.

"Dead," Iain said. "Fell off the cliff with an arrow in his throat."

"In truth?" Dirk glanced at the bow Torrin carried. "You shot him, MacLeod?"

"Aye." All he could focus on was seeing Jessie. Holding her. 'Twas all he cared about. By the time he limped to her, minutes later, he was out of breath and lightheaded, his vision blurring, the pain nigh overwhelming.

His men had helped Jessie move several yards away from the sea cliff's rim where she sat upon the grass. Torrin dropped to his knees beside her and pulled her into his arms. She would never know how precious she was to him.

"Thank God. I feared I'd lost you, Jessie."

Torrin felt himself falling and all went black.

***

"Retreat!" MacBain called out to his men. Damnation, they had lost at least eight men. But Haldane and his gang had disappeared, leaving the MacBains to fight the MacKays. The force that had just arrived by galley, along with the men from inside the castle walls, had combined to outnumber them. 'Twas a losing battle, and he couldn't allow more of his men to be slaughtered.

On foot, he and his clan scrambled up the hill and crossed the top. "Are they following?" he shouted back, gasping for breath.

"Nay, they're all headed in the opposite direction."

MacBain paused on top of the grassy hill and squinted, scanning the rocky headland in the distance where all the MacKays were running. Something was going on at the cliff's edge, but 'twas so far, he couldn't see who was involved.

Clearly, joining forces with Haldane MacKay had been a mistake. The lad had let on like he commanded a large faction of men who were scattered about. But he'd only had a few, mayhap half a dozen. Given the strength of the MacKay clan and how they fought for their chief, Dirk, they would never back Haldane as chief, anyway. 'Twas a lost cause.

MacBain had injured Torrin MacLeod in that sword dual, but he hadn't been able to kill him before his sword-bearer had engaged MacBain in a fight and driven him back. He'd had to retreat to save his own skin, but he'd escaped the bastard without much injury.

"Grab the horses and let's get out of here!" he ordered. "You two stay here, well hidden." He pointed to two of his stealthiest men. "Watch the castle, or find one of Haldane's men—if any of them survived—and see if Torrin MacLeod is alive or dead. Once you know for certain, head south. We'll wait for you just outside of Scourie."

"Aye, m'laird," they both murmured.

"We're headed to Scourie?" his sword-bearer asked.

"Aye. And if MacLeod lives, we go toward Munrick."

Moments later, they led the horses from the low-lying thicket where they'd hidden them earlier and mounted.

"What's your plan?" his sword-bearer asked.

"If MacLeod survives, he will head for home eventually.

We'll be waiting for him just north of his keep. He only had seven men with him, if you recall. And if Iain Stewart accompanies him, that will be five more, if they all survived the battle. We'll have them outnumbered. And if he brings Lady Jessie home with him, as his new bride, we'll kill the bastard and then grab her."

They took off, riding as if the devil were on their tails.

Aye, his plan was brilliant. He no longer cared about her dowry. 'Twas now about pride and revenge. No one got the best of Gregor MacBain.

***

"He still lives," Iain said, kneeling on the other side of Torrin, passed out on the grass.

"Thank the saints," Jessie whispered, the cooler air of gloaming and the harsh wind blasting the headland giving her a shiver. When Torrin had dropped to the ground beside her, she'd feared he was dead. He'd lost so much blood, his skin was pale. But thankfully, he still breathed.

They both rose and stood aside as three of Torrin's men moved in and hoisted him up onto their shoulders, then carried him toward the dunes leading to the castle. Iain followed them.

"Are you well, sister?" Dirk asked, limping toward her.

"Aye, are you hurt?" She glanced down at his leg, seeing no fresh injury below the bottom of his plaid.

"'Tis my calf, still healing from where Gil shot me with an arrow several weeks ago." Dirk shook his head. "When I saw you hanging off that cliff—" Fear sharpened his gaze. "I remember what 'tis like."

She nodded. But, thirteen years ago, Dirk had hung off the side of a cliff all night. She couldn't imagine the prolonged terror he must have felt. "Aye, I'm well. Thanks to McMurdo." Who would've ever imagined the murderer saving anyone's life? "But we must get MacLeod back to the keep and the healer," she said, still feeling jittery and weak from having almost fallen to her death.

"Indeed," her older brother said. "Let's go," he called out

to the MacKays.

Torrin's men carried him quickly, ahead of everyone else.

Please, God, keep him alive.

Dirk walked over and stood at the edge of the ravine, staring down toward the rocks and the sea where their youngest brother had met his death. A flash of grief cut through her, for no matter Haldane's crimes—and even though he would've killed her with no qualms—he had once been her wee brother. She knew Dirk felt the loss of one of their own, too.

She rushed to catch up to Torrin's men, transporting him through the sand dunes. The rest of the MacKays and Dirk's friends followed.

A quarter hour later, they entered Dunnakeil. The men carried Torrin to his chamber, while Jessie dashed to Erskine's room to get Nannag, but she wasn't there.

"Where is Nannag?" Jessie asked Flora, one of the healers-in-training who watched over the sleeping sword-bearer.

"In Lady Isobel's chamber."

Fear flashed through Jessie. "Why? Is she hurt?"

"She fainted while she was watching the battle and hit her head. She feared Chief Dirk had been hurt or killed."

"Saints." Jessie ran toward the laird's chamber, praying Isobel was not injured too badly. In the corridor, she found Nannag and her two helpers.

"Please go to Laird MacLeod's chamber. He is severely injured and has lost a lot of blood."

"Aye, m'lady," the ancient healer said. Carrying her medicine satchel filled with herbs and no telling what else, she and her two younger helpers quickened their pace.

While Jessie wanted to go with them immediately, she also needed to check on Isobel.

Upon bypassing the guard and entering the room, she found Isobel sitting before the hearth, Seona beside her.

"Were you injured badly?" Jessie asked.

"Where is Dirk?" Isobel demanded, leaping to her feet

and rushing forward, her eyes red.

"He was right behind me. He is well."

"Oh, thank the saints," Isobel whispered, pressing a hand to her chest and looking much relieved. "I saw him fall. After the guard brought me to my chamber, he wouldn't allow me to leave."

"And Keegan?" Seona asked, standing beside Isobel.

"Thankfully, he was unhurt, too. But Torrin was badly injured. He's out cold and has lost a lot of blood."

"Och, nay! I am sorry," Isobel said. "And here I have held you up."

"I wanted to see that you were well. I'll be in Torrin's room," Jessie said, dashing out the door.

When Jessie entered the crowded room, Torrin growled, his eyes closed, his teeth clenched in pain. Thank the saints he had awakened.

"Everyone out," Nannag ordered Torrin's men, and Iain. How could such a strong and commanding voice come from such an aged and tiny woman? The men obediently filed out, but when Nannag found Jessie still standing by the door, she said in a gentler tone, "You too, m'lady."

"I will help."

"You can help by going to fetch Flora for me. And tell her to bring some hot water." She smiled sweetly, then rushed back to Torrin's bedside. "Cut his doublet and shirt off," she murmured to one of her helpers.

What if Torrin died while Jessie was out of the room? *Nay, he cannot die!*

Praying the whole way, Jessie did as Nannag asked and retrieved Flora.

Back at Torrin's chamber a short time later, Jessie waited outside the door with Iain and Struan, though she felt uncomfortable doing so. She did not know the men well, and they sent her inquiring glances. Did they know how close she and Torrin had grown? What had he told them?

A pain-filled growl echoed from beyond the door and Jessie wanted to rush inside. Instead, she paced and clasped her hands together. A needle-like pain shot through them and she examined her palms. They were scraped raw from where she'd held onto the rocks. She would have to rub some salve on them. Her shoulders were also sore from being near wrenched from their sockets.

"Torrin is tough as a cliff-face," Iain said, his voice rough. "I'm certain he will be up and around in no time." Although, with that worried frown, Iain didn't look convinced.

Jessie nodded. "I hope you're right."

A string of loud male curses issued forth from the room. *Saints!* He had to be in horrible pain. She wished she could do something to help ease it.

During the ensuing half hour, Dirk and Isobel, and several others stopped by to see how Torrin was faring, and then left. All she knew was that he was in agony, given the noises emanating from inside the room. Soon, all grew quiet.

Too quiet.

Fear flashed through Jessie. She knocked at the door, then barged in.

"How is he?" she demanded, rushing to the bedside.

"Shh. He is sleeping," Nannag whispered. "You'll wake him."

'Twas true. His bare chest rose and fell evenly with his deep breaths. But she couldn't see his wounds for Flora held a linen bandage pressed firmly against them. "Did he pass out again?"

"Nay. 'Twas my sleeping potion, lass." Nannag gave a reassuring smile. "He but needs to rest for a few hours. Come back later. I'll watch over him closely."

"I don't mind staying and helping." In fact, she wanted to. She would enjoy watching him sleep and breathe, for it meant he was alive.

Nannag shook her head. "Go get yourself something to eat... and some wine. You need it."

Releasing a calming breath, Jessie glanced back at the open doorway, where Iain and Struan stood, staring into the room with much concern. She supposed everyone could see how distraught she was… which meant, everyone knew how much she cared for Torrin.

Jessie nodded. "I thank you."

"You're welcome. Flora and I will take good care of the lad for you," Nannag whispered so the men wouldn't hear, then winked.

"He will be well?" Jessie asked hesitantly, keeping her voice low.

"Oh, aye. He lost some blood, but he is a strong, young warrior. We stitched him up good, and the bleeding is slowing. He'll be like new soon." Nannag gave her a knowing smile.

Jessie's face heated. "Very well. I'll be back soon."

When she stepped into the corridor, Iain asked, "How is he?"

"Sleeping. Go in if you wish, but Nannag will likely run you off after a minute."

With a faint smile, he nodded and stepped into the room. A couple of Torrin's men followed him.

She found Aiden lurking further along the darkened corridor. "How is Torrin?" he asked.

"Sleeping. Nannag says he will recover. I pray she's right."

"Aye. I like him. And I'm so thankful you were unhurt, sister. Dirk told me what happened out there."

"He told you about Haldane?" she asked.

Aiden nodded. Dropping his gaze, he swallowed hard, his Adam's apple bobbing. "I'm just glad he didn't take you with him when he fell off that cliff."

Tears burned her eyes. "Me, too." She drew Aiden into a tight embrace. He was far too thin. "You need to eat more."

"Aye, sister." His tiny smirk reassured her.

"Well, if you will excuse me, I must go clean up. I'm a mess." She strode to her chamber and found her pup where she'd left him, asleep before the hearth. He leapt up and scurried toward her.

"Are you hungry, Greum?" She found some leftover hard cheese sitting on her bedside table and gave it to him. That would occupy him while she washed up and changed clothes. She didn't know where her maid was, but she was fully capable of taking care of herself.

Thankfully, the maid did show up a few minutes later, and Jessie asked her to take Greum out for a walk in the courtyard.

Heading toward the great hall a few minutes later, Jessie came upon Dirk and Isobel exiting their chamber.

"How is Torrin?" Dirk asked.

"He is sleeping, thanks to Nannag's potion. She says he will recover."

"Thank the saints," Dirk said.

"Jessie, you didn't tell me you almost died out there," Isobel said. "I'm so thankful you were unhurt." Isobel drew her into a fierce hug. "Oh, pray pardon. You must be sore."

"Just my shoulders a wee bit, and my hands." She showed them her scraped palms.

"Saints!" Isobel said. "I cannot imagine having to hold onto the rocks to avoid falling down a cliff."

"Aye, 'twas the most frightened I've ever been. And to think my own brother wanted me to die."

Isobel shook her head, blinking back tears. "I'm glad Haldane's dead, and I'm not going to apologize for saying that." She gave her husband a defiant look.

"As am I." Dirk raised an auburn brow. "He refused to change his evil ways, and he got what was coming to him. I always knew only death would stop him from trying to kill me. I'll have to thank Torrin when he feels better."

"McMurdo pulled you to safety?" Isobel asked her.

"Aye, 'twas unbelievable." Jessie had never been more shocked and grateful in her life.

"'Twas not out of the goodness of his heart. 'Tis simply that he wants the tomb in the church so badly."

Jessie nodded. "I wonder why?"

Dirk shrugged. "Who can guess what goes on in such a

twisted mind? But I believe he fears that the people of Durness will desecrate his remains after he dies unless they are sealed up safely in the church."

"I see. Well, I'm glad you had that to offer him. Aiden said you told him about Haldane."

"Aye." Dirk frowned, looking morose. "The lad took it hard, but he said he knew 'twas going to happen sooner or later. And though Aiden caused big problems for Erskine and the clan, he said he was glad he got to talk to Haldane one last time."

Jessie nodded, tears burning her eyes once again, more so for Aiden's grief than her own, because the two lads had always been so close.

"I've been meaning to ask you," Dirk said. "Why is Torrin here? Not that I mind him visiting."

Jessie glanced at the clan members passing by them in the corridor. "What do you think?" she said in a hushed voice.

"Come inside the room." Isobel pulled her into their chamber and Dirk entered, too, closing the door behind.

"I can guess why he's here, but I might be wrong," Dirk said. "When we stopped by Munrick a few weeks ago, he again asked for your hand."

Jessie's face felt scorched of a sudden. "He said he came to protect me from MacBain." Jessie explained how the two men had run into each other far south of Durness and traveled north together.

"And did he protect you?"

"Aye. He broke MacBain's nose when he tried to barge into my chamber in the middle of the night. Then, when MacBain tried to kidnap me, Torrin rescued me and had MacBain and his men thrown into the dungeon. The next day, he had his men, along with some of the MacKays, escort the brigands off MacKay lands."

"Saints! I'm glad he's here, then. Have you changed your mind about marrying him?" Dirk inquired.

"I'd rather not discuss it at the moment," Jessie said,

unwilling to share her conflictive feelings.

Dirk gave a wee smile. "Very well. We'll talk about it later."

"What happened on the ramparts when you fell?" Jessie asked Isobel, wanting to know, but also hoping to change the subject.

"After you left, Seona and I were watching that horrible battle below, on the beach." She shook her head. "Dirk fell and I thought McMurdo had stabbed him."

"'Tis my leg, you see," Dirk said. "My calf is still weak from where Gil's arrow went through it weeks ago. I stumbled and fell. Which was fortunate, for it allowed McMurdo's blade to miss me."

"Thank the saints. And I'm glad you were not hurt terribly when you passed out," Jessie told Isobel.

"Seona caught part of my fall, but my head slammed against the battlement." She gently rubbed the side of her head. "They helped me inside, though I wanted to go back out and see what'd happened to Dirk, but the guard wouldn't allow it. And then Nannag examined me and told me—" Isobel pressed her lips tight and glanced at Dirk. "Can I tell her?"

He smiled back, love shining in his pale blue eyes. "Aye, of course."

"Nannag told me I am with child," Isobel whispered.

Chapter Fourteen

Isobel was with child?

Jessie's mouth dropped open, and happy tears burned her eyes. "In truth? That is wonderful!" She embraced Isobel, knowing her friend had been worried for the past several months when she didn't conceive right after the wedding. Some had thought it could've been because Isobel had almost died from the deadly nightshade poisoning last winter.

"Aye." Isobel drew back, beaming.

Jessie turned to Dirk and embraced him. "Congratulations, brother. You will both make wonderful parents," she said, moving back.

"I thank you." He grinned.

She had never seen him look happier.

"We have not announced it to the clan as of yet," Isobel said. "Although Seona and Keegan know—Seona was with me when Nannag told me—but we wish to keep it a secret from the rest of the clan for now."

Jessie nodded. "I'll not murmur a word."

"We'll have a celebration feast, once everyone is more recovered from their injuries," Dirk said.

"Speaking of which, I'm starving," Isobel said, moving

toward the door. "Let's eat."

Dirk chuckled and joined her in the corridor. "I'd best order more supplies."

Isobel gasped and gave his arm a light swat.

"I only meant that my son will need a lot of food as he's growing." Grinning, he placed a hand upon her still flat belly.

"And what if the bairn is a dainty daughter, like me?" Isobel asked.

"I'll be thrilled, of course."

Watching the two stroll toward the great hall, Jessie smiled and shook her head at their playful exchange. She knew her brother would be overjoyed with either a healthy son or daughter, but men always had to brag that they were going to have a son, especially as a first born.

Jessie checked on Torrin again and found he was still sleeping. The bleeding was slowing, thanks be to God.

"I will watch over the laird," Flora said, ushering Jessie toward the door. "You go eat something afore you starve."

"I'll be back soon."

Flora nodded and closed the door behind her.

Jessie joined Dirk and Isobel at the high table in the great hall. Iain and a few others were already sitting there as well. She wanted to eat quickly, then go back and sit with Torrin. In truth, she had no appetite, but she was growing weak and jittery; it had been many hours since she'd last eaten. Isobel directed the servants to start serving supper. It was later than usual and everyone was famished.

Jessie was glad to see Seona and Keegan approaching the high table, her arm linked through his.

"'Tis good to see you again, cousin," Jessie said to Keegan, his long tawny hair freshly washed. "I hear you're married, now."

"Aye, indeed. I'm a lucky man." He grinned, his pale blue eyes alight as he pulled out a chair for Lady Seona.

She was beaming as she took her seat beside Jessie.

"Congratulations to you both. How did this come about?"

"Thank you. We'll have to tell you about it when we have more time," Keegan said, sitting beside Seona. "'Twill take two or three hours, I'm thinking."

"In truth? You must've had quite an adventure."

"We did. Although, not all of it was pleasant."

"Where is your sister?" Jessie asked Seona.

"In a guest chamber, sleeping. She is worn out from all the travel. And so is Aunt Patience."

Jessie nodded. "Was anyone else injured in the battle on the beach?"

"Most everyone had a few cuts and scrapes, but three of the MacKay guards had some bad wounds. Nannag and her helpers are seeing to them," Keegan said. "How is Chief MacLeod?"

"Sleeping at the moment, and Flora said the bleeding is slowing."

"'Tis good."

Jessie was happy to see Aiden come down the stairs and sit beside Keegan. She was glad he was moving past his withdrawn phase.

Two tall, dark-haired men entered from the bailey, Dirk's friend, Rebbie, and Isobel's brother, Cyrus. Rebbie asked about Torrin, then took the seat beside Dirk as the food was being served.

Jessie quickly ate the roast venison, along with onions, parsnips and oat bread. Although she loved eating with her friends and family, she missed Torrin sitting beside her and wished he was able to eat. Tears burning her eyes, she forced down a few more bites.

Moments later, Flora moved in behind Jessie and whispered in her ear. "Laird MacLeod is asking for you, m'lady."

A shock of icy fear went through her.

"Pray pardon," she told those sitting closest to her, leapt up from her chair and followed Flora.

"Is he worse?" Jessie asked on the way up the steps, her heart pounding in her throat.

"He's in great pain." Flora hastened along the corridor and opened the door to Torrin's chamber.

Jessie entered and rushed to his bedside. "What's wrong?"

"I wish to speak to the lady alone," Torrin told the healer, a fierce frown upon his ashen face.

Flora quickly vacated the room and closed the door.

"I'm sorry you're in such terrible pain," Jessie said, touching his arm. Saints, how she wished she could take away some of his agony.

"Never mind that," he said through clenched teeth, keeping his voice low. He took her hand into his. "You need to marry me now, in case you are with child and I die."

A jolt of alarm went through her. "What? Nay, you are not going to die," she said firmly.

"That remains to be seen." His eyes were dark with pain and more solemn than she could remember.

"Torrin, you must not say that," she said gently, her throat tightening. She stroked her hand along his bristly cheek. "You must get better."

He nodded. "Still, you could be carrying my heir, but only if we wed."

"Nay. You will simply have to recover. I'm not giving you an excuse to die."

His frown only deepened. "Are you mad? I don't want to die."

"Well then, you must grow strong and healthy again, and then... if I conceive..." She was afraid to even finish that sentence.

"Aye?" Torrin lifted his brows. "What?"

"I'll marry you," she whispered.

"You will?" he asked, hope lighting his eyes. "You will marry me?"

"If I am with child."

One side of his lips quirked up a wee bit. "You will be. I ken it."

She sent him a bittersweet smile. "I pray you're right."

His eyes widened. "You do?"

"Aye."

"You want to marry me. I knew it," he said with satisfaction.

She nodded, a mist of tears burning her eyes.

"But I want you to know, Jessie, I'll marry you even if you don't conceive."

She shook her head. "That means more to me than I can say, but your clan would hate us. You would grow to resent me if I couldn't provide you an heir."

"Nay. Never. I swear to you, Jessie—"

Someone knocked hard at the door.

Torrin muttered a curse.

"I'd better see who that is." She slipped her hand from his and went to open the door.

Iain waited in the corridor, his dark blue eyes concerned. "How is Torrin?"

"Come in," she said.

He advanced into the room and stood by the bed.

"I'm alive," Torrin told him, his face tight and pale.

"Thank the saints. I grew worried when I saw Lady Jessie rush from the great hall and follow the healer."

"You may need something else for the pain," Jessie told Torrin. "I should get Flora."

"Aye. The pain is growing worse," Torrin admitted.

His statement alone worried her, for she knew he wouldn't have said it if the pain wasn't severe.

***

"I will sit with Laird MacLeod tonight," Jessie said to Nannag an hour later. "You need some sleep." Though the elderly healer did not look near as exhausted as Jessie felt.

"Very well, lass." Nannag sent her a sweet smile. "Flora will sleep here on the pallet by the fireplace in case you need her."

"That will be good."

After Nannag left, Jessie pulled the straight chair closer to the bedside and, in the dim glow of the candle, watched

Torrin sleep. Whatever potion Flora had given him for pain had knocked him out. She studied his breathing—deep and even—and prayed that meant he was strong enough to pull through despite his severe injuries.

They had planned to spend the night together in her chamber. What a terrible turn of events. The main thing was he lived, for which she was exceedingly grateful. He had come to mean more to her than she would've ever thought possible. Aye, indeed, she loved him.

An hour or two later, he shifted and muttered something she couldn't understand. He thrashed about, then shivered. She touched his forehead.

"Saints, you are burning up," she whispered.

"Jessie?" he murmured.

"Aye, 'tis me."

His eyes remained closed.

She took the cloth from the basin of cold water, squeezed it out, and bathed his face with it.

He hissed and tried to draw away from her.

She pulled the blanket up to cover his bare shoulders. She had feared he would have a fever, but hoped it wouldn't be too severe. She might have to wake Flora and ask her what to do, for Jessie would never consider herself a healer. She hated to disturb the woman, who'd worked tirelessly for hours in her duties. But what if Torrin got too hot? Could such a fever kill him?

After rising from her chair, Jessie crouched by Flora and gently shook her.

Flora's eyes popped open. "Aye. What is it, m'lady?"

"He has a terrible fever."

"Och, nay." She scrambled up from the floor and poured some hot water, heating in the fireplace, into a cup. "We'll give him some willow bark tea, then," she whispered, sprinkling some ground up pieces of bark into the water. "And a bit more poppy for the pain." While it steeped, the healer pressed her hand against Torrin's forehead. "He is indeed scorching."

Jessie's stomach knotted, for she knew not what this meant. *Please God, heal him and help him recover,* she prayed, tears in her eyes. More than anything, she wanted to have a family with him.

When the tea was ready, Flora said, "Mayhap you can help him lean over this way a bit so he doesn't choke on the tea?"

"Of course." Jessie went to the back side of the bed. "Torrin?"

"Hmm."

"I'm going to help you turn over that way so you can drink some tea, aye?" She pushed at his shoulder.

When he tried to move, he grimaced terribly and growled a curse.

"I'm sorry," Jessie said.

"Och, m'laird, I ken it hurts," Flora said gently, as if to a child. "But if you drink this, 'twill help."

Jessie pushed harder at his shoulder so he could roll toward his right. 'Twas obvious that he was helping, for she couldn't have moved him so easily if he hadn't.

Flora held the cup to his mouth.

"Drink now, Torrin," Jessie whispered softly in his ear.

He swallowed several mouthfuls, took a few breaths, then drank the rest of the cup.

"Good. That will help," Flora said in an encouraging tone.

Torrin lay back, grinding his teeth together and hissing. Once he'd relaxed, he took several deep breaths. She stroked his forearm, lying on top of the blanket. He lifted his hand and closed it securely around Jessie's wrist.

Flora smiled slightly when she saw this, then returned to arranging the herbal remedies. Jessie pulled the blanket to his chin again but didn't remove his hand from around her wrist. Nay, she rather liked his tight, possessive hold, even in the face of such illness. 'Haps she could help give him the strength to pull through.

A half hour later, Flora was once again snoring beside

the hearth, and Torrin was sleeping peacefully. Jessie touched his face, his whisker stubble brushing her palm. He was still rather warm, but the fever was less severe than before.

The rough feel of his stubble sparked the memory of when he'd first kissed her in the chapel, and how he'd talked about his whiskers being prickly and growing back quickly despite his best efforts to keep them shaved off. Tears burning her eyes, she wished he could tease her now… kiss her, make her laugh… and a lot more.

When his grip on her wrist relaxed enough, she moved around the foot of the bed to the other side. Sitting in the chair, she took up the wet cloth again and stroked it over his face, then traced his attractive chestnut-colored brows with her fingertip. She always loved it when he raised one of them, giving her a mischievous look.

His eyes still closed, he grunted and gently took hold of her hand. "Jessie," he said, no louder than a breath.

"Aye."

"Love you," he said.

Tears filled Jessie's eyes. Her throat tightened, and she swallowed hard. Once she was able to speak, she whispered, "I love you, too."

One corner of his lips quirked upward in the barest hint of a smile, then disappeared.

Though she told the truth, she hoped he wouldn't remember it. Their feelings for each other were strong, but that wasn't the only factor. To a chief and his clan, the heir was of primary importance.

Holding her hand, Torrin lapsed into a deeper sleep.

Soon, dawn light gleamed silvery gray through the narrow window, and Jessie grew more and more sleepy. She would just lay her head down for a minute on the bed to rest her tight shoulders and neck.

The rattle of the door latch startled her awake and she sat upright. The room was lighter now and Iain stood on the threshold.

"How is he?" Iain whispered, then moved to stand at the

foot of the bed.

Truth be told, she'd been asleep and wasn't certain. She ran her gaze over Torrin, then laid her palm against his forehead. Still a bit too warm, but not scalding. His breathing was deep and even.

"Very well, I think."

"Thank the saints," Iain said, keeping his deep voice low. "You've taken excellent care of him, m'lady."

"God and the healers deserve all the credit. I merely sat here."

"You did far more than that," Iain said with a slight smile.

She wasn't sure what he was talking about, but she wasn't going to argue.

"Don't tell him I said so, but you, sitting here, holding his hand, will mean more to him than all the medicine in the world."

Her face burned, and she dropped her gaze to study Torrin. He moved a bit, a frown creasing his brow.

Torrin must have talked to Iain about his feelings for her. She wasn't sure whether to feel embarrassed or glad.

"I'll let you both rest," Iain whispered and slipped out the door.

Flora roused from her sleep by the hearth and pushed herself up. "How is the laird this morn?"

"Improving, I think. But mayhap you should check him over to be sure."

Moving to the other side of the bed, Flora placed a hand upon his forehead. "Aye. Still a mild fever, but I think he is doing well, all things considered."

"Thanks be to God," Jessie murmured.

"Aye, I think your prayers helped, m'lady." Flora went back to her herbal concoctions.

How did she know Jessie had prayed for Torrin? She had done so silently. Maybe the woman had simply assumed it, since 'twas obvious Jessie cared a great deal for Torrin.

Moments later, Nannag stole into the room, her footsteps so light, Jessie almost didn't hear them. Her white hair was confined beneath a red kertch, and her blue eyes were as bright as the morning sky.

"The lad is doing well, aye?" she asked in her papery thin whisper. "His color is better."

'Twas true. How had Jessie missed that? Last night, he had been so pale.

"Aye," Jessie said, feeling more hopeful.

Torrin shifted again with a low grunt.

"Mayhap you would like to get him some thin porridge while we check his wounds," Nannag suggested.

Jessie didn't see how a woman in her nineties could be so chipper and spry this early in the morn. She must have slept well.

Jessie stood and rubbed her low back; it ached from having sat in the same position so long.

"You need to eat something, too," Nannag told her. "'Twill take us about a half hour to re-bandage his wounds."

But would he miss her if she wasn't there when he woke up? Maybe she should go ahead and wake him now to tell him where she was going.

"Torrin?" She touched his forehead.

"Hmm?"

"I'm going to get food. I'll be back soon."

He opened his eyes, blinked a couple of times, a frown contorting his brow, then studied her. "Aye."

"How do you feel this morn?"

"Like hell... if you wish the truth." His deep voice was raspy.

"You are improving though." Aye, his face wasn't as pale, and he was not growling lengthy curses as he had been the evening before. She wanted to kiss his forehead to reassure him, but couldn't with Nannag and Flora watching. They'd make something of it, when she wanted to keep the true nature of their association secret.

"Aye," he agreed, but in a dull tone.

"They will take good care of you." She motioned to the

two healers.

"Come back soon," he whispered, his dark green gaze pleading with her.

"I will, and I'll bring you porridge, which you must eat," she said in a mock stern tone.

"I make no promises."

***

A half hour later, Torrin lay propped up against pillows in bed while he imagined Jessie. Thoughts of her were the only things that distracted him from the piercing agony in his abdomen. The healers were excellent, of course, but, since the evening before, they had inflicted prohibitive amounts of pain upon him. Only the younger one remained in the room at present. Thankfully, the bandages were changed and they'd given him some sort of bitter herbal tea to drink.

When someone entered the room, he opened his eyes.

Jessie. Thank the saints. He'd missed her. She carried a tray containing a bowl and cup. Hell, she was going to make him eat. The very thought of food made him want to retch.

"You are feeling better, aye?" she asked with a little smile.

"Indeed." He could lie if it made her happy.

She set the tray on the bedside table. "Flora, would you like to go break your fast?"

"Aye, if you think you can handle his lairdship."

"If he gets too unruly, I'll send someone for you," Jessie said.

The healer grinned and left the room.

"Och. As if I could be unruly," Torrin muttered.

"Once you eat, you will feel stronger."

He hoped she was right, for at the moment he felt weaker than a two-day-old bairn. Though he hated for her to see him like this, it couldn't be helped. He'd much rather have her at his bedside than not. He thought she had stayed with him all night. A couple of times when he'd awakened, she had been there. Either that or 'twas a fevered dream.

"Did you stay with me last night?" he asked.

"Aye, of course." Her blue eyes reflected such devotion, he could hardly believe it. "Do you not remember?" she asked.

Another memory flashed through his mind like lightning—she'd whispered: *I love you.* Saints! Was it really true? He had seen the tears glistening in her eyes and heard the emotion thick in her voice. But he was afraid if he mentioned it, she would retreat and become defensive again. He knew she was but trying to protect her vulnerable heart. Knowing she loved him, he was so thankful he could dance. Well… he'd best not do that now. He might do himself grievous harm.

"I remember some of it," he said vaguely. "And I thank you for being here with me."

"No need to thank me." Holding the bowl of porridge in her hand, she used a wooden spoon to scoop some up, then held it before his mouth.

"I can use my hand," he said, lifting it, though it was slightly sore and weak. He'd be mortified if Iain or another man came into the room and witnessed Jessie spoon-feeding him.

She cocked her head sideways. "You don't like the way I do it?"

"Of course, 'tis only…"

"I want to help you," she said, the sincerity in her tone, as well as the beautiful emotion in her eyes, clutched at his heart.

"Very well. But if Iain or any of the men come for a visit, you must stop. They'll think I'm a bairn."

Jessie grinned. "Oh, I see. Stubborn male pride rears its ugly head again."

"'Tis a hardship I must endure," he said drily.

Shaking her head, she offered him the bite of oat porridge again, and he opened his mouth to accept it. His stomach almost rebelled, but he closed his eyes and forced himself to swallow.

"Delicious," he said. 'Twas not a lie; the porridge was

slightly sweet and salty, with butter and honey, but his stomach felt like the pits of hell. He wasn't sure how many more bites he could tolerate.

He accepted another spoonful, and once he'd forced it down, he said, "While that digests, tell me what is happening around here."

She shrugged. "Three MacKay guards were injured in the same battle you were hurt in, but they are doing well. Erskine is still improving."

"Good."

"Iain came in to see you early this morn while you were sleeping."

"Very kind of him. He's a good friend."

"Keegan and Seona are happily married now."

"Indeed? How did that come about?"

"I'm not certain. 'Tis apparently a long story, but they've promised to tell me sometime."

When Dirk's party had stopped by Munrick several weeks ago, Torrin had suspected Keegan and Seona were more than a little smitten with each other. 'Twas obvious in the way Keegan attentively escorted her to the high table and pulled out the chair for her, and the way she smiled at him.

"I'm happy for them," Torrin said.

"Aye. Me, too." Jessie offered him another bite. His stomach was a little more settled now so he accepted the porridge.

"Would you like a sip of ale?" she asked.

"Aye. I like the ale here."

After giving him a drink of the bitter ale, she set it down and tore off a piece of bannock and held it before his lips. Leaning his head up, he opened his mouth and accepted it, his lips brushing her fingertips. Her touch was so soothing to him. He wished she would trail her fingers over every inch of his face and… the parts of his body that were not in profound pain at the moment. He remembered her stroking his face last night, both with the cool cloth and with her bare fingertips. It had taken his mind off the pain for a short time.

"I will have you up and around in no time," she said.

"Aye. Pull off your clothes and I might chase you across the room."

"Och. Rogue," she muttered, while trying to hide her smile.

"Just imagining that makes me feel ten times better."

She frowned and smiled at the same time, a fascinating expression that made him want to chuckle, but he couldn't. 'Twould be too painful.

"Now you *are* being unruly."

"'Tis what you like." He winked.

He was gratified to see the adorable pink blush spread over her cheeks.

"You're so bonny when you blush," he murmured.

"Cease your silver-tongued blather."

He started to laugh but a sharp pain struck his abdomen. "Saints, Jessie!" he growled. "Don't make me laugh. It hurts."

"I wasn't trying to make you laugh. Just lie back and relax. I'll be naught but morose and serious from now on."

Torrin ground his teeth. "You're doing it again!"

A knock sounded at the door.

"Come in," Jessie called.

Iain stuck his head in the door, then entered. "You two are arguing? You truly have performed a miracle, Lady Jessie."

"Nay, 'twas only…" Jessie's face reddened even more, and Torrin simply relaxed and enjoyed it for a moment.

"She was trying to make me laugh, but 'tis too painful by far," he said.

"I wasn't. I can't help that he laughs inappropriately at things."

Iain snickered and shook his head, then eyed the bannock in Jessie's hand. "Has she been feeding you?"

"Nay. I'm fully capable of eating on my own," Torrin assured him.

"She's spoiling you. I can tell."

"I deserve it," Torrin said.

Jessie smirked and rolled her eyes.

"Indeed you do," Iain said. "I'm happy to see you're feeling much better."

There was another light knock at the door.

"Come in," Jessie called.

Flora entered, along with Struan, Sim and Luag. He was glad to see his men, but the room was becoming crowded. And he'd much rather spend all day alone with Jessie.

"I'll leave you to your visitors and come back in a little while," Jessie told Torrin. "Flora will take care of you."

He nodded. "Hope you'll get some sleep." He was disappointed to see her go, but he knew she needed rest. She must have stayed awake, watching over him, all night. He would have to find a way to thank her for that.

Chapter Fifteen

Jessie truly hadn't wanted to leave Torrin's side, for she worried over him. But she also feared she was growing much too attached to him. Maybe they needed time apart, though that didn't feel comforting at all. Knowing he'd improved much this morn allowed her to relax enough to sleep a few hours.

After a nap with her puppy, and then a bath, Jessie felt better. Having put on clean clothes, she ventured out to see how Torrin was when she met Isobel in the corridor.

"How is Torrin?" Isobel asked.

"When last I saw him, he was much improved. He ate a few bites of porridge and bannock. He was even jesting, so I think he is recovering quickly. Iain and Torrin's men came for a visit, so I took a wee nap."

"'Tis wonderful to hear." Isobel smiled. "I'm sure he will be well soon."

"I hope so."

Isobel bit her lip, sending Jessie a look that was both affectionate and amused. "Could I talk to you for a moment?"

"Aye, of course." Jessie was curious as to what her friend wished to discuss.

Isobel led the way to her bedchamber. Once inside, with

the door closed, they took seats by the fireplace where a small fire warmed the room.

Isobel gave her that enigmatic, mischievous smile again. "Maybe I shouldn't ask. You will think I'm very nosy indeed."

"We're like sisters. You ken we can talk about anything."

Isobel tilted her head, giving her a sweet, warmhearted look. "You care for Torrin a great deal, do you not?"

"You can tell, aye?" Jessie asked in a dry tone. She'd known this was the subject her friend wished to discuss.

"Aye. After what happened when I introduced you two last winter, I feared you would never even talk to him again."

"Well, in truth, I didn't want to talk to him. And I had good reason." She told Isobel the story of how she had witnessed Torrin killing her foster brother years ago, and his reasoning for it.

"His poor sister," Isobel whispered, her dark brows furrowed. "In that situation, Cyrus or Dirk would do the same thing that Torrin did, seek justice for a sister's death."

"Aye. But I didn't understand at the time what was happening. I thought he was killing him for no reason. I was afraid to mention this to Torrin. If he knew I was a witness, I wondered what he would do. If I were to tell the Keiths, they would still seek revenge, even though Lyall was guilty of a horrid crime. Lyall's father, the chief, would especially want revenge, for he has never gotten over it."

Isobel's dark eyes widened. "You're not going to tell them, are you?"

"Nay, of course not. I'll do everything I can to protect Torrin."

Isobel frowned. "What of the lass Torrin supposedly loves who lives in the village near Munrick? Does he truly have children with her as Nolan told me?"

"Torrin said 'twas not true. He asked who had been spreading rumors about him. I didn't tell him that his brother had told you. We heard that Nolan had kidnapped you from your camp south of Munrick several weeks ago."

"Aye, 'twas horrible. I'd dropped my dagger, so I

couldn't even stab him. Dirk ended up killing him."

"We heard that as well. I'm glad you were not harmed."

Isobel's eyes widened. "So, Torrin knows about his brother?"

"Aye."

"Was he angry?"

"Nay. He was saddened to hear his brother is dead, of course, but he knew Dirk had done what he had to in order to rescue and protect you."

"Thank the saints. I would hate for Dirk and Torrin to be at odds." Her expression turning to inquisitive, Isobel asked, "So, has Torrin asked for your hand since he's been here?"

A clash of emotions made Jessie's heart beat harder. "Aye."

"Are you reconsidering?"

"'Tis not so simple," Jessie said, studying her broken, jagged nails. They looked the way she felt inside. "I didn't tell you the whole truth before."

"When?"

"Last winter, I told you that when I was handfasted to Gregor MacBain, we only shared a bed three times. That isn't true. We shared a bed for three months." Jessie's face heated. Blast! How she hated blushing.

"Oh." Isobel gave her an inquiring look.

Though Jessie trusted Isobel, she still found it difficult to hold her gaze while admitting such things. "I was ashamed because I was unable to conceive during that time. MacBain found another woman, and she bore him a son. He believed I was barren, and… I'm afraid he may be right."

"Nay," Isobel said firmly. "That may not be the case at all. Look how long it took me to conceive—seven months. So you must not give up hope. And you will, of course, have to allow Torrin to seduce you several times to know what the outcome will be." Isobel smiled.

Jessie's face felt scalded now. "Aye. You're right."

"Well then, has he? Seduced you?"

Trying to hold back her smile, Jessie drew in a deep breath, then nodded.

Isobel's grin grew wider as did her eyes. "How many times?"

"A few," she admitted.

"I'm glad."

"One morning, Uncle Conall came to my room early to tell me about Aiden, and Torrin answered my door. 'Twas horribly embarrassing. Then, my uncle had a talk with me about how I should marry Torrin."

Isobel chuckled. "The same thing happened to Dirk and me! Except Conall barged into the chamber early in the morn while I was half asleep. I have no idea what he said to Dirk about it. Thankfully, we were married soon after."

Jessie smiled.

"What have you decided about Torrin?"

Jessie shrugged. "I refuse to handfast again, and I won't wed him legally until I am with child. I can't put him in a situation where he'll be unable to sire his own heir."

"That's very selfless of you," Isobel said softly. "Too selfless, if you ask me."

"Well, 'tis for my benefit, too. I fear if I were to marry him and not produce an heir, he would grow to resent me and put me aside sometime in the future. Chiefs have been known to do that. For many of them, marriage is not permanent, no matter what the Church says. Some have four or five living wives, some of which they've divorced, as well as mistresses and paramours."

"Aye. 'Tis true. Some men are goats. But not Dirk, and I don't think Torrin would behave that way."

"I hope not, but I have a hard time trusting men." Jessie had already told her about the first man who'd abandoned her the day before their wedding years ago.

"I can understand that."

"Do you feel any different since you are with child?" Jessie asked.

"I often feel sick in the mornings. I don't think I've ever

fainted before either, but I did on the battlements when I was upset and afraid for Dirk."

Jessie nodded. "I don't feel sick in the mornings, so I don't think I'm with child."

"I'm not certain every woman feels that way. You might ask Nannag about it."

Jessie was too embarrassed to ask the healer about it now. Nannag always gave her that sweet, knowing smile every time Jessie and Torrin were together. Did Jessie really want her to know she and Torrin had been intimate? Nay. Jessie would just wait and see if she developed any of the symptoms Isobel talked about. But she was starting to fear she never would.

***

'Twas near noon and Torrin still lay in bed, thankful the pain was not as bad as it had been. The rest of his men and several others had visited during the morning, but Jessie had not yet returned. Though he would love to see her, he hoped she was having a good nap. Flora had just given him another half cup of the herbal tea for pain and fever when Dirk appeared at the open door.

"How are you feeling?" Dirk asked, entering the room.

"Better. I think you have the best healers in Scotland here at Dunnakeil."

Dirk gave a sharp nod and glanced at Flora. "I have to agree with you there."

Flora actually blushed, then executed a small curtsy. "I thank you both. Nannag is a skilled teacher. I'll just be in the corridor if you should need me." Flora exited and closed the door behind her.

"I must thank you for your hospitality these last few weeks," Torrin said. "I was not trying to impose. I wanted to protect Jessie from that knavish MacBain."

"Aye. She told me what an impressive job you did in rescuing her from MacBain in the attempted kidnapping, and when Haldane took you both hostage."

"'Twas the least I could do."

Dirk should know by now that Torrin would do anything to protect Jessie, even if it meant giving up his life for hers.

"I need to tell you something." Dirk appeared solemn, almost pained.

"I know what you're going to say. Haldane told me."

Dirk frowned. "About your brother?"

"Aye. I ken Nolan was an outlaw and deserved to die." Grief and regret sliced through Torrin again, despite all. "How did it happen?"

Dirk sat on the chair by the bed. "Well, he and the other outlaws attacked our camp in the middle of the night, about a day's ride south of Munrick. While I was fighting McMurdo at the front of our tent, Nolan cut into the back of the tent and abducted Isobel. He put her on a horse and rode away with her. I took out after them. There was no way in hell I was going to let him hurt my wife." Dirk's frown was fearsome, and Torrin could only imagine how furious the man had been. 'Twas the same rage he'd felt when both MacBain and Haldane had captured Jessie.

"'Tis what I would've done, too," Torrin said. In fact, he had killed Haldane for taking Jessie hostage.

"I caught up to Nolan and Isobel," Dirk continued. "We leapt off the horses and had a sword dual. 'Twas a fair and equal fight. I knocked his sword away and cut his throat. I didn't want to, but he gave me no choice." Anguish reflected in Dirk's pale blue eyes. "He was intent on raping and killing Isobel."

Torrin nodded, anger at his own brother twisting through him. He was ashamed of Nolan. "He would have if you hadn't stopped him."

"I had the men bury him in a small wood there," Dirk said solemnly. "And I brought his weapons and possessions to you. I have them downstairs in the armory."

Torrin cleared his throat, trying to shove away the constricting grief. "I thank you. You're a good man to do that."

"I hope you can forgive me, and that you and your clan

won't hold it against me."

Torrin shook his head. "Naught to forgive. I'd say we're even, because I had no choice but to kill your brother."

"Since he was bent on killing me, I must thank you for that—sad as I am to say it. And of a certainty, I must thank you for saving Jessie's life."

"You don't need to thank me for that. Jessie is… my life," Torrin said, his chest aching with love for her.

Dirk's sharp gaze searched his, and a bit of friendly amusement quirked one corner of his mouth. "She would do well to marry you. Have you convinced her yet?"

"Nay." Disappointment weighed heavily upon him. "She won't agree to it yet."

"Why?"

"I probably shouldn't tell you this, but… she thinks she's barren. I don't believe it. But because I'm a chief who needs an heir, she won't allow me to make that sacrifice. I'd marry her either way."

"Well, that's between you and Jessie. I'll not interfere."

"I wish you would. As her brother and the chief, you could force her to marry me." Torrin allowed a small smile, halfway teasing.

Dirk snorted. "I don't think anyone can force Jessie to do anything she doesn't want to. She's lethal with a knife, you ken."

"She is, indeed. I've seen her in action."

Dirk raised a brow.

"With a knife," Torrin added, wondering if Dirk would force Jessie to marry him, or kill him, if he knew they'd shared a bed. Torrin probably shouldn't risk it. Besides, it would embarrass Jessie. And of a certainty, he didn't want to tell Dirk that Jessie had knocked him to the ground when he wasn't paying attention.

"I also want to thank you for rescuing Aiden," Dirk said. "Without doubt, Haldane would've killed him, too, given the opportunity."

"I was glad to help. Aiden is a good man, even if he is a

wee bit naïve."

"He is that. He wants to believe, deep down, everyone is as kind-hearted as he is. We're going to have a brief funeral for Haldane out on the cliffs. Aiden wants to play the pipes as a final tribute."

Torrin nodded, imagining the clan out there with the wind off the North Sea whipping their plaids and carrying away the high skirl of the bagpipes. 'Twas far better than Haldane deserved, considering how horridly he'd treated his siblings and clan. But Torrin would do the same for his own brother, once he found his burial site.

"Since McMurdo and MacBain are still on the loose, I'm not allowing any of the ladies to attend the funeral," Dirk said.

"I'm glad."

"All the men will be heavily armed, except for Reverend MacMahon."

"Is Aiden angry with me for killing his brother?" Torrin asked.

"Nay. He knew someone would have to kill Haldane to stop him."

"What of the MacBains?" Torrin asked. Iain and his men had already told him Gregor MacBain was not among the dead on the beach, but he wondered if Dirk knew anything more about the knave.

"Eight of them died in the skirmish, and the rest fled over the hill. We found where they'd had their horses hidden in the trees and bushes in a small glen. They rode south. We also found Gil there, dead. One of the MacBains must have killed him."

"Haldane's archer?" Torrin asked, recalling how the lad had shot an arrow at him, then run away like a coward while Jessie hung off the cliff.

"Aye."

"I thought they were on the same side. Why would the MacBains kill him?"

"I have no inkling, unless they felt betrayed somehow."

Torrin shook his head. "I don't think I've seen the last of that Gregor MacBain bastard."

***

Three days later, Torrin was well enough to venture down to the great hall for the feast Dirk had ordered prepared. The servants had decorated the large room with heather, greenery and sweet-scented wildflowers. But his favorite part was sitting beside Jessie.

Though in horrible pain at times, as well as a bit lightheaded and queasy, Torrin had enjoyed spending time with Jessie during the last three days. Since he had improved quickly, she hadn't spent all night with him again. She'd brought him every meal, but he had insisted on feeding himself.

His men, Iain, Aiden, several of the MacKays, Rebbie, Cyrus, and even Erskine had visited him often. He was certain they'd all assisted in his recovery. Jessie had helped, especially, for each day he grew more and more certain that she loved him, though she hadn't said so again. She didn't need to; the affectionate look in her bright blue eyes said it all, as did her warm and caring touch.

Further along the high table, Dirk arose from his chair, tapping his knife against his silver goblet of wine, and everyone grew quiet. "We're extremely happy and thankful that Chief MacLeod, Erskine, Marston, Boyce, and Edwin are recovered from their injuries enough to join us in the great hall for supper." He raised his goblet. "*Slàinte*."

A cheer went up from the three dozen or so people in the great hall and everyone drank to their health.

"I have another announcement," Dirk said, a smile curving his lips. "Lady Isobel and I are greatly pleased to say we will soon be the proud parents of the possible next chief of Clan MacKay." Dirk leaned down and kissed Isobel's cheek.

Another loud cheer went up.

Saints! Torrin hadn't expected that announcement, but he was thrilled for them.

Torrin squeezed Jessie's hand beneath the table. She glanced at him, smiling, but he could see a wee bit of bittersweet sadness in her expression, and she didn't look the least bit surprised. He gave her a reassuring smile, hoping she would believe that one day they could share the same news with both their clans.

He leaned toward her and murmured, "You knew about this, didn't you?"

She nodded.

"And you didn't tell me?"

She shrugged. "Women talk about all sorts of things behind closed doors."

"Ah. I see. Does that mean you've talked about me?" he asked, keeping his voice low.

She grinned. "I'll never tell."

"You have," he accused, teasing. "I know you have."

From the corner of her eyes, she sent him an impish glance.

The meal was served and Torrin ate as much as he could. His appetite hadn't returned fully, but he was feeling stronger every day. Mostly, he wanted to take Jessie and escape the great hall.

Tarts and various kinds of sweets were served at the end of the meal. Torrin didn't want any, but he enjoyed watching Jessie consume the blueberry tart. Torrin was also glad to see Aiden take up his violin and head to the center of the room.

"For Lady Isobel!" Aiden announced over the loud roar of conversation, then he launched into a beautiful tune, his bow flying over the violin strings. Isobel clapped, a broad smile upon her face. It must have been her favorite song.

Once the dancing started a few minutes later, Torrin told Jessie, "I think I'll speak to Dirk and Isobel, then retire for the evening."

"Oh." She frowned. "Are you in pain?"

"No more than usual. Just tired." He pushed his chair back and stood. "Would you like to accompany me?" He hoped she would; he wanted a few moments alone with her while everyone else was occupied.

"Aye," she said, rising from her seat.

They made their way to Dirk and Isobel. Torrin offered Dirk his hand. "Congratulations, my friend. You will both make excellent parents."

Dirk gave him a firm handshake. "I thank you. And I want you to know I consider you a good friend and a strong ally."

Minutes later, Torrin and Jessie entered his chamber, and she closed the door.

"I'm truly happy for them," Torrin said. "And I hope you don't feel badly in any way. I pray that one day, we'll be able to make such an announcement."

She gave him a sad smile, tears glistening in her eyes. "I'm thrilled for them, too, of course. But, aye, I can't help but be a wee bit envious. I shouldn't be, for Dirk and Isobel have been married for seven months, and she's been worried the entire time about not conceiving more quickly. But you remember that Isobel was poisoned last winter from the tart."

"Aye, of course."

"Some thought that might have been the reason for the delay."

He nodded and drew Jessie into his arms. She slid her hands over his shoulders and around his neck.

"I don't want you to worry over it." He kissed her forehead.

She shook her head. "I won't."

"I don't believe you, but you're making a good effort."

She gave him a defiant smile. "I'm glad you were able to cat supper with us downstairs. It shows how much you've improved."

"Aye. Tomorrow, I may be well enough for jousting."

She snickered.

"What I truly want to be well enough for is… a different kind of sport." He lifted a brow, hoping she grasped his meaning.

She narrowed her eyes, but smiled all the same while her

cheeks turned rosy.

"Bedsport," he clarified.

"I'm well aware of your meaning, you rogue. But you are certainly not well enough for that yet."

"Nay, but 'haps tomorrow," he said.

She shook her head. "You're growing insensible. You'd best get into bed and drink some of Flora's tea."

"I'll need a kiss first. The real kind." Over the past few days, she had given him some affectionate kisses on the forehead when no one was looking, and he'd kissed her hand as often as he could grasp hold of it, but he was now ready for the kind of scorching kisses they'd shared before he'd been injured.

"Just a kiss. That's all," she said, stern but with a playful gleam in her eye.

"Though I hate to admit it, 'tis all I'm capable of at the moment." A certain part of him was willing and able, but 'twas the muscles of his abdomen that could not handle the task.

She rose up on her tiptoes and met his lips. "Mmm." Her mouth felt so good beneath his, he near went mad. He loved the way she always opened to him, and the way she teased his tongue with hers. She tasted of wine and sweet blueberry tart. He would devour every inch of her, given the chance.

His hands wandered up from her waist, and he stroked a thumb over her nipple, finding it hard and so enticing. *Saints!* How he wanted to draw it deeply into his mouth.

Someone screeched. "M'lady!" Then the door slammed.

Jessie jerked her arms from around his neck and spun to face the closed door.

"Who was that?" she demanded.

"I think 'twas Flora," he said, though he hadn't truly seen the woman. He'd been too caught up in the kiss to care.

"Now she thinks I'm a strumpet, I'm certain."

"Not if you would marry me."

She glared at him, though 'twas not a fully serious glare, merely one that warned him to not bring up the subject. But he couldn't help it. Much as it might pain her to discuss the matter, her refusal to marry him pained him just as much.

***

Torrin joined Dirk and the other men in the solar as they sipped whisky late one night. In the two weeks since his injury, Torrin had made a lot of progress. He was gaining strength every day and was able to stay up all day now. His abdomen was still sore from his wounds but the stitches had been removed and the cuts were healed closed. He knew 'twould take much longer to rebuild the strength of those muscles, but he'd already been working on it. He'd even practiced with his sword a bit, though he knew Iain had gone easy on him.

"We're off in the morn," Isobel's brother, Chief Cyrus MacKenzie said, referring to him, his younger brother, and their men.

"Och. I wish you'd stay longer," Dirk said.

"I'll be back in the spring for the birth of my new nephew, or niece." Though the man looked like a dark, hardened warlord, he obviously had a soft spot for the wee ones.

"We'll look forward to that," Dirk said.

"I'm going to head south with Cyrus," Rebbie said.

"You are?" Dirk asked, his eyes widening. And Torrin knew 'twas because Rebbie had been at Dirk's side most every day for more than a year. And that they'd been friends for over a decade.

"I think I'll pay our friend, Lachlan, a visit. I haven't seen him since November."

Dirk nodded, a nostalgic half-smile upon his face. "I'd like to see Lachlan. He's probably a proud da by now."

"Indeed." Rebbie grinned. "I'm looking forward to seeing if he's capable of holding a wee newborn bairn in those big paws of his."

Dirk laughed and shook his head. "In addition to a son, I hope he has ten daughters so he has to worry about rogues like he used to be."

Rebbie snickered. "I'll tell him you said that."

"Aye. Also tell him I wish him the best of health and happiness."

Rebbie nodded.

"And as for you," Dirk said, giving his friend a pointed look. "I hope you find a fiery lass who steals your heart and shows you unending happiness."

Rebbie shook his head. "I don't ken whether to thank you or give you the evil eye."

Torrin and the other men laughed.

"You'll thank me." Dirk sipped his whisky. "Isobel is the absolute best thing that's ever happened to me. Sorry, Torrin."

Torrin held up his hand. "I'm glad you came upon her in that snowstorm and rescued her. You two are perfect for each other." And if he hadn't, Torrin would've never met Jessie. Now, he knew Jessie was his destiny and his life. He simply had to convince her of that.

"He's a good man. He doesn't hold bride-thievery against you," Rebbie said.

Dirk nodded and raised his glass to Torrin. "I thank you for that."

"Aye. Now if only you can convince Jessie to marry me, all will be perfect," Torrin said.

"I'm afraid you are the only one who can do that, my friend," Dirk said.

"Indeed." But he needed far more time in bed with her in order to do that, since she wasn't willing to marry him until she was with child. They hadn't had any time alone because of his injury and, with so many people around, sneaking about the castle to spend the night together was difficult. Still, he must see her tonight.

"I'll travel to Dornie with Cyrus on his *bìrlinn*," Rebbie said. "Then hire one of his men to take me south to the port near Glasgow and travel overland toward Perth."

"I'll miss you, my friend," Dirk said. "I appreciate your help over these last several months."

"'Twas my pleasure. I'll probably come back to visit you in the spring. In the meantime, I'll send you a missive and let you know how Lachlan and Lady Angelique are doing."

"Aye. Good. We should get together every summer for a few weeks. Here or in Perth. We could travel by ship and *bìrlinn*."

"Sounds like a grand idea."

"But you have to get married first." Dirk grinned.

"What?" Rebbie's eyes rounded. "I'll not be getting married for a few more years, not until my da can truss me up like a wild boar and force some unsuspecting lass to marry me."

Dirk snickered. "Well, whoever she is, I hope she drives you mad."

After talking a short while longer, Torrin bid the other men goodnight. He needed to see Jessie. Was she in her room or elsewhere? He had to find out. Since no one else was about, he ventured down the corridor and knocked lightly at her door.

She opened it and smiled, hiding the rest of her body behind the door. That alone spiked his excitement.

"Can I come in?" he asked, keeping his voice low.

"Aye." She widened the door and he entered.

The candle on her bedside table revealed that she wore a thin white smock and naught else. Though it covered her body fully, he knew he could have it off her in an instant, revealing all her creamy skin and delicate curves.

"Don't give me that look, MacLeod," she said in mock warning.

He'd heard her say that before and knew it meant she was tempted. "What look?"

"That one." She pointed at him.

He grinned, remembering 'twas exactly what she'd said to him on the beach of Sango Bay before their first time.

"It means I want you," he murmured.

She dropped her gaze, looking demure of a sudden. "You're not well enough. I would hate for you to injure yourself further."

He shook his head and barred the door. "I'm well enough, if you'll… do some of the work."

Chapter Sixteen

Jessie lifted her gaze to Torrin's, unable to believe how sizzling and seductive he looked at the moment in the dim candlelight of her chamber. His green eyes were dark as midnight and wicked as sin. It had been over two weeks since they'd spent the night together, and she was feeling a bit shy. She was also hesitant to ask what he'd meant by *if you'll do some of the work*.

"How?" she asked.

"I'll be glad to show you." Wearing that crooked, mischievous grin that always lured her in, he pulled her close and kissed her.

She slid her arms around his neck and melted into the kiss, opening her mouth, wanting him to consume her utterly. His tongue teased and tempted hers. He tasted of whisky and virile, aroused male.

Slowly, he gathered up her smock until the hem was above her waist, then skimmed his hot hands over her hips.

"I want to undress you first," she said, not liking the idea of being naked while he was fully clothed.

"Very well." He unbuckled his belt, while she unpinned the brooch of the MacLeod Clan crest that held the top of his plaid in place over his shoulder, then unbuttoned his doublet and slipped it off. Once his plaid was removed, she carefully pulled his ivory linen shirt over his head.

Her eyes were drawn immediately to the wounds on his abdomen. Nannag had removed the stitches earlier that day and the cuts were healed shut, though still red. But not swollen, thankfully.

"I'm afraid 'twill hurt you," she said.

"Nay. But if it does, 'twill be a pleasurable pain." He lifted the smock over her head and flung it, then led her to the bed.

He stretched out on his back and held his hand up for her. She took it, lay down close beside him and brushed her lips over his.

Saints! How she had missed his sizzling kisses. He made all thoughts flit from her mind. All she could think about was how delicious he was. Turning onto his side, he pulled her tight against his heated body, though she tried to avoid putting pressure on his injury.

With his stone-hard shaft pressed against her lower belly, all she could focus on was her growing need for him. She already knew he would feel heavenly sliding into her.

He stroked a warm hand up and down her back, over her hip and along her thigh.

It suddenly struck her that Torrin was well, and she was so thankful tears sprang to her eyes. "I love you," she whispered.

He pulled back a few inches, looking deep into her eyes with an affectionate smile. He stroked his fingers over her face. "And I love you, Lady Jessie. I have since the first moment I saw you."

She bit her lip and stared down at his chest, for she knew not how to respond to that. She could not believe how lucky she was to have such devotion from a man like him.

With a finger, he lifted her chin, telling her without words to look into his eyes. She did, amazed at the emotion she saw there once again.

"You are the most remarkable man I've ever met," she

said.

He shook his head. "I doubt that, but no other man could ever love you as much as I do."

"I believe that," she whispered. "And I want you to know that I love you no matter what, even if—"

He placed a finger upon her lips, halting her words. "Do not say it, Jessie MacKay."

Sliding his finger away, he pressed his lips against hers, forcing any remaining thoughts from her mind. If he kept kissing her like this, she'd go along with almost anything he said. But she knew she couldn't lose her head completely… the way she'd lost her heart.

His hand again trailed over her back, her hip, her thighs, turning her body into a bonfire of sensation. He stroked his thumb over her breast, then leaned down and drew her nipple into his mouth, sparking off thousands of fiery sensations inside her. She buried her fingers in his hair and pulled him closer.

After treating her other nipple to the same delicious torment, and sending her mind toward the stars, he said, "Climb on top of me."

"What?" Her eyes sprang open. Surely she'd misheard.

He grinned, looking more roguish than ever. "You said you would help with the work, aye?"

She nodded.

"I need for you to get on top. Just put one knee on either side of my hips."

"Oh." She did as he asked, realizing this was the most wanton position she'd ever been in. He smiled up at her, and she immediately knew she was going to love this.

"Lean up this way and put your hands on either side of my shoulders." He helped her get into position and lifted his shaft to stroke it against her. "Now, slowly sit back," he whispered.

She moved backward a tiny bit and the head of his shaft slipped inside her. She gasped.

He gave a slight thrust, then growled. She couldn't tell if

it was a passionate growl or a pain-filled one. "More," he said between clenched teeth.

She pressed down upon him as he slid deeper. "Am I hurting you?" she asked.

"Nay. You feel so good," he ground out.

"You do, too." She loved the sensation of him filling her.

"Now, ride me," he said.

"Do you mean like…?" She slowly lifted herself, near rendered senseless by the feel of him gliding from her body.

"Aye," he breathed. His hands at her hips, he pushed her down again. "Faster."

Need possessing her, she followed his directions, finding that the more rapidly she moved, the more intense the pleasure. Breathless anticipation stole over her and when the intense delight of climax seized her, she felt she would collapse.

Growling, Torrin tugged her to him, kissing her while his body trembled against hers.

"Saints," she hissed, moments later when her breath returned. "I didn't even ken that was possible."

He grinned. "I'm glad I taught you something, then."

She bit his earlobe in punishment for his impertinent mouth.

He chuckled and she moved to lie beside him.

"Give me five minutes and we'll do that again," he said.

"In truth?"

"You doubt me?" he asked, incredulous, but grinning.

"Nay. 'Tis only… you are not fully recovered."

"I'm recovered enough."

She stroked her fingers over his chest and arms, appreciating each hard curve and flat plane of muscle. She wanted him to heal completely, of course, but she knew once he grew strong again, he would leave Dunnakeil and head for home. Then, she would be utterly lost without him.

***

A week later, Jessie slipped into Torrin's chamber. Thrilled, he grinned and barred the door.

They had secretly spent every night together in one of their rooms, and Torrin had enjoyed every moment of it. But he could not stay at Dunnakeil forever. His clan would start wondering where he was and whether he was ever going to return to Munrick. He was much more recovered now and able to travel.

After they made love, they lay in bed, snuggled together in the candlelight.

"Jessie, I have to leave in the morn," he said, though the very idea made him feel wretched. "I have to go to Munrick and tell Nolan's widow and the rest of the clan of his death. Then, two of Dirk's men are going to show me where Nolan's grave is."

Jessie nodded, her eyes misting. "I understand."

"Please, will you marry me and come with me?" he asked, trying not to sound as if he were begging, though he would if it would convince her.

Closing her eyes, she shook her head. "You know I cannot do that. I've already told you why."

Disappointment engulfed him as it always did when she refused. "You might be carrying my bairn, even now." 'Twas his only argument.

She gave a sad smile. "I wish I was."

His heart pounded with hope. "Is that truly what you want?"

"Of course."

"Why do you not ask the healer to examine you and see?"

"I have. Flora said she didn't see any sign of a bairn yet." Tears filled Jessie's eyes.

"Saints, lass." He pulled her to him, just as disappointed as she was. "I'm sorry."

She shook her head.

He kissed her forehead. "I love you."

"I love you, too."

"Stay here with me tonight."

She nodded.

He would get her with child or die trying, but 'twas no hardship. Making love to her was like heaven on earth.

But, once he left, he feared he might go mad without her.

***

The next day, Torrin rode away from Dunnakeil with a heavy heart. He was not looking forward to going home to Munrick without Jessie. He'd told her he would return in a fortnight, or as soon as possible. He had to believe something would change her mind between now and then. Either she would be with child, or she would miss him so badly, she would agree to go with him.

He could just imagine her riding with him now, commenting on how beautiful the purple drifts of bell heather were upon the green and rocky hills. 'Twas a warm, sunny day, reminding him of the unforgettable days they'd spent on the beaches around Durness. Aye, the best days of his life, so far. He hoped better ones were to come… if only she would marry him.

Dirk had sent a dozen of his clansmen with them because 'twas unsafe for only a few people to travel alone with McMurdo and MacBain still roaming about. Some of the MacKays with them were the ones who had buried Nolan, and they were going to show Torrin the gravesite in the small wood south of Munrick.

Iain rode beside Torrin, glancing at him from time to time.

"Stop worrying about me," Torrin said.

Iain smirked. "I'm not worried about you."

His friend was lying, but he expected that.

"I ken you're disappointed," Iain said. "In your situation, I would be, too. But when you return to Dunnakeil in a couple of weeks, you may well find that she is with child and eager to marry you."

"I hope so." But he also knew there were no guarantees.

***

Since Torrin had left the day before, Jessie had tried to

keep herself busy by helping Isobel oversee the serving staff, especially in the mornings when Isobel wasn't feeling well. But Jessie was often distracted. She thought about all the places she'd had conversations with Torrin, or more intimate encounters.

Now, she found herself in the third floor bedchamber with the broken window where she and Torrin had one of their first conversations of any length. The pigeon had scared her and Torrin had rushed to her rescue. She should've known then that he was honorable and heroic.

She stared out at the view over Balnakeil Bay and the golden sand beach where they'd talked, wrestled, and practiced archery, the distant cliffs on each side, protecting the bay. Cliffs that looked far more ominous now, for she'd almost lost her life out there.

With the MacBains and McMurdo skulking about, she couldn't walk on the beach anymore. She missed it. But she missed Torrin far more. It felt like he was a thousand miles away now. Tears burned her eyes, and she prayed he would be safe and return soon.

The sky was heavily overcast and the water of the bay dark, so unlike the sunny day she'd spent with Torrin out there. She still couldn't believe she'd been stealthy enough to knock him to the ground. She smiled, tears in her eyes, remembering the priceless look of shock on his face. 'Twas the day he'd first kissed her… and the day she'd fallen in love with him. Though she hadn't realized it until later.

Why did life have to be so difficult? Why couldn't she simply marry him, conceive and give birth like a normal woman? She would give anything to be normal, and the type of wife he needed.

He was the best of men, accepting, understanding and always affectionate with her. He hadn't faltered in his pursuit of her. Weeks ago, when she'd seen him on the opposite side of that ravine, barely able to stand, his clothing drenched in his own blood, while Haldane held the knife to her throat, she'd known then that Torrin's heart was true. And that he would give his life for her if he had to.

But to marry him would be too much of a risk. If she were to do that and then be unable to provide him an heir, she would be devastated. If only she knew what the future held. She could certainly envision a joyful future with him. She could dream of making love to him every night, and several months from now, holding a healthy newborn babe in her arms, while he smiled proudly and kissed her.

But 'twas only a dream.

***

After spending the night in Scourie, Torrin, Iain and the rest of their party drew closer to Munrick that evening. 'Twas only a couple of miles away. They had been traveling for two days through rough, rocky terrain, and Torrin was sick of riding. All the men and horses having to be ferried across a loch had also slowed their progress.

Maybe 'twas because of his recent injury that riding was tiring him more easily. *Saints!* He had to toughen himself up again. Or maybe 'twas because he missed Jessie so profoundly that he'd gotten little sleep the night before. He'd become used to her sleeping in his arms for the past week, and for her to suddenly not be there anymore was hell.

The sun was sinking low over the mountains, gleaming through the rosy clouds and sparkling off Loch Assynt below. Torrin would love for Jessie to see this view, for it would mean she was coming home with him.

Shouting and war cries snagged his attention. From the opposite direction, Highland warriors with swords and targes stormed down from the crest of the hill on foot.

Torrin's horse reared unexpectedly and almost unseated him.

"Damnation." He held on. Once the horse was on all fours again, he drew his sword and slashed at the marauders nearest him. "MacBain," Torrin growled, recognizing the knave amongst those fighting.

Torrin's abdomen was still healing, and therefore still weak and sore from the wounds, but he would not allow this miscreant to defeat him. Thankfully, with the dozen MacKays, Iain's men and Torrin's men, they were evenly matched.

Once Gregor MacBain had felled one of the MacKays, he charged Torrin. When he slashed Torrin's horse's flank, fury consumed Torrin. With a scream, the horse kicked at MacBain and spun. Torrin brought his sword down across MacBain's shoulder, slicing through his doublet and shirt. The man cried out and leapt back, blood soaking his clothing.

After grabbing his targe from his saddle, Torrin jumped to the ground, for an injured horse was unpredictable. The animal bolted away from the fighting.

Torrin was disappointed to see that he hadn't cut MacBain's sword arm, but the opposite one. Still, the cut would slow him down. The bastard's face was red and his teeth clenched. Good. Now he knew what Torrin had suffered. With his shoulder injured, MacBain had a difficult time holding his targe and dirk in fighting position, which left him vulnerable.

After sliding the leather straps of the targe onto his forearm and yanking his dirk from the scabbard on his belt, Torrin stabbed his sword toward MacBain's stomach, but he deflected the blow with his own blade.

MacBain bared his teeth and sliced at Torrin. He easily blocked it. Shoving his targe and dirk toward MacBain, he trapped the man's sword arm and jabbed his own sword toward MacBain's side. The blade slid deep into the flesh at near the same place MacBain had wounded him three weeks ago. MacBain screeched and stumbled back.

Pain burned across Torrin's leg. Damnation, the bastard had cut his thigh. Torrin redoubled his efforts and stabbed MacBain in the chest with his dirk, then again in the side.

Wide-eyed, the man cried out and dropped to the ground.

One of MacBain's men attacked Torrin from his right. He blocked his sword slash just in time. Seconds later, Torrin stabbed the man in the gut and cut his throat.

A horrid pain sliced across Torrin's back. Growling, he spun to find another of MacBain's men behind him.

"Coward!" Torrin yelled. He blocked his next blow with the targe, then drove the shorter man back with strike after strike. He shoved at the bastard with his targe, then used his dirk to stab him in the sword arm. The man howled in pain and tried to escape, but 'twas too late. Torrin slashed and stabbed with his sword, sending the bleeding man to the ground seconds later.

He turned to find some of the MacBains fleeing into the bush and up the hill. Several of them lay on the ground, dead or dying.

"How many did we lose?" he asked Struan, thirty feet away.

"Saints, Chief! You're badly injured again. We need to stop the bleeding."

Iain ran toward him, his shirt and doublet bloody.

"Are you wounded?" Torrin asked him.

"Only a few minor cuts."

Iain glanced down at Torrin's leg, below his sliced plaid. "You were cut badly. We have to get that bleeding stopped."

"Luag's dead!" Struan yelled, kneeling by him.

"Nay!" Torrin limped toward them, seeing that indeed his guard was unmoving, and drenched in blood, his eyes staring sightlessly. "Damnation." Luag had been by his side most every day since he'd become chief.

"Two of the MacKay guards were killed," Iain said. "And eleven of the MacBains."

Torrin shook his head, saddened by the death of Luag and also two of their allies. How he hated the MacBains. "Bastards," he growled. But at least he had killed their leader.

"Sit on the ground and let me see your wound," Iain said.

Torrin did, pulling up his plaid to bare the deep cut on his thigh. "One of the bastards sliced my back, too."

Iain muttered curses and pulled off his own shirt. He wrapped it around Torrin's leg twice and tied it tight. "That might slow the bleeding a little. Let me see your back."

Torrin pushed himself up, but when he stumbled, Iain helped him stand. He ripped the fabric of his shirt where it was sliced to better see the cut. "'Tis not as bad as the other one," Iain said. "But we need to get you to Munrick quick so the healer can stitch you up. We're only a couple of miles away."

"Aye," Torrin said, suddenly going lightheaded.

Sim found Torrin's horse and led him forward. Pain lancing through his leg and his back, Torrin examined the cut to the horse's flank. It had bled some but was not terribly deep. He believed the horse would recover.

Agony bore through him, making mounting seem an impossible task. Dizziness assailed him and he caught against the horse and saddle. The bandage on his thigh felt saturated with hot blood.

"Struan!" he shouted at his sword-bearer, and though he tried to hold onto the saddle to keep upright, he felt himself sliding to the ground as all around him went black.

***

Torrin dreamed he was searching for Jessie in the night. Someone had stolen her away, MacBain or Haldane, he wasn't sure which. But all was dark, and he couldn't see. He couldn't find her.

"Jessie!" he yelled.

A strong hand on his shoulder pushed him back. "Torrin. She's not here right now."

"Iain?"

"Aye."

"Where is she?" Torrin opened his eyes to see that he lay in his own bedchamber at Munrick, a few candles lighting the dark room.

"Still at Dunnakeil."

Burning pain consumed his leg and his lower back. The skirmish. He remembered killing MacBain.

"You lost too much blood in a short amount of time," Iain said. "You were not fully recovered from your earlier injury when you got these."

"Aye." He well knew that, but was he going to survive? Would he ever see Jessie again? He slid down into the darkness yet again.

Chapter Seventeen

At Dunnakeil, Jessie forced herself to eat supper at the high table. Though her family and friends surrounded her, she was intensely lonely. Torrin had been gone four days, and she missed him terribly.

One of the guards rushed across the great hall to the high table. "The MacKay guards who went south with MacLeod are returning. We saw them in the distance," he told Dirk.

"Why are they coming back so soon?" Dirk shoved up from his chair and strode quickly across the great hall with the guard. Several others followed, including Jessie and Isobel. Was Torrin returning, too? What had happened? The MacKays had planned to travel south with Torrin to show him where Nolan was buried. They wouldn't have had time to do that.

When the soldiers rode through the portcullis, she was shocked to see two dead bodies, completely wrapped in plaid including their heads, lying stiff and straight, tied to the horses' backs. A cold chill shook her, and tears filled her eyes.

"Who is this?" Dirk demanded, motioning to the dead bodies. "What happened?"

"Henry and Ross," Dougal said, his blue eyes pain-filled.

"MacBain and his clan attacked us just this side of Munrick. 'Twas a terrible skirmish. One of the MacLeods was killed, too."

Nay! Jessie hurried forward. "Who?"

"The one they called Luag. Chief MacLeod was injured badly."

Icy fear poured through her. "Nay," Jessie whispered. Isobel put an arm around Jessie and held her close.

"MacLeod has two wounds and lost more blood. Iain told us that he was out cold for most of the night while we were there, and he has a fever."

Devastation crashed in upon Jessie, making her feel as if she were suffocating. "Saints," she hissed, her heart breaking. Tears filling her eyes, she felt herself trembling, but was unable to stop. She was so far away from him when he needed her.

"We killed eleven of the MacBains," Dougal continued. "Chief MacLeod killed Gregor MacBain."

Jessie pressed her eyes closed. She was glad that bastard MacBain was dead, but more importantly, she had to see Torrin. Having so many severe injuries only weeks apart might be more than his body could deal with.

After Dirk gave his men orders, he headed toward Jessie.

"I have to go to Torrin," she said.

Dirk nodded. "I'll take you. We'll leave at first light. I'm glad you weren't with him. You could've been killed."

That was true, but she wished she was at Munrick now. It had likely been two days since Dougal and the other MacKays had left Munrick. Had Torrin grown worse during that time? Was he still alive?

***

"Dirk and Keegan will keep you safe," Isobel told Jessie in the solar that night.

"Aye." Too nervous to sit, Jessie paced before the fire-place, wishing they could leave this very instant, though she knew they couldn't travel very well in the dark. Too dangerous.

She had packed a few changes of clothes and had the servants prepare foods that wouldn't spoil during the trip. She prayed they could make the journey quickly for she had to reach Torrin as soon as possible. Flora would go, as well, and take her healing herbs. Jessie didn't know how skilled the healers were at Munrick. Aiden was going to take care of her puppy, Greum, so she didn't have to worry about him.

"I pray Torrin is much improved by the time you arrive at Munrick," Isobel said, sitting on the settle, her dark eyes worried.

Jessie nodded. "It kills me not knowing how he is at this very moment."

"I pray there will be no more attacks," Seona said. She turned from the window, tears in her eyes.

"Indeed." Isobel faced her. "Are you well, Seona?"

"Aye. But…" Seona wrung her hands and averted her gaze.

"What is it?" Isobel joined Seona at the window and took her hands.

Seona swallowed hard and smiled through her tears. "This may not be the best time to tell you this, but… I am with child."

"What?" Isobel exclaimed, then hugged Seona. "Why didn't you tell us?"

"I only learned of it this morn. I wasn't feeling well and Keegan sent Nannag in to check on me. She thinks I am with child."

"Saints!" Isobel said. "Keegan does fast work."

Jessie forced a smile and embraced Seona. Though she was truly thrilled for her, she was still too devastated by the news of Torrin's injuries to give a real smile. "Congratulations. I'm happy for you and Keegan." She pulled back. "I'll ask him and Dirk to stay here for their own safety. You both need them now more than ever, since you will soon be parents. The MacKay guards and a couple of Keegan's brothers can take me safely to Munrick."

"Nay! Dirk wouldn't hear of it," Isobel said.

"I'm certain they will be safe and fight off any attackers," Seona said, though she still looked worried. "They did on our long journey across Scotland."

Isobel nodded. "Dirk and Keegan are two of the best at fighting."

"I just pray that we make it in time," Jessie whispered.

***

Two days later, Jessie and over twenty of the MacKays traveled south through the rugged granite mountains and along the green moors, interspersed with lochs and bogs. She had gotten little sleep the previous two nights, being terribly worried about Torrin. Last night, they'd stayed in Scourie with Lewis MacLeod, a friend of Dirk's.

Today, she rode between Dirk and Keegan. Half of the MacKays rode in front of them and half behind. Uncle Conall, Dougal, and Little Conall accompanied them. Jessie had also brought along her young maid, Dolina, and Flora.

Heather bloomed on the hills but Jessie barely noticed. Though she normally loved looking at the purple heather, all she could think about was taking a walk through it with Torrin. Tears filled her eyes. Annoyed, she wiped them away and hoped the men didn't notice. Dirk and Keegan would understand, of course, but she didn't want to appear weak.

She knew the two would much rather be back with their wives at Dunnakeil.

"I thank you both for bringing me," she said.

"No thanks needed," Dirk said.

"Indeed," Keegan agreed.

Though she had hoped they would talk more, to take her thoughts off her dark fears, they didn't. Did they suspect that Torrin wouldn't be alive when they arrived?

She bowed her head and tears dripped from her eyes. *Please God, keep him alive.*

As late afternoon approached, Jessie could not believe how tired and sore she was. It had been a long time since she had ridden a horse for more than a few minutes. She feared she would be unable to walk once she dismounted.

A glistening loch reflecting the blue sky came into view in the distance as they rode carefully down a rocky incline.

"'Tis Loch Assynt," Dirk said.

"We are close?" she asked.

"Aye."

Her heart rate sped up and her stomach knotted. Pressing her eyes closed, she said another prayer.

Minutes later, they arrived at a smoother trail by the loch's edge and kicked their horses into a gallop, her heart pounding at the same quick pace.

A castle came into view in the distance. That had to be Munrick. As they approached, she saw that the gray stone castle had three towers and sat on a small island in the loch. 'Twas a beautiful, magical setting with the green hills in the background.

She imagined Torrin inside the walls. Would he be better or worse?

As they drew nearer the guard house and drawbridge, the men riding in front of them moved aside, allowing Dirk and Jessie to approach first.

Sim was one of the first people she recognized.

"Chief MacKay, Lady Jessie! Am I glad to see you," he greeted, his eyes wide with excitement. "Lower the bridge," he told the other guards.

"Are you certain?" one of them demanded, frowning and eying Dirk suspiciously.

"Aye, these are our allies, and they're here to help the chief."

"How is Laird MacLeod?" Jessie asked.

"He's alive but ailing something fierce. Thank the saints you've come. You can help him recover as you did last time."

"I hope so." She blinked back the tears burning her eyes once again.

The gate opened and the drawbridge was lowered. She, Dirk and the rest of the MacKays proceeded across into the walled cobblestone bailey.

Jessie quickly dismounted, her legs and derriere so sore

she could hardly move. But she forced herself to walk stiffly toward the entrance. Where was Flora? She stopped and turned, seeing that one of the men was helping her dismount. The healer, completely unaccustomed to riding a horse, waddled forward. "I'm coming, m'lady," she said, carrying her satchel.

"Lady Jessie! Thank the saints."

She turned to find Iain standing in the portal.

"Come inside." He offered his hand to help her up the steps, then helped Flora. "Torrin needs you and your healer now more than ever."

"Is he bad?" Jessie asked.

Iain frowned. "Aye. I'm afraid so."

Please, God, don't let him be too far gone. She followed Iain along one end of the great hall and up a narrow turnpike stairwell, Flora and Dolina trailing behind. At the end of a short corridor, Iain opened a door and motioned her inside. "Let me know if you need anything. I'll send a maid to assist you."

Jessie rushed into the bedchamber. Torrin lay in a large four-poster bed with his eyes closed, his skin was so pale. "Saints!" She touched his feverish brow. "Torrin?"

His eyelids fluttered and then he moved his head. "Jessie?" 'Twas naught more than a breath.

"Aye, I am here."

Frowning, and with seemingly great effort, he opened his eyes a crack. "Missed you."

Tears filled her eyes. "I missed you, too. You must get better."

"Aye."

"I've brought Flora, the healer, with me."

At the moment, she was conversing with another woman in the corner of the room, near the door. Another healer, perhaps.

Torrin's hand moved from beneath the layers of blankets and clasped onto hers.

"Have you eaten anything?" she asked, holding his hand

tight.

"Not hungry."

"How long has it been?"

He shook his head a little and frowned. *Saints!* Could he not even remember when he'd last eaten? "Would one of you go see if there is any fresh broth in the kitchen?" she asked the two women. "And if there is, bring some. Some ale, too."

"Aye, m'lady. My name's Margie. We tried to get him to eat, but he'd have none of it." She hurried out the door.

Well, at least they'd tried. He would have to eat for her; she'd make him.

"Is she the healer for Munrick?" Jessie whispered.

"Aye. Their main healer passed a few months ago. Margie admits she isn't well trained."

"Saints! Torrin, why on earth did you not hire a competent healer?"

"Didn't ken I'd need one," he whispered.

She shook her head.

"I need to examine his wounds and see if they are festered," Flora said.

"Aye." Jessie said. "I'll help you." Knowing one of the injuries was on his left thigh, Jessie moved the blankets aside while trying to keep his groin covered, although she was certain Flora had seen countless naked men while performing her healing duties.

Flora removed the bloody linen bandage from his thigh, revealing a swollen, angry gash. It had been roughly stitched up. Jessie wanted to mutter several curse words, but kept her lips sealed tight.

"'Tis a festering wound. I must bathe it, then apply a poultice." Flora turned to the MacLeod maid who waited near the door. "I'll need a kettle of boiled water if you please."

"Aye." The maid hastened away.

"It looks bad, does it not?" Jessie asked.

Flora nodded.

"You can help him though, aye?"

"I will certainly try, m'lady. But you must pray. Your

prayers seem to work miracles." Flora dug into her satchel and pulled out several wee cloth pouches of dried herbs.

Jessie nodded, her throat closing. Her prayers had been answered thus far. Torrin was alive, as she'd asked. Now, she must ask for his rapid healing.

Holding his hand, she kissed his overheated forehead, then silently said a swift but heartfelt prayer.

"Don't cry, Jessie," Torrin whispered. "Don't like it when you cry."

She wiped her tears away. "Then you must recover quickly."

"Don't leave me," he said.

"I won't."

"Ever," he added, his pain-filled gaze locked on her.

Realizing what he was saying, she bit her lip. He was asking her to stay with him permanently. Was that what it would take to give him the strength to fight for his life? She would do anything to keep him alive.

"I will stay with you… always," she said.

"In truth?" He frowned, his eyes searching hers.

"Aye. I love you," she whispered, stroking his cheek, sporting a weeks' worth of beard stubble.

"Love you, too." He turned his head slightly and kissed her palm.

Margie and the maid rushed into the room, one carrying a kettle of hot water and the other a tray of food.

Flora set about making an herbal tea. While it steeped, Jessie fed Torrin a couple of spoonfuls of warm venison broth. It smelled fresh and delicious. It had been many hours since she'd eaten and she was hungry. But Torrin's well-being was far more important than her own.

"'Tis all I can stomach," he said after another sip.

Flora and Jessie helped him turn onto his side so they might check the wound on his back. It was healing well because it hadn't been as deep a cut.

Once Jessie forced him to drink the tea containing the poppy, willow bark, thyme, red clover blossom and several other things, Flora bathed the wound on his thigh with hot water containing herbs over the basin. She then gently applied a poultice of plantain, red clover, comfrey and calendula to the wound and covered it with clean linen.

A few minutes later, Torrin dropped off to sleep and his fever seemed diminished.

"Go get yourself something to eat, m'lady," Flora whispered.

Before Jessie could say anything, Dolina entered the room, carrying a tray filled with food. "Margie sent this up for you both."

"Oh, I thank you," Jessie said.

While Jessie was eating, Dirk, Keegan and Iain entered the room. "How is he?" Dirk asked, keeping his voice low.

"Flora has attended to the wound on his thigh and given him a tea to help him sleep and recover. The cut on his back is already healing well."

Dirk nodded, still looking worried as his gaze scanned over Torrin.

"I'm so thankful you've all come," Iain said in a hushed tone. "I'm not a healer. I knew not what to do. I knew Flora and Lady Jessie could help him more than anyone."

"We'll do our best," Flora said. "But he'll need a lot of prayers."

***

Jessie woke up, a bit disoriented for a moment, then realized she was sitting in the padded chair by Torrin's bed. Bright morning light filtered through the two narrow windows. Her gaze darting to Torrin, she found him watching her. It had been two days since she'd arrived, and Torrin had been either sleeping or feverishly delirious most of the time.

"I like to watch you sleep," he murmured.

Thank the saints he was lucid and alert. "Are you feeling better?" she asked.

"Aye."

"Good." She stood, then sat on the edge of the bed,

careful not to bump his leg, and pressed her palm to his forehead. Still a bit too warm, but his gaze was clear green, not glassy as it had been the day before. "Thank God you're improving." She smiled, a mist of happy tears burning her eyes.

"And thank you, too." He stared at her intently, but then his stomach growled.

She grinned. "Sounds like you're hungry."

"Mayhap."

At a rustling sound behind her, she turned to find Flora rising from her pallet near the fireplace. Jessie moved across the room, awoke Dolina and sent her after Torrin's breakfast, while Flora changed the poultice on his leg.

A half hour later, Jessie fed Torrin porridge. She enjoyed the task of giving him sustenance. He had argued and insisted he was capable of feeding himself, but she refused to let him. She simply wanted to help him in any way she could.

A knock sounded at the door. Dolina answered it, and a pretty, young, dark-haired woman entered the room, dressed as a lady rather than a servant.

"Good morn. I'm Rhona, Nolan's wife," she told Jessie, a solemn expression on her face. "How are you feeling this morn, m'laird?" she asked Torrin, moving closer.

"Better. This is Lady Jessie MacKay," Torrin said.

After pleasantries were exchanged, Torrin frowned and asked, "Has anyone told you about Nolan?"

"Aye, Sir Iain did. 'Twas one reason I wished to speak to you."

"I wanted to tell you myself, but I was blacked out and had a fever for… I don't ken how long it has been."

"Just over a week," Jessie said.

"Saints! That long?" he asked.

"I know," Rhona said. "I'm simply glad you are feeling better today. Sir Iain didn't tell me everything. When did Nolan die, and how did it happen?"

Jessie detected no emotion or tears in the young woman's gaze, which she found interesting and unusual.

"Several weeks ago, south of here," Torrin said. "He kidnapped Lady Isobel, and Chief MacKay killed him. 'Twas only a couple of nights after they stayed here on their journey. 'Twas a fair fight. Nolan was an outlaw."

"Aye," Rhona said, frowning. "I knew someone would kill him."

"When I'm up to it, some of the MacKays are going to take me to his gravesite. I ken you probably cannot go to the grave, because of wee Lainie, but we'll have a funeral for him here in the kirk."

She nodded. "After the funeral, with your permission, I would like to take Lainie and go stay with my mother and father for a while."

"Of course. Whatever you wish," Torrin said.

"I'll come back later and bring Lainie to see you." She gave a hint of a smile.

Torrin nodded. "My niece," he said to Jessie.

She forced a tight smile and watched Rhona leave the room. Once the door was closed, Jessie gave Torrin another bite of porridge. "She did not seem terribly upset over the death of her husband."

Torrin shook his head. "'Twas not a love match. Nolan seduced her, the daughter of a chieftain, got her with child and was forced to marry her. They were miserable together."

"I see." Each of the young women Jessie knew either had a bairn or were expecting a bairn, even those who'd had unhappy marriages. She felt completely lacking.

***

"Come, lie on the bed with me and get some sleep," Torrin said to Jessie late that night when they were alone.

As far as he could tell, she had slept very little since she'd been here at Munrick, for every time he awoke, she was there. Thank the saints for that, but she needed rest, too.

"Nay. Are you mad?" she asked in a loud whisper. "Someone might come in."

Flora and the maid had moved to the small chamber next door, but 'twas possible Flora would come in and give him more herbal tea later.

"Bar the door," he said. "That way you can open the door for them and they won't see us in bed together."

"Rogue," she muttered and tried to hide her smile.

He winked. "I promise not to molest you."

She narrowed her eyes, giving him a mock glare, but then her smile came through. "Very well." She rose from the chair and barred the door.

As she was walking back toward him and climbing onto the bed, excitement stampeded through him. Even though she was fully clothed and he was certainly in no condition to do anything about beautiful Jessie in his bed, 'twas still like seeing one of his dreams come true.

He took her hand and pulled her closer.

"I'll stay on top of the covers," she said.

"If you insist," he whispered, wishing more than anything she was nude, but he knew he would have to save that treat for later. "Lie right next to me."

She scooted and wiggled closer, and he put his arm around her.

"I don't want to hurt you," she whispered.

"You're not. Lay your head on my shoulder."

She did, turning toward him and placing her hand on his chest.

"Aye, that's it." He sighed, simply enjoying the feel of her curled next to him.

She'd promised to stay with him forever, and he wanted to know when they could marry. But he wouldn't bring the subject up now; it might make her tense.

"Get some sleep," he murmured and kissed her forehead.

"Aye. You, too."

Thanks to the herbal tea Flora had given him, he was soon asleep. When he awoke, early dawn light seeped through the windows. Jessie was still next to him, asleep. Saints, but she was lovely when she slept, and she fit perfectly in his bed.

Her presence alone made him want to leap from the bed and declare himself healed. But he couldn't yet. Still, he felt far better than he had yesterday and his thigh didn't pain him as much.

He wished he could stroke his fingers over Jessie's face and her lovely auburn brows, but he would likely wake her.

The door rattled, as if someone had tried to open it. Then, a knock sounded.

Jessie startled awake, glancing at him and blinking as if confused. A second later, she leapt from the bed, unbarred the door, and opened it.

Flora waited outside. "Is everything all right, m'lady?"

"Aye. I simply didn't want anyone coming in while I was asleep."

"Oh. I see." Flora's gaze flew to Torrin. "And how are you this morn, m'laird?"

"Fine as a fiddle."

"Glad I am to know that!"

Jessie watched Flora, preparing Torrin's herbal tea and a fresh poultice for his leg. She broke out into a cold sweat and, minute by minute, she felt more and more nauseous. She could not tolerate the scent of the herbs. What on earth? She slipped out into the corridor, then dashed to the garderobe. Thankfully, it was empty. She retched, though she had little on her stomach at this early hour. A couple of minutes later, she felt better.

She then remembered how sick Isobel was every morning.

"Saints!" she whispered. *Am I with child?*

Chapter Eighteen

Moisture filled Jessie's eyes, and she burst into happy and hopeful tears. As she cried, she prayed the nausea truly meant she was with child.

"M'lady is something wrong?" Flora asked from the other side of the curtain.

Wiping her tears, Jessie pushed the curtain aside. "I'm sick," she whispered with a mad chuckle.

Flora's eyes rounded, her concern obvious. "Sick, m'lady?"

"Aye," Jessie whispered. "Do you think you could tell if I'm with child?"

Flora's eyes grew even wider as she searched her face. "Is it the morning sickness you've got, then?"

"I think so. You must keep it a secret until we know for certain," Jessie said. "Promise me."

"I promise."

For the next three mornings, Jessie awoke nauseous. And although she was miserable, she was thrilled. She was fortunate to be able to rush to the garderobe each time.

On the fourth morning, she went to the chamber Torrin had told the maids to clean for her, so that she might nap there when she wasn't watching after him. She washed her face and rinsed her mouth, then took a sponge bath and changed clothes.

Her stomach felt much more settled now. She uncovered the bannocks Flora had left for her the night before and ate one. Flora had assured her that she was with child. She could hardly eat for smiling, happy tears filling her eyes. She needed to tell Torrin.

Minutes later, Jessie entered Torrin's room and found him propped against the pillows while he ate porridge.

"The maid brought you a bowl of porridge, too, m'lady," Flora said, giving her a smile.

"Good. I'm hungry."

"I'll be back in a few minutes," Flora said, then left the room.

"You're bright-eyed this morn," Jessie told Torrin.

"I'm looking at you."

She smiled and sat on the edge of the bed, watching him eat.

"Are you not going to eat?"

"Aye, but I wanted to tell you something first."

He eyed her suspiciously and lowered his bowl. "What is it?"

"I've been sick several mornings this week."

He frowned. "Sick?"

She nodded, smiling.

"Why? Are you well now? I've noticed you hurry out of the room each morn when you awake, but I thought you merely needed to… relieve yourself."

"Getting sick in the morn is a sign that… I am with child," she said, tears filling her eyes.

"What!" He almost dropped the bowl of porridge.

She took it from him and set it on the bedside table.

"With child?" he asked, raising his voice, his eyes wide.

"Shh. We don't want everyone to know yet," she whispered.

"You're with child?" he demanded, though in a quieter tone, a smile spreading across his face.

"Flora says 'tis likely. I've had the morning sickness for four mornings. Isobel has this ailment also."

"Saints, Jessie!" Torrin pulled her close and kissed her lips. 'Twas a quick but fierce kiss. His gaze searched hers for several seconds, his excitement as obvious as hers. "I cannot arise from this bed as of yet, nor get down on one knee. But, Lady Jessie, will you marry me?"

"Aye." She threw her arms around his neck, hugging him close, and he did the same, near squeezing the breath from her. She found herself laughing and crying at the same time.

He pulled back and brushed her tears away with his thumb. "Shh," he hissed but she detected a hint of moisture in his own eyes. "I love you," he whispered, then kissed her.

"And I love you," she said.

"Let's get married today." His eyes were alight with more eagerness than she'd ever seen.

She frowned. "Today! Are you mad?"

"Aye, why not? I believe I can stand." Moving his injured leg a bit, he grimaced.

"I don't want you to overdo it."

"I won't. But a man must stand for his own wedding."

"Nay. You do not have to. The minister can come in here."

He shook his head, looking disappointed. "That won't do at all. I'm the chief. The whole clan will want to witness our wedding."

"We'll wait until you're a bit better, then," she said, trying to calm him.

His eyes lit up again. "Tomorrow."

"Are you certain 'tis not still too soon? You must not injure yourself further."

"Nay. For you, Jessie, I could climb that mountain to the north of the castle. Let me get up."

"'Tis too soon, Torrin. In truth. You might start falling and I wouldn't be able to hold you up."

"I'll hold onto the bed."

She stood two feet from the bed, while he threw back

the blankets. Today he wore a long-tailed shirt that came to mid-thigh and naught else. He slowly moved his injured leg. When it slid over the edge, he winced and clamped his teeth together. His knee bent and he growled, his face going white.

"Torrin, I told you, 'tis too soon!" Jessie said, grabbing onto his arm.

Flora rushed in the door. "What on earth are you doing, m'laird?"

"Getting married," he said through clenched teeth.

Flora gave Jessie a wide-eyed quizzical look, and Jessie's face felt scalded.

"I told him," Jessie said. "And this is what I get… Torrin trying to kill himself."

"Och! I'm not trying to kill myself. You said yourself my wound is looking better this morn," he told Flora. "The swelling is going down."

"Aye, but…"

"Nay. I intend to stand while I marry Lady Jessie." He lowered his healthy leg to the floor and pushed himself up. Holding onto the bed, he stood for a moment, getting his bearings, then he took a step, a loud growl of pain issuing forth.

Jessie draped his arm around her shoulder so she might act as a sort of crutch for him. He made it to the end of the bed and grasped onto the tall, carved post, but he wasn't done there. He rounded the foot of the bed and limped along to the other post.

"What in blazes is going on in here?" Iain asked from the open doorway, shock written upon his face.

"He insisted on walking," Jessie said.

"Iain," Torrin said, breathing hard, his face white and drenched with sweat.

"Aye." Iain came forward, concern clear on his face.

"Will you stand up with me tomorrow and be my best man?"

"What?" He frowned.

"Lady Jessie and I are to be wed tomorrow."

"In truth?" He looked to Jessie for confirmation.

She nodded. "If Torrin is up to it."

"I'm up to it, trust me," Torrin said in a near growl. Clearly, the pain was terrible.

"I told him we could wait a few days," Jessie said.

"Of course, I'll be your best man anytime you wish."

"But you must not overdo it today, if you want to feel well tomorrow," Jessie said.

Torrin nodded and turned to walk back to the other side of the bed, a horrid scowl on his face the entire time.

"Can I tell everyone?" Iain asked.

"Aye. Tell the servants to prepare a feast and decorate the great hall. Tell the whole of the clan to be ready to witness me marrying this beautiful lady tomorrow." Torrin sat on the edge of the bed and threw his good leg onto the mattress. Jessie helped him lift his wounded leg, and then covered him with the blankets.

"I need to talk to Dirk," Torrin said. "I'll need his permission."

"I'll have him come to visit you after you rest a while," Jessie said.

"I don't need to rest. I've rested for a fortnight."

"I can go get him," Iain said.

"Aye, if you would please," Torrin said, relaxing back.

"You haven't even finished eating," Jessie said after Iain left. She wiped Torrin's sweaty face with a cool cloth, then handed him the porridge again. After he caught his breath, he ate a few more bites, then she set the bowl aside.

Five minutes later, Dirk entered the room, a curious look in his eyes. "How are you, Torrin?"

"Almost better." He took Jessie's hand. "I want to ask you once more for your lovely sister's hand in marriage."

"Oh?" Dirk looked to Jessie.

She nodded and smiled, happiness misting her eyes.

His brows shot up. "Aye, well, if Jessie is agreeable to the marriage, I certainly give my permission and my blessing."

"I thank you," Torrin said, kissing Jessie's hand. "I want

you to know, I love this woman more than life itself. I'll protect her and make her as happy as I'm able."

Jessie's heart melted with Torrin's confession.

"I know you will," Dirk said, smiling. "Would you like me to draw up a contract?"

"Indeed. You can use my official chamber if you wish. You'll find paper, ink and anything you might need on the desk. Iain can show you where it is. We've decided that tomorrow is the day."

"That soon?"

"Aye. I've waited long enough to make this lady my wife."

"I'll set to work right away on the marriage contract, then." Dirk grinned. "Congratulations to you both. I've been hoping Jessie would finally get past her stubborn streak and marry you." He left the room.

"I wasn't being stubborn," Jessie muttered when she was alone with Torrin again.

"Call it what you will." Torrin smirked. "I agree with Dirk; you were stubborn."

Much to Jessie's annoyance, Torrin walked around the bed twice more that day. He assured her each time 'twas a bit easier, but she could not tell this by his horrid grimaces, curses and groans.

That night, Jessie slept in the guest chamber the servants had prepared for her. Several women of the clan insisted 'twould be for the best, for they should not see each other before the wedding. Flora slept on the pallet in Torrin's room, should he need anything.

A knock sounded at the door, waking Jessie. Morning sunlight streamed through the narrow window. Had she overslept?

She leapt up and the nausea struck her. She quickly found the empty chamber pot and retched into it. Flora rushed in. "Och! M'lady, I'm so sorry."

"'Tis all right." She arose and rinsed her mouth with the watered down wine from the jug on her bedside table.

"Laird MacLeod is all dressed and ready."

"What? This early?"

"Aye. Woke me at the crack of dawn, he did, insisting on a bath in the tub. His manservant came in and helped him dress in his finest plaid and doublet. He's a right handsome sight." She grinned.

"'Twill take me a wee bit to get ready," Jessie said, the nausea still tormenting her, though not as bad as before.

"I'll tell him to be patient, and then I'll send in the maids. I brought you two bannocks to help settle your stomach." She set a plate on the bedside table.

"I thank you."

While she ate, a crew of servants brought in a tub and filled it with buckets of hot water. It had been a while since she'd had anything more than a sponge bath. 'Twould feel heavenly to sink into that warm water.

An hour later, she was squeaky clean from her head to her toes, and dressed in a fine royal-blue gown she'd brought. When she'd packed it, she'd had no inkling she would be using it as her wedding dress… or did she? Why else would she bring her best gown?

Dolina braided sections of her drying hair and created a lovely hairstyle where some of her wavy hair remained down on her shoulders. She thought Torrin would like it this way.

"Och!" Flora exclaimed upon entering the room. "How lovely you look, m'lady!"

Jessie smiled. "I thank you, Flora."

"Are you feeling better?"

"Aye. Where is Torrin?"

"He's in the great hall with the rest of the men. They're all dressed in their finest."

Jessie's mouth dropped open. "Did he walk down there?"

"Aye, with the help of Iain and a walking stick."

Jessie shook her head, unable to believe how eager he was, and how much improvement he'd shown since yesterday.

She was eager, too, for she would soon be Torrin's wife.

***

Sitting in the great hall, Torrin kept glancing at the doorway leading to the staircase, hoping each time to see Jessie.

'Twas unfortunate that it was too early in the day to drink whisky. He could use a dram to take the edge off the sharp ache in his leg. But more, he needed to be fully himself when Jessie walked down those steps, and when he said his vows. He could endure a bit more pain in order to see his dreams come true.

His clan was happy that he was finally marrying, and that he was recovering. Each of them had congratulated him that morn when he'd entered the great hall. Female servants had decorated the large room with flowers and greenery, but mostly with sweet-smelling heather, which he knew Jessie would love. Musicians were playing various ballads from the elevated alcove at the opposite end of the great hall. Dirk, Keegan, Conall, Iain, and several more men sat at the high table, talking and drinking ale.

Torrin and Dirk had already signed the marriage contract. He truly did not care about the land in her dowry—he would've been just as happy without it—but it would benefit the clan, for they could grow more crops.

Dirk had already decided that he, Keegan and several others would leave the next morn for Dunnakeil, but a half dozen of the MacKays would stay until Torrin was able to travel south in a few weeks to find Nolan's grave.

"Women are hellishly slow when getting ready for their weddings," Dirk said, giving Torrin a sympathetic look.

Torrin nodded. "I remember, last winter, when you were awaiting Isobel." Dirk had been fidgety, pacing back and forth. Torrin felt like pacing, but couldn't at the moment. He had to save his strength for the wedding itself, which would be held here in the great hall instead of the chapel. This room was bigger; the whole clan and several villagers could attend, and he wouldn't have to walk down more steps.

"The waiting was torture," Dirk admitted.

"Mayhap you could go hurry her along a bit," Torrin suggested hopefully.

Dirk grinned and stood. "I'll try." He headed up the stairs.

A few minutes later, Flora emerged from the stairwell and whispered in Iain's ear. He grinned and stood. "'Tis time," he said to Torrin, while Flora ran back toward the stairs.

His heart pounding with excitement, Torrin pushed up from his chair and, using his walking stick, limped toward the area in front of the decorated fireplace where the wedding was to take place. He ground his teeth, determined to ignore the stabbing pains in his leg. Reverend MacPherson joined him and Iain.

Dirk emerged from the narrow stairwell, stepped aside, and Jessie appeared next. Saints, she was more beautiful than Torrin had ever seen her. Her fiery hair was down upon her shoulders, and the braids woven through with wee flowers. The blue gown hugged her slender curves. Again, he was overjoyed that she carried his bairn, though no one would guess by looking at her.

Her bright blue eyes held his, her love written clearly on her face, as her brother escorted her toward them. When she took his hand, she smiled, tears welling in her eyes.

"Don't cry," he whispered quiet as a breath. Because if she cried, he might be tempted to do so himself. And a chief simply couldn't cry before his clan.

He kissed her hand, then held it while Reverend MacPherson began the ceremony. Torrin heard a word here and there, enough to know that 'twas indeed a marriage ceremony, but the main focus of his attention was Jessie. She nervously glanced at him from time to time.

"You are blood of my blood, and bone of my bone. I give you my body, that we two might be one. I give you my spirit, 'til our life shall be done." Looking into her eyes, he repeated the rest of the vow after the minister.

As she said her vows, he listened to every word. Though 'twas the standard Gaelic vows, he knew she meant them with all her heart.

When it was time for the ring, he pulled the circle of gold from his sporran. He'd had it specially made for Jessie in the spring, when he'd become determined that he would marry her. The gold band was encrusted with several sapphires, rubies, and emeralds.

When he slid it onto her finger, she gasped, her eyes widening. 'Twas indeed a lovely ring that reminded him of her colorful beauty.

"With this ring, I thee wed," Torrin said. "With my body, I thee worship, and with all my worldly goods, I thee endow, in the name of the Father, and of the Son, and of the Holy Ghost. Amen."

Jessie smiled and tears glistened in her eyes.

"Chief MacLeod, you may kiss your bride to seal the vows," the minister announced.

Finally, they were married. Torrin smiled and leaned down to kiss Jessie. Her lips were warm, sweet and welcoming beneath his.

A cheer went up loud enough to rattle the rafters. Jessie pulled back and laughed. Grinning, he pulled her close and kissed her again.

"You'll have to heal quickly, Chief, if you're to give your bride a proper wedding night," Struan said, giving rise to lots of laughter from the rest of the men.

Torrin grinned, knowing a secret they didn't. Jessie didn't mind doing some of the *work*. "Don't you worry about that. She'll enjoy the wedding night."

Epilogue

Munrick Castle, April, 1620

Jessie held their newborn babe, wee Liam, in her arms. He'd just finished eating and was snoozing peacefully, his tiny hand clasped around her finger.

"He's such a strong and fine-looking lad, Jessie," Torrin whispered, sitting beside her on the padded settle near the fireplace in their bedchamber, while a spring snowstorm raged outside. Torrin slid his arm around her and kissed her cheek.

She nodded. "He is. He favors his father, you ken." 'Twas true; the babe had Torrin's dark hair and green eyes and most of his features. Jessie was thankful that Torrin had healed from all of his injuries and was now as strong as he had been before. He trained with the other men most every day, when the weather permitted.

"Our next one will look exactly like you, with beautiful flaming red hair and sky blue eyes," he said.

"Mayhap." She smiled, imagining a wee lad or lass who resembled her, but if they all looked like Torrin, she would be just as thrilled and grateful.

Dirk and Isobel had sent a missive a few weeks before,

saying that their babe had been born and 'twas a healthy lad. Keegan's and Seona's bairn had been born four days afterward, a beautiful lass. Jessie couldn't wait until the summer when she could see them all again.

Greum got up from where he'd been sleeping by the hearth and padded closer. The pup had grown by leaps and bounds since last summer and was now near up to Jessie's waist. Greum sniffed the babe's head, then gave Jessie a look filled with doggie love.

"I know you love him, too, Greum. Don't you?"

He sat back on his haunches, panting, his long pink tongue lolling and a grin on his furry lips.

"He can't wait to play with the lad," Torrin said.

"'Twill be a while. He's ten times bigger than Liam."

Torrin chuckled. "In a year or two, he'll be trying to ride Greum like a horse."

Jessie laughed at that image, though not too loudly, for she didn't want to wake the babe.

After their laughter had quieted into a comfortable silence, Torrin asked, "Do you ken how happy you make me?"

Taking in his delighted and proud expression, she realized once again that her dreams had come true. Tears filled her eyes. "Not as happy as you make me," she said.

"Och. Far happier." He leaned close and kissed her. "I love you."

"And I love you."

***

Please look for My Rebel Highlander (Rebbie's story) next in the Highland Adventure Series.

***

The Highland Adventure Series

My Fierce Highlander
My Wild Highlander
My Brave Highlander
My Daring Highlander
My Notorious Highlander
My Rebel Highlander

About the Author

Vonda Sinclair's favorite indulgent pastime is exploring Scotland, from Edinburgh to the untamed and windblown north coast. She also enjoys creating hot, Highland heroes and spirited lasses to drive them mad. Her books have won an EPIC Award and a National Readers' Choice Award. She lives with her amazing and supportive husband in the mountains of North Carolina where she is no doubt creating another Scottish story. Please visit her website to learn more. www.vondasinclair.com

Author's Note

Donald McMurdo was a real highwayman and assassin who resided in Durness. He died in 1623 and was buried in Balnakeil Church.

Made in the USA
Middletown, DE
07 October 2018